SAVAGE TEXAS

SAVAGE TEXAS SERIES, BOOK 1

SAVAGE TEXAS

3727 8609

WILLIAM W. JOHNSTONE
WITH J. A. JOHNSTONE

WHEELER PUBLISHING
A part of Gale, Cengage Learning

GALE
CENGAGE Learning·

Detroit • New York • San Francisco • New Haven, Conn • Waterville, Maine • London

GALE
CENGAGE Learning

LIBRARY OF CONGRESS CATALOGING-IN-PUBLICATION DATA

Johnstone, William W.
    Savage Texas / by William W. Johnstone ; with J. A. Johnstone. — Large print ed.
        p. cm. — (Wheeler Publishing large print western)
    ISBN-13: 978-1-4104-4550-6 (softcover)
    ISBN-10: 1-4104-4550-X (softcover)
    1. Texas—Fiction. 2. Large type books. I. Johnstone, J. A. II. Title.
PS3560.O415S335 2012
813'.54—dc23   2011044196

Published in 2012 by arrangement with Pinnacle Books, an imprint of Kensington Publishing Corp.

Printed in the United States of America
2 3 4 5 6   16 15 14 13 12
FD073

"Texas . . . Texas . . ."

— Last words of Sam Houston,
soldier, patriot, and founder and
president of the Republic of Texas

ONE

Some towns play out and fade away. Others die hard.

By midnight Midvale was ablaze. The light of its burning was a fire on a darkling plain.

It was a night in late March 1866. Early spring. The earth was quickening as Midvale was dying.

The well-watered grazing lands of Long Valley in north central Texas supported many widely scattered ranches. Midvale had come into being at a strategic site where key trails came together. The town supplied the needs of local ranchers and farmers for things they couldn't make or grow but couldn't do without.

A cluster of several square blocks of wooden frame buildings, it had a handful of shops and stores, several saloons, a small café, a boardinghouse or two, and a residential neighborhood.

Tonight Midvale had reached its end. Its

passing was violent. The killers had come to usher it into extinction. Raiders they were, a band of cutthroats, savage and merciless. They came under cover of darkness and fell on the town like ravening wolves — gun wolves.

The folk of Midvale were no sheep for the slaughter. The Texas frontier is no place for weaklings. For a generation, settlers had fought Comanche, Kiowa, and Lipan Apache war parties, Mexican bandits and homegrown outlaws. The battle fury of the recent War Between the States had left this part of Texas untouched, but there was not a family in the valley that hadn't given husbands and sons to the armies of the Confederacy. Few had returned.

The folk of Midvale were not weaklings. Not fools, either. They were undone by treachery, by a vicious attack that struck without warning, like a bolt out of the blue. By the time they knew what hit them, it was too late to mount any kind of defense.

Ringing the town, the raiders swooped down on it, shooting, stabbing, and slaying. No fight, this — it was a massacre.

After the killing came the plundering. Then the burning, as Midvale was put to the torch.

The scene was an inferno, as if a vent of

hell had opened up, bursting out of the dark ground in a fiery gusher. Shots rang out, shrieks sounded, and hoofbeats drummed through the red night as the killers hunted down the scant few who'd survived the initial onslaught.

All were slain outright; all but the young women and children, boys and girls. Captives are wealth.

The church was the last of Midvale to burn. It stood apart from the rest of the town, a modest distance separating it from worldlier precincts. A handful of townsfolk had fled to it, huddling together at the foot of the pulpit.

That's where the raiders found them. Their screams were silenced by hammering gunfire.

The church was set on fire, its bell tower spire a flaming dagger thrusting into night-black sky. Wooden beams gave, collapsing, sending the church bell tumbling down the shaft into the interior space.

It bounced around, clanging. Dull, heavy, leaden tones tolled Midvale's death knell.

The marauders rode out, well satisfied with this night's work. They left behind nearly a hundred dead men, women and children. It was a good start, but riper targets and richer pickings lay ahead.

The war had been over for almost a year, but there was no peace to be found on the Texas frontier. No peace short of the grave.

But for the ravagers and pillagers who scourge this earth, the mysterious and unseen workings of fate sometimes send a nemesis of righteous vengeance. . . .

Two

From out of the north came a lone rider, trailing southwest across the hill country down into the prairie. A smiling stranger mounted on a tough, scrappy steel-dust stallion.

Man and mount were covered with trail dust from long days and nights of hard riding.

Texas is big and likes bigness. The stranger was no Texan but he was big. He was six feet, two inches tall, raw-boned and long-limbed, his broad shoulders axe-handle wide. A dark brown slouch hat topped a yellow-haired head with the face of a current-day Viking. He wore his hair long, shoulder-length, scout-style, a way of putting warlike Indians on notice that its owner had no fear of losing his scalp to them. A man of many ways, he'd been a scout before and might yet be again. The iciness of his sharp blue eyes was belied by the laugh-lines nestled in their corners.

No ordinary gun would do for this yellow-haired wanderer. Strapped to his right hip was a cut-down Winchester repeating rifle with a sawed-off barrel and chopped stock: a "mule's-leg," as such a weapon was popularly known. It had a kick that could knock its recipient from this world clear into the next. It rested in a special long-sheath holster that reached from hip to below mid-thigh.

Bandoliers lined with cartridges for the sawed-off carbine were worn across the stranger's torso in an X shape. A six-gun was tucked butt-out into his waistband on his left side. A Green River knife with a foot-long blade was sheathed on his left hip.

Some time around mid-morning, the rider came down off the edge of the Edwards plateau with its wooded hills and twisty ravines. Ahead lay a vast open expanse, the rolling plains of north central Texas.

No marker, no signpost noted that he had crossed a boundary, an invisible line. But indeed he had.

Sam Heller had come to Hangtree County.

THREE

Monday noon, the first day of April 1866. A hot sun topped the cloudless blue sky. Below lay empty tableland, vast, covered with the bright green grass of early spring and broken by sparsely scattered stands of timber. A line of wooded hills rose some miles to the north.

The flat was divided by a dirt road running east-west. It ran as straight as if it had been drawn by a ruler. No other sign of human habitation presented itself as far as the eye could see.

An antlike blur of motion inched with painful slowness across that wide, sprawling plain. It was a man alone, afoot on the dirt road. A lurching, ragged scarecrow of a figure.

Texas is big. Big sky, big land. And no place for a walking man. Especially if he's only got one leg.

Luke Pettigrew was that man, painfully

and painstakingly making his way west along the road to Hangtown.

He was lean, weathered, with long, lank brown hair and a beard. His young-old face, carved with lines of suffering, was now stoically expressionless except for a certain grim determination.

He was dressed in gray, the gray of a soldier of the army of the Confederate States of America. The Confederacy was now defunct a few weeks short of a year ago, since General Robert E. Lee had signed the articles of surrender at the Appomatox courthouse. Texas had joined with the South in seceding from the Union, sending its sons to fight in the War Between the States. Many had fallen, never to return.

Luke Pettigrew had returned. Minus his left leg below the knee.

A crooked tree branch served him for a crutch. A stick with a Y-shaped fork at one end, said fork being jammed under his left arm and helping to keep him upright. Strips of shredded rags were wrapped around the fork to cushion it as best they could. Which wasn't much. A clawlike left hand clutched the rough-barked shaft with a white-knuckled grip.

A battered, shapeless hat covered his head. It was faded to colorlessness by time and the elements. A bullethole showed in the top of the crown and a few nicks marked the brim.

Luke wore his uniform, what was left of it. A gray tunic, unbuttoned and open, revealed a threadbare, sun-faded red flannel shirt beneath it. Baggy gray trousers were held in place by a brown leather belt whose dulled metal buckle bore the legend: CSA. Many extra holes had been punched in the belt to coincide with his weight loss. He was thin, half-starved.

His garments had seen much hard use. They were worn, tattered. His left trouser leg was knotted together below the knee, to keep the empty pantleg from getting in his way. His good right foot was shod by a rough, handmade rawhide moccasin.

Luke Pettigrew was unarmed, without rifle, pistol or knife. And Texas is no place for an unarmed man. But there he was, minus horse, gun — and the lower part of his left leg — doggedly closing on Hangtown.

The capital of Hangtree County is the town of Hangtree, known far and wide as Hangtown.

From head to toe, Luke was powdered with fine dust from the dirt road. Sweat cut sharp lines through the powder covering his face. Grimacing, grunting between clenched teeth, he advanced another step with the crutch.

How many hundreds, thousands of such steps had he taken on his solitary trek? How many more such steps must he take before reaching his destination? He didn't know.

He was without a canteen. He'd been a long time without water under the hot Texas sun. Somewhere beyond the western horizon lay Swift Creek with its fresh, cool waters. On the far side of the creek: Hangtown.

Neither was yet in sight. Luke trudged on ahead. One thing he had plenty of was determination. Grit. The same doggedness that had seen him through battles without number in the war, endless forced marches, hunger, privation. It had kept him alive after the wound that took off the lower half of his left leg while others, far less seriously wounded, gave up the ghost and died.

That said, he sure was almighty sick and tired of walking.

Along came a rider, out of the east.

Absorbed with his own struggles, Luke was unaware of the newcomer's approach until the other was quite near. The sound of hoofbeats gave him pause. Halting, he looked back over his shoulder.

The single rider advanced at an easy lope.

Luke walked in the middle of the road because there the danger of rocks, holes and ditches was less than at the sidelines. A sound caught in his throat, something between a groan and a sigh, in anticipation of spending more of his meager reserves of energy in getting out of the way.

He angled toward the left-hand side of the road. It was a measure of the time and place that he unquestioningly accepted the likelihood of a perfect stranger riding down a crippled war veteran.

The rider was mounted on a chestnut horse. He slowed the animal to an easy walk, drawing abreast of Luke, keeping pace with him. Luke kept going, looking straight ahead, making a show of minding his own business in hopes that the newcomer would do the same.

"Howdy," the rider said, his voice soft-spoken, with a Texas twang.

At least he wasn't no damned Yankee, thought Luke. Not that that made much difference. His fellow Texans had given him plenty of grief lately. Luke grunted, acknowledging that the other had spoken and committing himself to no more than that acknowledgment.

"Long way to town," the rider said. He sounded friendly enough, for whatever that was worth, Luke told himself.

"Room up here for two to ride," the other said.

"I'm getting along, thanks," muttered Luke, not wanting to be beholden to anybody.

The rider laughed, laughter that was free and easy with no malice in it. Still, the sound of it raced like wildfire along Luke's strained nerves.

"You always was a hard-headed cuss, Luke Pettigrew," the rider said.

Luke, stunned, looked to see who it was that was calling out his name.

The rider was about his age, in his early twenties. He still had his youth, though, what was left of it, unlike Luke, who felt himself prematurely aged, one of the oldest men alive.

Luke peered up at him. Something familiar in the other's tone of voice . . .

A dark, flat-crowned, broad-brimmed hat with a snakeskin hatband shadowed the rider's face. The sun was behind him, in Luke's eyes. Luke squinted, peering, at first unable to make out the other's features. The rider tilted his head, causing the light to fall on his face.

"Good gawd! — Johnny Cross!" Luke's outcry was a croak, his throat parched from lack of water.

"Long time no see, Luke," Johnny Cross said.

"Well I'll be good to gawd-damned! I never expected to see you again," said Luke. "Huh! So you made it through the war."

"Looks like. And you, too."

"Mostly," Luke said, indicating with a tilt of his head and a sour twist of his mouth his missing lower leg.

"Reckon we're both going in the same direction. Climb on up," Johnny Cross said. Gripping the saddle horn with his right hand, he leaned over and down, extending his left hand.

He was lean and wiry, with strength in him. He took hold of Luke's right hand in an iron grip and hefted him up, swinging him onto the horse behind him. It helped that Luke didn't weigh much.

Luke got himself settled. "I want to keep hold of this crutch for now," he said.

"I'll tie it to the saddle, leave you with both hands free," Johnny said. He used a rawhide thong to lash the tree branch in place out of the way. A touch of Johnny's bootheels to the chestnut's flanks started the animal forward.

"Much obliged, Johnny."

"You'd do the same for me."

"What good would that do? I ain't got no horse."

"Man, things must be tough in Hangtree County."

"Like always. Only more so since the war."

They set out for Hangtown.

Johnny Cross was of medium height, compact, trim, athletic. He had black hair and clean-lined, well-formed features. His hazel eyes varied in color from brown to yellow depending on the light. He had a deep tan and a three-day beard. There was something catlike about him with his restless yellow eyes, self-contained alertness and lithe, easy way of moving.

He wore a sunbleached maroon shirt, black jeans and good boots. A pair of guns were strapped to his hips. Good guns.

Luke noticed several things right off. Johnny Cross had done some long, hard riding. His clothes were trailworn, dusty; his guns, what Luke could see of them in their holsters, were clean, polished. Their inset dark wooden handles were smooth, well worn with use. A late-model carbine was sheathed in the saddle scabbard.

The chestnut horse was a fine-looking

animal. Judging by its lines it was fast and strong, with plenty of endurance. The kind of mount favored by one on the dodge. One thing was sure: Johnny Cross was returning to Hangtree in better shape than when he'd left it.

The Cross family had always been dirt-poor, honest but penniless. Throughout his youth up till the time he went off to war, Johnny had worn mostly patched, outgrown clothes and gone shoeless for long periods of time.

Johnny Cross handed the other a canteen. "Here, Luke, cut the dust some."

"Don't mind if I do, thanks." Luke fought to still the trembling in his hands as he took hold of the canteen and fumbled open the cap. The water was as warm as blood. He took a mouthful and held it there, letting the welcome wetness refresh the dust-dry inside of his mouth.

His throat was so dry that at first he had trouble swallowing. He took a couple of mouthfuls, stopping though still thirsty. He didn't want to be a hog or show how great his need was. "Thank you kindly," he said, returning the canteen.

Johnny put it away. "Sorry I don't have something stronger."

"That's plenty fine," Luke said.

"Been back long?"

"Since last fall."

"How's your folks, Luke?"

"Pa got drowned two years ago trying to cross the Liberty River when it was running high at flood time."

"Sorry to hear that. He was a good man," Johnny said.

Luke nodded. "Hardworking and God-fearing . . . for all the good it done him."

"Your brothers?"

"Finn joined up with Ben McCullough and got kilt at Pea Ridge. Heck got it in Chicamagua."

"That's a damned shame. They was good ol' boys."

"War kilt off a lot of good ol' boys."

"Ain't it the truth."

The two were silent for a spell.

"Sue Ellen's married to a fellow over to Dennison way," Luke went on. "Got two young'uns, a boy and a girl. Named the boy after Pa. Ma's living with them."

"Imagine that! Last time I saw Sue Ellen she was a pretty little slip of a thing, and now she's got two young'uns of her own," Johnny said, shaking his head. "Time sure does fly. . . ."

"Four years is a long time, Johnny."

"How was your war, Luke?"

"I been around. I was with Hood's Brigade."

"Good outfit."

Luke nodded. "We fought our way all over the South. Reckon we was in just about every big battle there was. I was with 'em right through almost to the finish at the front lines of Richmond, till a cannonball took off the bottom part of my leg."

"That must've hurt some," Johnny said.

"It didn't tickle," Luke deadpanned. "They patched me up in a Yankee prison camp where I set for a few months until after Appomatox in April of Sixty-Five, when they set us all a-loose. I made my way back here, walking most of the way.

"What about you, Johnny? Seems I heard something about you riding with Bill Anderson."

"Did you? Well, you heard right."

Hard-riding, hard-fighting Bill Anderson had led a band of fellow Texans up into Missouri to join up with William Clarke Quantrill, onetime schoolteacher turned leader of a ferociously effective mounted force of Confederate irregulars in the Border States. The fighting there was guerrilla warfare at its worst: an unending series of ambushes, raids, flight, pursuit and counterattack — an ever-escalating spiral of brutalities and atrocities on both sides.

"We was with Quantrill," Johnny Cross said.

"How was it?" Luke asked.

"We gave those Yankees pure hell," Johnny said, smiling with his lips, a self-contained, secretive smile.

His alert, yellow-eyed gaze turned momentarily inward, bemused by cascading memories of hard riding and hard fighting. He tossed his head, as if physically shaking off the mood of reverie and returning to the present.

"Didn't work out too well in the end, though," Johnny said at last. "After Bill's sister got killed — she and a bunch of women, children and old folks was being held hostage by the Yanks in a house that collapsed on 'em — Bill went off the deep end. He always had a mean streak but after that he went plumb loco, kill crazy. That's when they started calling him Bloody Bill."

"You at Lawrence?" asked Luke.

Lawrence, Kansas, longtime abolitionist center and home base for Jim Lane's Red-legs, a band of Yankee marauders who'd shot, hanged and burned their way through pro-Confederate counties in Missouri. In retaliation, Quantrill had led a raid on Lawrence that became one of the bloodiest and most notorious massacres of the war.

"It wasn't good, Luke. I came to kill Yankee soldiers. This business of shooting down unarmed men — and boys — it ain't sporting."

"No more'n what the Redlegs done to our people."

"I stuck with Quantrill until the end, long after Bill split off from him to lead his own bunch. They're both dead now, shot down by the blue-bellies."

"I'd appreciate it if you'd keep that to yourself," Johnny said, after a pause. "The Federals still got a grudge on about Quantrill and ain't too keen on amnestying any of our bunch."

"You one of them pistol-fighters, Johnny?"

Johnny shrugged. "I'm like you, just another Reb looking for a place to light."

"You always was good with a gun. I see you're toting a mighty fine-looking pair of the plow handles in that gun belt," Luke said.

"That's about all I've got after four years of war, some good guns and a horse."

Johnny cut an involuntary glance at the empty space below Luke's left knee.

"Not that I'm complaining, mind you," he added quickly.

"Hold on to them guns and keep 'em

close. Now that you're back, you're gonna need 'em," Luke said.

"Yanks been throwing their weight around?" Johnny asked.

Luke shook his head. " 'T'ain't the Yanks that's the problem. Not yet, anyhow. They's around some but they're stretched kind of thin. There's a company of them in Fort Pardee up in the Breaks."

"They closed that at the start of the war, along with all them forts up and down the frontier line," Johnny said.

"It's up and running now, manned by a company of bluebelly horse soldiers. But that ain't the problem — not that I got any truck with a bunch of damn Yankees," Luke said.

" 'Course not."

"What with no cavalry around and most of the menfolk away during the war, no home guard and no Ranger companies, things have gone to rot and ruin hereabouts. The Indians have run wild, the Comanches and the Kiowas. Comanches, mostly. Wahtonka's been spending pretty much half the year riding the warpaths between Kansas and Mexico. Sometimes as far east as Fort Worth and even Dallas."

"Wahtonka? That ol' devil ain't dead yet?"

Luke shook his head. "Full of piss and

26

vinegar and more ornery than ever. And then there's Red Hand."

"I recollect him. A troublemaker, a real bad 'un. He was just starting to make a name for himself when I went north."

"He's a big noise nowadays, Johnny. Got hisself a following among the young bucks of the tribe. Red Hand's been raising holy hell for the last four years with no Army or Rangers to crack down on him. There's some other smaller fry, but them two are the real hellbenders.

"But that's not the least of it. The red-skins raid and move on. But the white bad-men just set. The county's thick with 'em. Thicker'n flies swarming a manure pile in a cow pasture on a hot summer day. Deserters from both armies, renegades, outlaws. Comancheros selling guns and whiskey to the Indians. Backshooters, women-killers. The lowest. Bluecoats are too busy chasing the Indians to bother with them. Folks're so broke that there ain't hardly nothing left worth stealing any more, but that don't matter to some hombres. They's up to all kinds of devilments out of pure meanness.

"Hell, I got robbed right here on this road not more than a day ago. In broad daylight. I didn't have nothing worth stealing but they took it anyhow. It'd been different if

I'd had me a six-gun. Or a good double-barreled sawed-off."

"Who done it, Luke?"

"Well, I'll tell you. First off, I been living out at the old family place, what's left of it," Luke said. "Somebody put the torch to it while I was away. Burned down the ranch house and barn."

"Yanks?" Johnny asked.

Luke shook his head. "Federals never got to Hangtree County during the war. Probably figured it wasn't worth bothering with. No, the ranch must've been burned by some no-goods, probably just for the hell of it.

"Anyhow, I scrounged up enough unburnt planks and shacks to build me a little shack; I been living there since I come back. Place is thick with maverick cattle — the whole range is. Strays that have been gone wild during the war and now there's hundreds, thousands of them running around loose. Every now and then I catch and kill me one for food. I'd've starved without.

"I had me some hides I'd cleaned and cured. I was bringing 'em into town to sell or barter at the general store. Some fish-hooks, chaw of tobacco, seeds . . ."

"And whiskey," Johnny said.

"Hell, yes," Luke said. "Had my old rifled musket and mule. Never made it to Hangtown — I got held up along the way. Bunch of no-accounts come up, got the drop on me. Five of them."

"Who?"

"Strangers, I never seen 'em before. But when I seen 'em again — Well, never mind about that now. Lot of outsiders horning in around here lately. I ain't forgetting a one of 'em. Led by a mean son name of Monty."

"Monty," Johnny echoed, committing the name to memory.

"That's what they called him, Monty. Big ol' boy with a round fat face and little piggy eyes. Cornsilk hair so fine and pale it was white. Got him a gold front tooth a-shining and a-sparkling away in the middle of his mouth," Luke said. "Him and his crowd gave me a whomping. Busted my musket against a tree. Shot my poor ol' mule dead for the fun of it. Busted my crutch over my head. It hurt, too."

Luke took off his hat, pointing out a big fat lump in the middle of his crown.

"That's some goose egg. Like I said, you always was a hardheaded fellow. Lucky for you," Johnny said.

"Yeh, lucky." Luke put his hat back on, gingerly settling it on his head. "While I was out cold they stole everything I had: my hides, my knife, even my wooden leg. Can you beat that? Stealing a man's wooden leg! Them things don't grow on trees, you know. That's what really hurt. I walked from hell to Texas on that leg. Yes, you could say I was attached to it."

"You could. I wouldn't."

"When I come to, them owlhoots was talking about if'n they should kill me or not. Only reason they didn't gun me down on the spot is 'cause Monty thought it would be funny to leave me alive to go crawling across the countryside."

"Yankees?"

"Hell no, they was Southerners just like us. Texans, some of 'em, from the way they talked," said Luke.

His face set in lines of grim determination. "I'll find 'em, I got time. When I do, I'll even up with 'em. And then some. That gold tooth of Monty's is gonna make me a good watch fob. Once I get me a watch."

He waved a hand dismissively, shooing away the topic as if it were a troublesome insect. "Not that I want to bother you with my troubles. Just giving you the lay of the land, so to speak. And you, Johnny, what're you doing back here?"

Johnny Cross shrugged. "I came home for a little peace and quiet, Luke. That's all."

"You come to the wrong place."

"And to lay low. The Border States ain't too healthy for any of Quantrill's crowd."

"You wanted, Johnny?"

"Not in Texas." After a pause, he said, "Not in this part of Texas."

"You could do worse. Hangtree's a big county with lots of room to get lost in. The Yanks are quartered forty miles northwest at Fort Pardee in the Breaks. They don't come to Hangtown much, and when they do they's just passing through. They got their hands full chasing Indians."

"They catch any?"

Luke laughed. "From what I hear, they got to look sharp to keep the Indians from catching them."

"Good, that'll keep 'em out of my hair."

"What're your plans, Johnny?"

"One thing I know is horses. Mustangs still running at Wild Horse Gulch?"

"More now than ever, since nobody was rounding 'em up during the war."

"Figured I'd collect a string and sell 'em. Folks always need horses, even in hard times. Maybe I'll sell 'em to those bluebellies at the fort."

Luke was shocked. "You wouldn't!"

"Gold's gold and the Yanks are the ones that got it nowadays," said Johnny Cross.

Something in the air made him look back.

A dust cloud showed in the distance east on the road, a brown smudge on the lip of the blue bowl of sky. Johnny reined in, turning the horse to face back the way they came. "Company's coming," he said.

"Generally that means trouble in these parts," Luke said.

"Ain't necessarily so, but that's the way to bet it," he added.

Johnny Cross unfastened the catch of the saddlebag on his right-hand side, reaching in and pulling out a revolver. A big .44 front-loading cap-and-ball six-gun like the ones worn on his hips: new, clean and potent.

"Here," he said, holding it out to Luke. "Take it," he said when the other hesitated.

Luke took it. The gun had a satisfying heft and balance in his hand. "A six-gun! One of them repeating revolvers," Luke marveled.

"Know how to use it?" Johnny asked.

"After four years with Hood's Brigade?" Luke said in disbelief.

"In that case I'd better show you how it works, then. I wouldn't want you shooting me or yourself by accident," Johnny said, straightfaced.

Luke's scowl broke into a twisted grin. "Shucks, you're joshing me," he said.

"I am? That's news to me."

"You're still doing it, dang you."

Johnny Cross flashed him a quick grin, strong white teeth gleaming, laugh-lines curling up around the corners of his hazel eyes. A boyish grin, likable somehow, with nothing mean in it.

Sure, Johnny was funning Luke. Hood's Brigade of Texans was one of the hardest-fighting outfits of the Confederacy, whose army had been distinguished by a host of fierce and valiant fighters.

Johnny turned the horse's head, pointing it west, urging it forward into a fast walk.

Luke stuck the pistol into the top of his waistband on his left side, butt-out. "It's good to have something to fill the hand with. Been feeling half-nekkid without one," he said.

"With what's left of that uniform, you are half-nekkid," Johnny said.

"How many more of them ventilators you got tucked in them saddlebags?"

"Never enough."

"You must have been traveling in some fast company, Johnny. I heard Quantrill's men rode into battle with a half-dozen guns or more. That true?"

"And more. Reloading takes time. A fellow wants a gun to hand when he wants it."

Luke was enthusiastic. "Man, what we

couldn't have done with a brace of these for every man in the old outfit!"

"If only," Johnny said flatly. His eyes were hard, cold.

A couple of hundred yards farther west, a stand of timber grew on the left side of the road. A grove of cottonwood trees.

East, the brown dust cloud grew. "Fair amount of riders from the dust they're kicking up. Coming pretty fast, too," said Luke, looking back.

"Wouldn't it be something if it was that bunch who cleaned you out?"

"It sure would. Any chance it's somebody on your trail, Johnny?"

"I ain't been back long enough."

Luke laughed. "Don't feel bad about it, hoss," he said. "It's early yet."

Johnny Cross turned the horse left, off the dirt road into the cottonwood grove. The shade felt good, thin though it was. The Texas sun was plenty fierce, even at the start of spring. Sunlight shining through spaces in the canopy of trees dappled the ground with a mosaic of light and shade. A wild hare started, springing across the glade for the cover of tall grass.

Johnny took the horse in deep behind a concealing screen of brush. "We'll just let these rannies have the right of way so we can get a looksee at 'em."

Luke was serious, in dead earnest. "Johnny — if it is that pack that tore into me — Monty is mine."

"Whoa, boy. Don't go getting ahead of yourself, Luke. Even if it is your bunch — especially if it is — don't throw down on 'em without my say-so. They'll get what's coming to 'em, I promise you that. But we'll pick the time and place. Two men shooting off the back of one horse ain't the most advantageous layout for a showdown.

"I know you got a hard head, but beware a hot one. It should have cooled some after four years of war," Johnny said.

"Well — it ain't," said Luke.

Johnny grinned. "Me neither," he said.

The blur at the base of the dust cloud sweeping west along the road resolved itself into a column of riders. About a dozen men or so.

They came in tandem: four pairs in front, then the wagon, then two horsemen bringing up the rear. Hardbitten men doing some hard traveling, as indicated by the trail dust covering them and the sweat-streaked flanks of their horses. They wore civilian clothes, broad-brimmed hats, flannel shirts, denim pants. Each rider was armed with a holstered sidearm and a carbine in a saddle-scabbard.

A team of six horses yoked in tandem drew the wagon. Two men rode up front at the head of the wagon: the driver and a shotgun messenger. A freight wagon with an oblong-shaped hopper, it was ten feet long, four feet wide, and three feet high. A canvas tarpaulin tied down over the top of the hopper concealed its contents. Crates, judging by the shape of them under the tarp.

The column came along at a brisk pace, kicking up plenty of dust. There was the pounding of hoofbeats, the hard breathing of the horses, the creak of saddle leather. Wagon wheels rumbled, clattering.

The driver wore his hat teamster-style, with the brim turned up in front. The men of the escort were hard-eyed, grim-faced, wary. They glanced at the cottonwood grove but spotted no sign of the duo on horseback.

On they rode, dragging a plume of brown dirt in their wake. It obscured the scene long after its creators had departed it. Some of the dust drifted into the glade, fine powder falling on Johnny, Luke, and the horse. Some dust got in the chestnut's nostrils and he sneezed.

Luke cleared his throat, hawked up a glob of phlegm and spat. Johnny took a swig from his canteen to wash the dust out out of his mouth and throat, then passed the canteen to Luke. "What do you make of that?" he asked.

"You tell me," Luke said.

"You're the one who's been back for a while."

"I never saw that bunch before. But I don't get into town much."

"I'll tell you this: they was loaded for bear."

"They must've been Yankees."

"How can you tell? They don't wear signs, Luke."

"They looked like they was doing all right. Well-fed, good guns and mounts, clothes that wasn't rags. Only folks getting along in these parts are Yankees and outlaws.

"They was escorting the wagon, doing a job of work. Outlaws don't work. So they must be Yanks, damn their eyes."

"Could be."

"They got the right idea, though. Nothing gets nowhere in Hangtree less'n it's well-guarded," said Luke. "Wonder what was in that wagon?"

"I wonder," Johnny Cross said, thoughtfully stroking his chin. A hard, predatory gleam came to his narrowed eyes as they gazed in the direction where the convoy had gone.

FOUR

The wagon and its mounted guards rode west toward Hangtown. Ahead lay a ridge running north-south. It met the road at right angles. The ridge was long, low, and rounded, blocking the view of the landscape beyond.

The convoy came to a halt A rider left the others and went on ahead. He was a scout named Dawkins. He was round-shouldered, beefy. Watery blue eyes bracketed his turnip-shaped nose.

He climbed the east side of the slope, cresting the ridge, stopping. The slope tilted down into a wide, flat trough with a water-course running through it. The watercourse ran parallel to the ridge. This was Swift Creek. Winding out of the northern hill country, it ran south across the valley.

A dirt road descended the west slope of the ridge to the creek. Here the creek ran fast and deep. It could have passed for a fairly respectable-size river. The shallow valley was marshy bottomland, tree-lined on both banks by willows and cottonwoods. On both sides the water's edge was thick with brakes and rushes.

"Nice country — for an ambush," Dawkins said to himself.

On the far side of the creek, a long, gentle slope rose to a tree-topped table. The road climbed the hill and disappeared into the trees. Several miles beyond, screened from view by the brush, lay the town of Hangtree, capital of Hangtree county:

Hangtown.

A wooden plank bridge spanned the river. Flatbridge, it was called. Only it wasn't there anymore. A hole gaped where the center of the span had been, showing only fast-flowing blue water.

This gave Dawkins pause. "What happened to the bridge?" he wondered aloud.

He took off his hat and scratched his head. His skin was shiny with sweat. He used the hat to fan himself. "Only one way to find out," he said.

He put his hat back on and rode downhill. On the near side of the creek, on the left-hand side of the road, stood a grove of willow trees, their boughs yellow-green. The grass was dark green, the creek sapphire, the sky turquoise.

Under the willow trees, in the shade, were a man and a horse. The man was sitting and the horse was standing. The horse was tied to a tree; it browsed contentedly on new green shoots and leaves. The man sat on a fallen tree trunk, smoking a cigar. He stood up, facing Dawkins.

The smoker wore cavalry blue and held a rifle at his side, muzzle pointing at the ground. A cigar stuck out of one side of his mouth. He stood there, smoking and waiting, as Dawkins approached.

The scout halted a few paces away. The two men eyed each other. The cavalryman broke the silence. "Looking for something, Mister?" he asked.

"Yeh — the bridge," Dawkins said.

"It ain't here no more."

"I can see that. What happened to it?"

"Comanches," the soldier said.

Dawkins couldn't help but give a start. He stiffened, stoop shoulders hunching as if anticipating a heavy blow. His eyes widened, trying to see everywhere all at once. No Comanches were to be seen.

Dawkins got a grip on himself after that first rush of belly-knotting body terror, pure and instinctive. He'd knew what the Comanches could do, particularly to any poor bastard unlucky enough to be taken alive by them.

Sense returned. If Comanches were anywhere around, the soldier would hardly be sitting under a tree smoking a cigar. He'd be making tracks for somewhere else, pronto.

The trooper looked like a tough customer. He had a good size on him, blotting out a fair amount of landscape. A hogshead-barrel torso with sloping shoulders and thick arms was supported by a pair of squat bowlegs. A short-brimmed cavalryman's cap perched at a jaunty angle on the back of his pumpkin head. Thick, curly black hair was cut close to the scalp, topping a gargoyle face.

A blue uniform tunic with dull brass buttons lay draped over a broken branch projecting from the fallen tree. The trooper wore a brick-red flannel shirt, sleeves rolled up past the elbows. His gun belt was worn low on his right hip, pistol facing butt-out in its holster, cavalry style. Its top flap was unbuttoned for quick and easy access. In his massive, pawlike hands the rifle looked like a carbine. His blue pants bore the yellow vertical side-stripes of the cavalry. They were tucked into the tops of knee-high brown leather riding boots.

An ugly, powerful brute, thought Dawkins,

a bull of a man. Reassuring to have around when the Comanches were on the warpath.

"You must be the man I'm looking for," he said. "I'm Dawkins, out of Fort Wolters — with the wagon."

"I don't see no wagon," the soldier said. If a buffalo could talk, its voice might sound something like that, Dawkins thought.

"It's on the other side of the hill. They sent me on ahead to meet up with our escort, a patrol from Fort Pardee," said Dawkins.

The cavalryman was silent. "Where is it?" Dawkins asked. "The escort from Fort Pardee?"

"You're looking at it," the soldier said.

"Eh? What's that you say?"

"The rest of the troop is way to hell and gone, scouring the countryside in search of a war party of Comanche bucks," the cavalryman said. Leaning his rifle against the fallen tree, he pulled on his tunic. It was several sizes too small for him, bursting at the seams. The sleeves were each blazoned with a set of sergeant's stripes. He didn't bother buttoning up.

He went to Dawkins. "I'm Sergeant Sales from Fort Pardee," he said. "If you was an officer, they wouldn't have sent you on ahead. You ain't so I won't bother to salute."

43

Reaching into a side pocket, the noncom pulled out a sheet of notepaper folded into a square and held it out to the other. "Here's my orders," Sales said.

Dawkins took the document, eyeing it. It was topped by a U.S. Army letterhead and stamped with the seal of the commanding officer of Fort Pardee. It bore a handwritten note.

Dawkins squinted blearily at it. "Looks okay to me," he said.

" 'Course, I can't read too good," he added. He returned the document to Sales.

"Give it to Lieutenant Greer, he's heading up this detail," Dawkins said.

"How many are you?" Sales asked.

"Twelve, counting the driver and shotgun rider."

Sales swore, a heartfelt obscenity. "That's all?"

"Lucky to get that many, we're stretched so thin at Fort Wolters," Dawkins said. "Nobody knew we were gonna run smack into a Comanche rampage!"

"What do you think we're doing up in the Breaks, practicing parade ground drill? We got Comanche war parties coming and going — Kiowas and Lipan Apaches, too!"

"Lieutenant Greer ain't gonna like this," Dawkins said mournfully. "He's a green shavetail on his first posting out West," he confided.

Sergeant Sales shrugged his massive shoulders, further straining the already over-stressed fabric of the tunic. "Tough," he said.

He crossed to his horse, sheathing the rifle in its saddle-scabbard. Untying the reins, he gathered them up in one hand. Still-lit cigar stub chomped in the corner of his mouth, he swung up into the saddle. His horse grunted from the burden of the big man's weight. He moved alongside of Dawkins. "Let's go," he said.

Dawkins a-hemmed. "A word to the wise," he said. "The Lieutenant's kind of a stickler for army discipline. Soldierly deportment and whatnot. You might want to spruce up some before meeting him."

"Me? What about you? Hell, you ain't even in uniform," Sales countered.

"That's different. The wagon guard detail's all in civilian clothes, to call less attention to the mission."

The noncom barked out a derisive laugh. "The Comanches'll lift your scalp all the same if they catch you."

"When that first looie of yours finds out how things lay, he'll change his tune pretty damned quick," he added.

"Well, mebbe," Dawkins said, "but I doubt it."

The convoy was on the other side of the ridge, at the foot of the eastern slope. The men were at ease, taking a break. They were watchful, wary. The sun was at its zenith. It was hot. Insects buzzed in the brush. Some of the men idled in the shade, what shade there was to be found, smoking, sipping warm water from their canteens, chatting low-voiced.

Sergeant Sales had shaped up to some extent before meeting Lieutenant Greer. His cap was screwed on tight to the top of his head. The cigar-stub had been discarded along the way. He and Dawkins dismounted, handing the reins of their mounts to a horse-holder. Dawkins led the way, Sales following.

Their arrival — rather, that of the single, solitary noncom — had sparked muted interest among the detail, whose members stared in frank, open curiosity. They were trail-worn and weary but looked spruce compared to the sergeant.

Lieutenant Greer had brown hair, dark eyes, and a well-trimmed mustache. He was in his early twenties, still shiny and fresh-faced, the Texas sun not yet having baked all the youth out of him. He looked like a schoolboy beside burly, brutish Sergeant Ben Sales.

"This here's Lieutenant Greer," Dawkins said by way of introduction before quickly sidestepping out of the scene.

The sergeant managed to pop a stiff-backed brace and fire off a sharp salute at the young first lieutenant. "Sergeant Sales reporting for duty, sir!"

Greer returned the salute. "As you were, Sergeant."

Sales handed him the document he'd earlier shown to Dawkins. Greer studied it. It seemed in order. It was a handwritten note from Captain Ted Harrison, commander of Fort Pardee, identifying the bearer as Sergeant Sales, heading the troops detailed to escort the convoy the rest of the way to the outpost.

Greer carefully refolded the note, putting it into the right breast pocket of his shirt. "Where are your men, Sergeant? Securing the bridge?"

"That's a problem, sir," Sales said. "The bridge is wrecked and my men are off chasing the Comanches who did it."

Greer's eyes looked ready to pop. Catching himself, he scowled, narrowing them.

Sergeant Sales explained that a Comanche

war party was running riot in Hangtree County, that they'd destroyed the bridge, and that Swift Creek was too fast and deep to allow for a crossing.

Greer's flushed face reddened, his lower lip quivering. "How can that be? I was told that the Comanches wouldn't start raiding south from their home grounds for another month or two!"

"I'm afraid they ain't holding to schedule this year, sir," Sales said. "Comanches is like that — ornery."

Greer scrutinized the other for some hint of mockery or insubordination, but the sergeant kept a poker face.

Sales said, "Wahtonka — he's the big man of the Comanche war chiefs —"

"Yes, yes, I know who he is, I'm not totally uninformed about local conditions!" Greer snapped. "Go on, man!"

"The war between North and South never quite registered on the savages out here. They got the crazy idea that it was them that caused the army to pull up stakes back in Sixty-One and abandon the line of forts along the frontier that was keeping them red devils in check. The Comanches don't know or won't believe that the troops were being pulled back East to put down the Rebs. They figure they got us on the run.

"Now Wahtonka aims to finish the job. He wants all the whites pushed back off the plains, leaving them free and clear like they used to be. He and his bucks started their killing and burning early this year. They hit hard two weeks ago farther south, wiping the town of Midvale off the map.

"A few nights ago they struck below the south fork of Liberty River, hitting some ranches, raping, raiding, killing. We don't know if it's the same bunch that sacked Midvale or if this is a whole 'nother war party. They tore up the bridge across Swift Creek to slow pursuit. I sent my men after them and stayed behind to guide you to the fort."

Lieutenant Greer was taken aback. "You decided — ?! But that's a violation of orders — dereliction of duty! Your mission is to escort this detail to Fort Pardee," he said, sputtering, outraged.

Sales was blandly, patronizingly composed, in the timeless mode of veteran soldiers explaining the facts of life to green, untried junior officers. "Begging the lieutenant's pardon, but that just ain't so," he said. "Standing orders from Captain Harrison and the district military commandant is that we're charged to fight and kill the savages and protect the civilian population. That mission trumps all others."

Greer sniffed. Under trail dust his face blazed red. "If there's one thing I detest, it's a barracks-room lawyer, Sergeant."

"I'd be facing a court-martial if I disobeyed Captain Harrison and missed the chance to take some Comanche scalps, sir."

"Don't be too sure of that, Sales. You may be facing that court-martial sooner than you think."

Sales faced that prospect with calm self-assurance. "It's the lieutenant's privilege to prefer charges — once we reach Fort Pardee. If we reach it. If the Comanches knew what this wagon is carrying they'd ride hell bent for leather to have it. By sending my men after them I took the inititiative, buying us some time."

"All very well and good, Sergeant. But the bridge is out, remember? And according to you, Swift Creek is too fast and deep to ford!"

"Yes, sir. It is, here. But several miles upstream the creek widens out. We can cross at Mace's Ford and strike out west along the Old Mission Trail, then angle northwest through the Breaks to the fort."

"All right, then," Lieutenant Greer said. "Very well, Sergeant. We move out now!"

FIVE

A dirt road ran along the foot of the eastern slope of the ridge east of Swift Creek. The wagon convoy followed it five, six miles north until they came to a trail cutting it at right angles. The convoy halted.

Sergeant Sales and Scout Dawkins rode to the top of the ridge. On the far side, in the valley below, Swift Creek widened, becoming more shallow, its current slowing. It was a broad, flat, lazy band, gently twisting and bending. Downstream at Flatbridge it had been dark blue, but here it was greenish-brown.

"Mace's Ford," Sergeant Sales said.

There was a mounted man on the east bank and a man on foot with a horse nearby on the west.

"Those two are mine. I sent them on ahead to make sure that there's no surprises waiting for us," said Sales. He took off his hat and waved it over his head. The man on

51

the near side of the ford held a rifle in one hand, pumping it up and down in the air several times in response.

"Looks okay. Let's go down to make sure," Sales said. He and Dawkins rode down to the creek. The ground was thick with tall grass, rushes, willow trees. Everything was green and moist. Small streams and rivulets webbed the flat, tufts and hummocks thrusting up between them. There was a smell of damp earth, water. The air was a little hazy.

The trail was hardpacked, but not as dusty as it had been on the slope. It ran right straight to the water's edge. A man in a cavalry uniform sat his horse near the creek. He had narrow eyes and a close-cropped blue-black beard. His jacket was unbuttoned and open and he sat slouching in the saddle. Sales and Dawkins reined in, facing him.

"Dawkins — Corporal Reese. Dawkins is a scout for the convoy," Sales said, indicating the cavalryman. "How's it look, Reese?"

"Okay, Sarge," Reese said.

"No Comanches?"

"Ain't seen an Injin all day."

"You won't see them till they lift your scalp."

"I still got my hair and so does Fenner, so

I guess we're in the clear."

"Good." The creek was about fifty feet wide here. Sales put a hand to the side of his mouth and shouted to the man on the west bank. "Okay on your end, Fenner?"

"All set, Sarge!" Fenner shouted back.

Dawkins frowned. "Hell, he sounds like a Johnny Reb."

"He was. He's been galvanized," Sales said, using the term for a former Confederate soldier who'd been recruited into the service of the Union. "The army don't much care who's fighting the Comanches as long as they get the job done. As for Fenner, he likes eating regular — even if it is Yankee mess-hall chow."

Sales turned to Reese. "Button up that tunic and get yourself squared away. It's time to start looking like a soldier. We got us a first lieutenant who's all spit-and-polish."

Reese saluted jauntily. "Yes, sir!"

Sales's face clouded. His expression, always stony, was now glowering. "Don't call me 'sir,' you dumb son of a bitch. I'm no officer. Get smart with me and I'll kick your butt so hard your tail-bone'll be coming out the top of your head."

That wiped the smirk off Reese's face. He straightened up in the saddle.

"Sorry, Sarge —"

"Shaddup. Never mind that you been up all night and day chasing Indians, we got to show the lieutenant something." Sales faced Dawkins. "You can tell Greer it's safe to make the crossing."

"All right," Dawkins said.

"And make it quick — there's a Comanche war party on the loose and we're still a long way off from Fort Pardee."

Dawkins nodded. He turned his horse, riding uphill, disappearing on the other side of the ridge.

Presently the convoy came into view, descending the trail to the creek. Lieutenant Greer rode at the head of the column of armed guards, followed by the wagon. The horses could see and smell the water. Some of them got antsy, nostrils flaring, ears twitching. They had to be held in.

Sales rode over to Lieutenant Greer and saluted. "My men have scouted the area, sir. The way is clear."

Greer acknowledged the report with a curt nod. "Thank you, Sergeant."

One of his men rode up. "It's been a long, dry journey, sir. The horses could use some water," he said.

"Get them across the creek first," Greer said. "I want to make the crossing as soon as possible. We've already lost too much time thanks to this detour. Once we're on the other side we'll water the animals. But don't let them drink too much. I don't want them swelled up so they slow us down."

"Yes, sir," the other said. He went to pass the word to the rest of the men.

The convoy started across the creek, horses kicking up little splashes and spumes of water. The stream was less than three feet deep at its center and much shallower for most of its width. A mild current swirled around the horses and wagon, chuckling and purling. A light breeze lifted, rustling through the rushes, making them wave their tops.

Crossings are always a bit disordered. The line got stretched out, making a noisy hub-bub. The wagon's harnessed team lurched forward, heaving and pulling. The horses wanted to stop and drink. The driver handling the traces fought them, grunting and cursing, cracking the whip over their heads to keep them moving. The wagon bounced and jostled on its springs. Even at midstream, the water level was well below the bottom of the wagon bed.

Sergeant Sales rode alongside Lieutenant Greer. He had to shout to be heard over the racket. "Hey, Lieutenant!"

Greer glanced his way, turning a cold eye on the noncom. "What is it, Sergeant?"

"I want to tell you something."

"Yes?"

"If there's one thing I hate, it's officers," Sergeant Sales said. He drew his gun and shot Greer in the side. Greer crumpled like he was imploding, shrinking into himself.

Sales pumped a slug into the officer's belly. Greer grabbed his middle and fell sideways off his horse into the water.

Sales's opening shots were a signal triggering an answering fusillade from both sides of the creek, where gunmen were hidden in the tall grass. The murderous volley took out a number of the wagon's escort riders.

"Ambush!"

"Bushwhackers — !"

All hell broke loose. Startled shouts from the guards were drowned out by racketing gunfire. Frightened birds burst out of the trees, taking flight in droves.

On the far bank, Fenner swung his rifle up and shot the guard nearest him off his horse.

Dawkins, cursing, clawed for his pistol, fumbling with the top flap of the holster. Before it could clear leather, Sales shot the top of his head off.

The shotgun rider on the wagon swung his weapon up. Riding up from behind, Reese shot him in the back. The shotgunner's dying spasm caused him to jerk both double triggers at once, discharging a shattering blast to the side that caught two more mounted guards, peppering them ragged with shot.

Seven ambushers lurked on the west bank, four on the east. They popped up from behind rocks and trees, potting away at the guards fording the creek. Horses reared and circled, whinnying and nickering, eyes rolling in fright. The men of the convoy cursed, shouted, screamed and died. All was chaos, confusion.

The wagon driver jerked and shuddered under the impact of slug after slug ripping into him from different directions.

Sales emptied his revolver into nearby wagon guards, burning them down. He clutched the reins tightly in his other fist, holding the horse's head down, wheeling it this way and that in search of new targets.

Reese was on the opposite side of the column, gunning down guards.

The hammer of Sales's gun clicked on empty chambers. The gun dropped from his hand as he freed it to shuck his rifle out of its saddle-scabbard. He bit down, holding the reins between his teeth as he worked the long-levered gun with both hands.

Something tugged at his tunic below his right arm — a slug passing through. It came not from a wagon guard but rather from one of the shooters on the far bank. Sales didn't see who it was. He cursed under his breath.

A guard rider wheeled, breaking for the east bank. Sales leveled the rifle and shot him off his horse. The rider's foot snagged in the stirrup causing him to be dragged a short distance before the corpse tumbled free on shore. The horse kept running.

It was all over in a minute or two. A passel of riderless horses milled about in the creek. Sales guided his horse a half-dozen paces upstream. He yelled, "Cease firing!"

The shooting did not stop at once but raggedly died down. Bodies bobbed floating facedown in the water, the gentle tug of the current starting to move them downstream. A pall of gunsmoke hung over the ford. Random shots continued to erupt from both banks of the creek.

"Stop shooting, you sons of bitches!" Sales bawled, red-faced. The firing stopped.

Reese rode up alongside the wagon, transferring to it from his horse. The shotgunner had fallen out but the driver lay sprawled across the seat. Reese planted a booted foot against the driver's side and push-kicked him into the water. Plunking down into the driver's seat, he gathered up the traces and took control of the team.

The man with the sergeant's stripes spoke again:

"Get the wagon across to the other side!"

"Okay, Brock!" said Reese.

"Sergeant Ben Sales" was an alias. There was a real Sergeant Sales on the rolls at Fort Pardee, but the man calling the shots wasn't him. That man was Brock Harper, one of the most dangerous bandit chiefs west of the Mississippi, or east of it, for that matter. Hailing from California, he'd shot his way across the map to surface in Hangtree County, Texas.

"Reese" was no alias; it was the phony corporal's real name but it was his Christian name, not his surname. His full name was Reese Kimbro — better known as Killer Kimbro. Killer Kimbro was the name bannered on the many Wanted posters and circulars bearing his likeness that were papered throughout Texas and the Southwest. Luckily, the drawing accompanying them was generic enough to fit any one of a thousand men.

Kimbro was Harper's trusted aide, his right-hand man.

The shooters on both sides of the creek began emerging from their places of concealment. They were a rough bunch: robbers and killers, armed with rifles, shotguns and six-guns.

Fenner took off his hat and howled a Rebel yell, echoing the defiant cry that had sounded across every battlefield of the late war. Some of the men joined in, whooping it up. Some, not all.

The bushwhackers were a mixed bag, some Southerners, some Northerners. There were a couple of Mexicans, several persons of mixed blood, a full-blooded Kiowa Indian, a Canadian, and even one transplanted Australian.

What they had in common was a lust for gold and, at best, an indifference to taking human life to get it. "At best" — some of them liked to kill for the pure fun of it.

Kimbro drove the wagon across the creek up on to the west bank, reining the team to a halt.

"Some of you men get in the water and keep those bodies from drifting too far downstream!" commanded Brock Harper. He had a big braying voice and a pair of leather lungs for bawling out commands.

He turned in the saddle, facing the east bank. Four men stood there, holding rifles and shotguns whose muzzles still trailed strings and wisps of gunsmoke. "You bastards have to get wet crossing back over anyhow, so make yourselves useful and corral those deaders," Harper said. "Move!"

The quartet splashed into the creek to obey. There was blood in the water. Swirling, spiraling clouds of the red stuff spread among the strata of green and brown water. The creek was murkier than ever due to the bottom having been churned up by hooves and wagon wheels during the action. The four outlaws took hold of floating corpses, herding them to shore.

Brock Harper rode up on to the west bank. It was thickly wooded. The trail resumed at the water's edge and continued west, making a tunnel through the brush. Farther down the trail, around a bend and out of sight of anyone crossing the ford from the east bank, was a clearing.

The gang's horses were hidden there, tethered and watched by two men designated as horse-holders. Nothing was more embarrassing or potentially fatal than having horses run off when their riders were dismounted. A flatbed wagon hitched to a four-horse team was hidden around the bend, too.

Fenner was gangly, thin-faced, with long, lank hair, sunken eyes and buck teeth. He went to Harper. He crowed, "Whoo-whee! What a turkey shoot! Did the feathers fly!"

Harper held a flap of his blue tunic out and away from himself, showing where a bullet hole had pierced it. "One of you jackasses almost shot me. It came from over here. Who did it?" he demanded.

Nobody stepped forward to own up. Fenner snickered, wiping his nose with the back of his hand. "Must be that blue uniform, Boss. Folks just naturally like to shoot at it. You can't blame 'em for it."

"Think it's so funny, you'll be laughing out of the other side of your mouth if I get a notion to straighten you out," Harper said.

"Weren't me, Brock! If I was shooting at you I wouldn't have missed," Fenner said.

"Not that I ever would," he added quickly.

"You're damned right about that, you Ozark pecker wood." Harper swung down out of the saddle. Relieved of his weight, his horse seemed to gain several inches in height.

The empty holster at his hip nagged at him. "Somebody give me a gun," he said.

Most of the gang carried more than one six-gun. Somebody handed Harper a pistol.

"Here go, Brock."

"Thanks." Harper checked to make sure it was loaded — he took nothing on faith. Loaded it was. He weighed it in his hand, checking the balance. He fired a test shot, knocking a pinecone off a tree.

The gun passed muster. Harper stuffed it into his empty holster. He looked around, his eye falling on the nearest of his men. He called them out by name.

"Wilse! Gordy! Digger! Mart! Mount up and round up those army horses! They're loot. Any of them gets away, it's like throwing away money," he said. Those singled out by him went down the trail to the clearing around the bend to get their horses.

Harper shucked off the blue tunic, throwing it to the ground. "Feels good to be rid of that. It was as tight as a sausage skin."

"You just about busted out of the seams," Reese Kimbro said.

"We were lucky to get those uniforms at all, thanks to our inside man at Fort Pardee. But they don't hardly field troopers in my size."

"No they don't, and that's a fact."

"That reminds me," Harper said, "where's the lieutenant?"

"The one you gut-shot? Somewhere in with the rest of 'em," Reese said.

Harper went down to the edge of the creek. A row of bodies lay sprawled along the muddy bank, twisted by the contortions of violent death. Harper went along the line from one victim to the next, searching. Sometimes he used the toe of his boot to turn a body faceup.

He stopped when he found Lieutenant Greer. The body lay there dripping, pale, white-faced. There was a big dark blotch from the hole in its belly and another one in the side where Harper's first bullet had tagged him.

Harper squatted down, tearing open Greer's right breast shirt pocket. He didn't bother opening the pocket; he just tore it loose from the shirt. A square of sodden folded paper tumbled out. Harper picked it up.

"What's that, Brock?" somebody asked.

"A fake document my friend at Fort Pardee gave me to establish my bona fides with the shave-tail." The paper tore as Harper unfolded it. The handwriting was blurred and smeary from the water, but the Army letterhead and Fort Pardee red stamp were still legible.

He tore up the paper into little pieces and threw them away. "That'll protect our inside man at the fort. I might need him again."

Some of the fragments stuck to his thick strangler's fingers. He wiped them clean on his pants.

Riders on horseback, the men Harper had singled out earlier, came down the trail out of the woods. They rode into the creek, fanning out to round up the wagon guards' stray horses.

"Long as I'm in this neck of the woods, might as well make a thorough job of it," Harper said, turning out the rest of Greer's pockets. He came up with a thin wad of greenbacks and a few — not many — gold coins.

The search also yielded a pocket-watch. It was still ticking. Harper opened the watch. On the inside of the lid was an oval miniature painting of a young woman, an attractive brunette. A couple of outlaws crowded in to take a look.

"What's that, Brock?"

Harper shrugged. "I dunno. His sweetheart, maybe. Pretty gal."

"Let's see," somebody said.

Harper closed the watchcase lid with a snap. The money he pocketed.

"What happened to sharing out the profits equally like we always do?" asked Kimbro, frowning fiercely.

"That's my bonus for nearly getting shot

by my own compadres," Harper said.

"I ran the same risk," Kimbro said, "so I'll take the watch."

Harper shrugged massive shoulders. He tossed Kimbro the watch. Kimbro snatched it out of the air. "Thanks," he said.

A number of outlaws rushed toward the bodies. Harper barked at them, "Back off, you buzzards!"

The others halted in mid-stride.

"Me and Kimbro took ours off the top as a bonus for running the extra risk. The rest of the spoils will be handled in an orderly fashion. Dump it all in a hat and we'll divvy up later at the hideout," Harper said.

He knew his men. They were like kids, greedy kids. A full-course meal was laid out on the table and all they could think of was getting their grubby hands on the penny candy. Whatever pittance lay in the pockets of the dead men was as nothing compared to the wagon's cargo. But if the badmen didn't have at it they'd be sore and bellyaching. Better to get it over with now, the quicker to get at the real job at hand.

"Get to it and make it fast, we haven't got all day," Harper said. "And remember — anybody dragging down loot for himself is robbing the rest of you. Having you scavengers watching each other is the best way to keep you honest — you should pardon the expression," he went on, chuckling to himself.

The outlaws fell on the corpses like starving dogs on a juicy bone. They turned out the dead men's pockets, divesting them of their valuables, such as they were. They weren't much.

Something tugged on Harper's sleeve. "What do you want, Fenner?" he asked.

"What about me, Brock?"

"What about you?"

"I deserve something, I took a risk, too."

Harper laughed, without humor. "Risk? You were safe here on the far side of the creek while Kimbro and me were in the thick of it."

"Aw, Brockie, don't be like that . . ."

"Shaddup." Fenner wore a high-crowned hat. Harper snatched it off his head.

"Hey! What're you doing?! —"

"Take it easy, Fenner. This hat of yours will fit the bill," Harper said. He turned it upside-down. "Here, men, put the loot in Fenner's hat. Anybody holds out, I'll shoot him. And make it quick! There's work to do and daylight's burning."

Scavenging the dead men's pockets yielded a meager take. "Them soldier boys don't carry much in the way of hard currency," somebody said.

"Pay's almost as little as cow punching," another groused.

The corpses' yield of money, watches and such was not enough to fill the inside of Fenner's hat to the brim.

"Kaw, get up here," Harper said. Kaw came forward. He was a full-blooded Kiowa, an outcast from his tribe who now rode the outlaw trail. Harper handed him the hat filled with loot.

"Take care of this, Kaw. Put it in your saddlebag," Harper said.

"Why him, Brock?" somebody asked.

"Because he's the only honest man here. Everybody knows Kaw's not in it for the loot, but for the pure hell of it. He's the only one you can trust not to steal from you because he doesn't give a damn about money."

Nods and murmurs from the men indicated their general agreement with the statement.

"Stow it away now, Kaw. We've already wasted too much time on this chicken feed," said Harper.

"Every little bit helps, Brock," Kimbro said.

Kaw turned, starting down the trail toward where the horses were picketed. Fenner trotted after him.

"Where you going, Fenner?" asked Harper.

"I want my hat back. It's my hat and I want it."

Kimbro said, "Watch him, Kaw, and make sure none of that loot sticks to his fingers."

A new voice made itself heard:

"That's penny-ante stuff. How about a looksee at what's in the wagon?"

The speaker was Hap Englehardt. Balding, with a beaky nose and vulture face, he was lean, spare and as tough as a strip of beef jerky. A lifetime in the saddle had left him so bowlegged that a hogshead barrel could have passed lengthwise between them without touching the insides of his thighs.

He was in his late fifties, old for an outlaw. That meant he was good at what he did because he'd been at the business of robbing and killing since boyhood days, and few men in his peculiar trade lived long enough to grow ripe and full in years. "Hap" was short for "Happy," a moniker that had been hung on him long ago by some sagebrush wag, in the same humor as calling a big man "Tiny."

He looked around at some of the others. "We'd like to see what we been working so hard for," Englehardt said.

"You speaking for this bunch now, Hap? What do you think is in the crates, eggs?"

"I sure as hell hope not, Brock. If we come all this way for nothing —" Engelhardt broke off, swearing, swiping a fist in the air.

Harper faced him, hands on hips. "Yeh? What'll you do then, Hap?"

". . . I'll be purely disappointed, Brock," Engelhardt said, backing off.

Harper grinned. "What I thought. You were born sour, Hap, and whatever's in that wagon, honey or horse turds, you'll stay sour."

He eyed the rest of the gang. They were taut, keyed-up. Feral dogs straining at the leash. "I suppose none of you will rest easy until you've had a look so let's get it over with," Harper said, growling.

He went to the wagon, the others swarming around it, crowding in. Their faces were eager, rapt, like players at a gambling table intent on a turn of the wheel. Some of them were breathing hard as if they were running a race.

Down came the freight wagon's tailgate. The ropes tying down the canvas tarpaulin over the cargo were cut loose and the tarp folded back, baring stacked wooden crates.

"You like to brag on your strength, Neal.

Get up there and haul one of those crates down."

"Right, Brock." Neal was a strongback, big, beefy, athletic. He clambered up on the tailgate. Squaring his stance, he took hold of one of the topmost crates and wrestled it loose from the stack.

"Easy does it. Lower it down, don't drop it," Harper said.

Words in big black letters were stenciled on the top and sides of the crate. A rail-thin gunman in his late teens squinted at it, Adam's apple bobbing in a turkey neck. "What's that say?"

"Whatsa' matter, Dewey, can't you read?" a badman demanded.

"No, can you?"

"Well . . . no."

"It says, 'Property of U.S. Army,' " Harper said.

"Not no more, it ain't," Kimbro said quickly.

That got a laugh all around. Neal manhandled the crate, red-faced, veins bulging, breathing hard. He started lowering it down from the tailgate and lost his grip. The crate fell heavily to the ground, breaking open a corner of the nailed-down lid.

"Damn it, Neal, I told you to be careful!"

"Sorry, Brock, it got away from me."

"Use your knife to pry it open the rest of the way, Dewey," Harper said.

Dewey used a long-bladed sheath knife to lever open the lid. It came undone with a shriek of pulled nails and a splintering of wood. Dewey threw back the lid, exposing the contents.

The crate was filled with brand-new repeating rifles.

The outlaws pressed inward, all avid, eager acquisitiveness. The prettiest young whore in the territory might have been stripped naked and sprawling before them, for all the oohs and aahs rising up from their number. A magical moment for the bad-men.

Brock Harper himself was not immune to the lure of the loot, the seductive siren call of that much prime lethal hardware laid out at his feet. The corners of his eyes and mouth turned up. He reached into the crate and hauled out a weapon, holding it up for all to see.

"Take a look, boys: one brand-spanking-new Henry repeating rifle. Twelve to a box, twelve boxes in all. With thousands of cartridges in some of the other crates. There's more massed firepower in that wagon than anywhere else on the frontier," Harper said.

"Now — what kind of hell do you think you can raise with that?!"

All of the outlaw band were appropriately enthused and excited. There were shouts of appreciation, roaring laughter, backslapping. Even Hap Englehard's sour-faced expression looked a little bit less funereal than usual.

Harper crowed, "What do I always say? — 'Trust Brock Harper.' Well, seeing is believing. When Harper tells you something is so, it's so! You can take it to the bank."

He paused for effect, then went on:

"I should say, you can take the bank — every bank in the Southwest! And every town those banks are in! Bust them wide open like ripe melons and rip out all the meat and juices until you've had your fill!"

That raised a cheer.

"You said a mouthful, Brock!"

"You're the bull of the woods, boss!"

"Sure called the tune on that one, Brock!"

Harper handed the rifle around so the others could examine it. It was passed from hand to hand, stroked with all the tenderness that none of these hard cases would ever expend on a lover. They fondled it possessively, caressing its smooth lines and well-wrought workings. When someone had held it for too long, the next in line was sure to demand his turn.

Dutchie Hiltz reached over the shoulders of some of the others, proffering a bottle of red whiskey. "Here go, Brock!"

Harper grabbed the bottle. It was one-third full. "Didn't leave me much did you, ya greedy bastards," he said.

"It's a wondernation that there's any left a-tall," Fenner said. His hat was back on his head.

Harper pulled the cork out with his teeth and spat it out. He upended the bottle, taking a long pull, gulping greedily, draining the bottle. Gripping the empty bottle by the neck, he flung it out high over the creek.

He drew his gun and fired, one lightning-fast move. The bottle exploded in midair, raining shards of broken glass into the water.

"Now that I have your attention," Harper said, "let's get back to work. There's plenty that needs doing. You've all had a chance to paw that gun. Now give it here. Come on, give it up!"

Groans and protests sounded from those complaining they hadn't had time to examine the goods.

"There'll be plenty of time for that later," Harper said. "Every mother's son of you will each get his own personal rifle at the share-up at the hideout, along with plenty of cartridges. I know you'll put them to good use!"

The rifle was passed hand over hand to Harper, who put it back in the crate from which it came. He closed the broken lid as best he could, hammering it into place with a thud from his club-like fist. "Load it back in the hopper," he said.

A couple of men hefted the crate into the wagon. The tailgate was closed, locked in place. The flap of the tarp was pulled down, covering the crates.

"We're taking the gun wagon to Ghost Canyon," Harper said. "Too bad we've got to travel by day but there's nothing for it but to do it. Those of you picked for the cleanup — you know who you are — will have to load the bodies on the flatbed wagon, cover 'em up, take them north into the hills and get rid of them. Then join us at the hideout.

"Kimbro! Fenner! We've got to get rid of these bluebelly duds, get them all gathered up for burning later. That's important. Make a clean sweep of it. Any scrap or rag of bluecoat is a ticket for a oneway ride to the gallows.

"Remember that, all of you — no mistakes! No slip-ups! Each must do his part

else all of us will have our heads in the
noose!

"Move!"

Six

Seven men stayed behind at Mace's Ford for the mopping up of the massacre site. Jeff Parr, one of Kimbro's sidemen, headed the crew. With him were Neal, Remy Ballew, Wilse, Gordy, Ralph and Dutchie Hiltz.

Brock Harper and the rest of the bunch were gone. They mounted up and rode out, taking with them the gun wagon and a string of horses that had belonged to the dead men. They went west on the trail and were soon lost from view.

The blood in the creek took care of itself. The current carried it away downstream, leaving no trace of the gore that had been spilled. That was the good thing about using the creek for a killing ground: it was self-cleaning.

The flatbed wagon which had been hidden around a bend in the woods trail now stood on the muddy creek bank near the bodies. The four-horse team harnessed to it was unnerved by the presence of blood and violent death. They snorted, pawing the ground. The handbrake on the wagon was set tight.

A wooden keg was stowed up front in the boot of the wagon. Handpainted red lettering identified its contents: GUNPOWDER.

"Move that black powder out of the way," Jeff Parr said. He was big, tough, stolid — a hard case. They were all hard cases, the outlaws of Harper's Raiders. Jeff was harder than most. He had brown hair and a brown beard and wore leather chaps and a gun on his left hip. He was a left-handed draw.

Neal hefted the keg with a grunt. "Where you want it?" he asked.

"Put it on top of that rock for now," Jeff said. "Out of the way where no damn fool can touch off the powder with a stray match or careless cigar butt."

Neal toted the keg to a grassy shoulder on the north side of the trail and set it on top of a flat-topped, waist-high boulder.

"That'll do," Jeff said.

Wilse pushed his hat forward and scratched the back of his head. "What's the gunpowder for?"

"You feel like digging a grave deep enough for all these bodies?" Jeff countered.

"Hell, no!"

78

"That's what the gunpowder is for. We take the bodies north into the hills, dump them in some ravine and blow it up, bringing the sides down on it."

"Huh. I get it," Wilse said. "Pretty good."

"The boss'll be glad to know it meets with your approval," Parr said. He addressed the others:

"You men start loading them bodies on the wagon. And be quick about it! We don't want to spend all day here. Not when the others'll be long back at the hideout eating up all the grub and drinking all the whiskey."

It was early afternoon, hot. There were a lot of bodies, twelve in all. They were dead weight and smelled bad. Fat black flies were starting to swarm them. The buzzing sounded loud as a sawmill.

Wilse stood at one end of the pile of bodies, the one nearest the wagon. "Somebody lend a hand here. I ain't gonna do it all by my lonesome."

Dutchie Hiltz took up a stance opposite Wilse at the head of the body. Wilse stooped down to take hold of the dead man's legs. His gun fell out of his holster to the ground. "Damn!"

He picked up the gun and wiped the mud off on the side of his pants. Holstering the sidearm, he fastened the rawhide loop over the top of the gun to keep it in place.

He and Dutchie picked up the corpse, Wilse holding it by the feet, Dutchie hooking his hands under the dead man's arms. Handling it like a heavy feed sack, they heaved the corpse up on to the flatbed wagon.

"I don't need no help, I can do it all by myself," Neal announced.

"What are you waiting for, applause? Get to it," Jeff said.

One of Neal's big hands grabbed a fistful of a dead man's shirtfront, the other gripping its belt at the middle. With a grunt Neal lifted and jerked, hefting the body off the ground and swinging it up and onto the flatbed, where it landed with a thud.

Gordy and Ralph slung-heaved a third body up on the wagon. Wilse and Dutchie returned to the corpse mound for another.

Remy Ballew stood around with his nose in the air and his arms folded across his chest. "You ain't working, Remy," Jeff said.

"Neither are you."

"I'm ramrodding this job."

Remy Ballew held up his hands in front of him, palms-out. They were white and smooth, uncallused. "I can't damage these," he said.

Somebody swore and another made a rude noise.

Ballew, sharp-eyed and sharp-featured, with what seemed to be a permanent sneer on his thin-lipped mouth, wore a black hat, black jeans, and a black leather gun belt with twin holstered .44s. The holsters were tied down. He fancied himself a gunslinger. He showed his hands palms-out, turning them over to display the backs of them, as if exhibiting them for admiration.

"These hands are my stock in trade. I can't risk anything that might affect the speed of my draw," he said.

Jeff Parr laughed, a harsh cawing noise. Remy's face colored. The back of his neck reddened. He was touchy.

"We all depend on our gun hands. What makes you so special?" Jeff asked.

"I'm fast," Remy said.

"Not that fast," Jeff said, resting a hand on his gun butt.

Remy thought it over, making quick calculations. He thought he was faster than Jeff, he was sure of it. Trouble was, Jeff didn't seem to share that surety. Remy toted up the pluses and minuses and reached a decision not to press the point.

He reached into the side pockets of his vest, pulling out a pair of wrist-length black leather riding gloves. He pulled them onto his hands. The gloves were thin, tight. He flexed his fingers in them.

He stood over a corpse. "I can't do it by myself."

"Help him out, Neal," Jeff Parr said.

"Okay," Neal said. He and Remy loaded the corpse on the flatbed, Remy huffing and puffing.

"Whew! This is hard work —"

"How would you know, Remy? You never did an honest day's work in your life," Jeff said.

"No, and this is a hell of a time to start!"

"It'll give you something to tell your grandkids. If you have any."

Most of the outlaws wore bandannas tied over their noses and mouths to mask the stink. They worked up a pretty good sweat loading the corpse cargo on the flatbed wagon. The more bodies that were loaded on the wagon, the harder the job got, because the flatbed filled up pretty quick and each successive body had to be thrown on top of an ever-higher pile.

Jeff eyed the results with a critical eye. "You're getting sloppy, men. Them deaders are all over the place. Soon as the wagon crosses a rough patch of ground, some'll start to fall off. Dress 'em up, there."

Gordy, a gangly, raggedy man out of Natchez, demanded, "What'd you get a flatbed for? It's no good for the job. You need something with a hopper to hold the load in place."

"That's the only wagon we could find to steal on the way over here," Jeff said.

"This is no work for honest outlaws, Jeff," Dutchie Hiltz complained.

"Quit bellyaching!"

The work got done. Jeff Parr circled the flatbed, studying it from different angles. "Tie 'em down with some rope so they don't fall off."

This was done.

"Best cover 'em up, too. Can't go traipsing around the countryside in broad daylight with a wagonload of corpses," Jeff said.

"Why not? Anybody sees us, it'll be their tough luck," Remy said. "We'll burn them down — what's another body more or less?"

Jeff thought there was some merit in that view, but since Remy had said it he was moved to take a contrary position. "No sense asking for trouble. We'll cover 'em with a horse blanket or two," he said.

This, too, was done. Blankets secured by ropes masked the flatbed's unsightly load. Mostly. A few hands and legs stuck out past the edges of the covering.

Remy Ballew went to the creek, hunkering down beside it. He took off his bandanna, dipped it in the water, and mopped his face with it. He rose, a flicker of motion on the other side of the ford catching his eye.

He whistled softly. "Get a load of this," he said

A rider was approaching the edge of the eastern bank. A lone rider on a gray horse.

Remy turned, calling to the others. "Somebody's coming!"

"How many?" Jeff Parr asked.

"One man, alone."

"One of ours?"

"No, a stranger."

"Too bad for him," Jeff said. "You boys know what to do."

Gordy said, "I'll get my rifle and drop him from here."

"Wait'll he crosses over and comes to us. That'll be one more for the pile," said Jeff. "Come back here, Remy, before he sees you and gets suspicious."

Remy joined the others in the shadows of the overgrown trail. He took off his gloves, pocketing them. He flexed his fingers, working some of the stiffness out, loosening them up.

The stranger on the gray crossed the ford, coming at a walk.

"He don't suspicion nothing," Gordy said, smirking.

The gray stepped out of the creek, climbing up on to the west bank, advancing several paces into the shade under the trees. The outlaws stood in a loose line across the trail, blocking it.

The stranger reined in. He blinked a couple of times; otherwise his face was utterly impassive, betraying no sign of surprise or alarm. He was a blond, blue-eyed giant.

The badmen's faces were cruel, mocking. Remy Ballew took it on himself to do the talking. He liked to run his mouth. "Hello, friend," he said.

"Howdy, gents," the stranger said. "This the road to Hangtree town?"

"A Yankee!" Gordy exclaimed. Some of the others laughed.

The stranger's eyes were restless, in constant motion scanning the scene. They took in the number and weaponry of those who faced him; the arms and legs protruding out from under the blankets covering the mound on the flatbed wagon; and, on top of a boulder, the wooden keg with the legend GUNPOWDER blazoned across it in red letters.

"The road to Hangtown? That depends, friend," Remy said.

"Depends on what?"

"On who you are."

"And who might you be?" the stranger asked, pleasantly enough.

"Us? Why, you might call us the toll keepers." Remy was playing to his compadres.

"Didn't know this was a toll road. What's the fare?"

"Your life," said Remy.

That got a laugh from some of the others. Not Jeff Parr, though. He was all business. "Cut the cat-and-mouse crud and get on with it," he said.

The stranger must have reached a similar conclusion. He struck first. His hand streaked to the pistol stuck butt-out in the top of his pants on his left side, drawing and firing it. He put two slugs into the keg of gunpowder.

A tremendous booming blast followed, as if a lightning bolt had suddenly emerged from out of the clear blue sky, smashing into the west bank with a thunderclap.

Earlier, Sam Heller had come southwest out of the hills across the plains to Swift Creek. His path struck the more northerly Mace's Ford rather than Flatbridge. That suited him fine. He preferred to make a

86

quiet entrance into the country by a round-about route, rather than approach Hang-town directly.

He'd neared the ford well after the carnage was over. Shadows hid the depths of the trail tunneling through the trees on the west bank.

One thing he could see from a long way off, though: buzzards circling high above the site. A half-dozen or so of them hung way up in the sky, black V shapes wheeling and soaring on the thermals. Hovering. Waiting.

Sam knew what that meant well enough — death. Buzzards have keen eyesight. They can sight dead meat from a long way off. They're scavengers, carrion eaters, shunning live prey in favor of the remains of another's fresh kill.

Their gathering over the west bank meant that there was something dead below. That they still remained aloft, rather than descending to feast on the remains, meant that the predator that had made the kill was still in place.

Sam decided to investigate, crossing the creek to the other side. The gray advanced steadily. It was a war horse, used to blood, violence and death through long exposure.

The clearing in the trees was full of all

three. Sam saw that it was thick with armed men, lurking back in the shadows. He made out seven of them. Gunmen. Outlaws. Cocky bastards, sure of themselves. A type he knew and didn't like.

He could feel the rage within him, ever-present just below the surface, begin to freeze into a ball of burning ice.

There were more of them than he expected, but he didn't find their numbers particularly daunting. He trusted to skill and nerve to see him through. And if not — what the hell?

The keg of gunpowder on top of a boulder decided him on his play. The stopper in its tophole indicated that it was full.

Sam took a mental picture of the layout, memorizing the positions of his foes relative to himself, the clearing and each other. He didn't wait for Remy to run out his taunting line. He stole a march on him and the others, taking the initiative.

He drew and put two balls of hot lead into the keg. Came a flash of blinding glare, intolerable heat, noise, pressure — a big boom!

Sam was ready for it, having already worked his booted feet clear of the stirrups. He threw himself off the saddle to the right.

Choking masses of gray-white smoke boiled through the clearing, veiling the scene. Sam hit the ground with a jarring thud, rolling to the side to avoid the horse's stamping hooves. He lay flat as debris rained down around him, tree-branches and boughs pelting the ground. The gun was still gripped in his hand. The blast left him temporarily half-deaf.

The smoke began to break up. Cries, shouts and shots erupted. Wild bursts of gunfire. The sounds were muffled in Sam's ringing ears, taking on a curious air of unreality.

Slugs speared through the smoke, zipping past. Somebody shrieked in pain, the cry suddenly choked off.

A voice — Jeff Parr's — shouted, "Stop firing, you blamed fools! You're only shooting each other —"

The smokescreen thinned, rifts appearing in the murk, showing glimpses of shadowy, indistinct figures stumbling around.

Sam rose, standing on one knee. He stuffed the gun in his belt and unlimbered the mule's-leg, holding it leveled with both hands. A gap opened in the gray-white billows. A figure stumbled forward, gun in hand, staggering blindly.

It was Wilse. Coughing, choking, waving

his arms in front of him, trying to clear away the smoke.

Sam saw him first. The sawed-off Winchester spat, a flat, cracking sound. Drilling Wilse with a center shot. Wilse screamed, falling, the gun skittering from his hand.

Not staying in the same place after firing, Sam rose into a crouch, moving a few paces forward and to the side.

Wilse rolled around on the ground, screaming. "Oh god I'm gut-shot! Somebody help —"

A breeze lifted, blowing masses of smoke east out of the clearing across the creek. The pall thinned, bringing more of the surroundings into view.

Ralph prowled around in a half-crouch, gun swinging from side to side in search of a target. Somebody — not Sam — cut loose, burning Ralph down.

"I got him!" the shooter crowed.

Jeff Parr shouted and stormed, trying to get his men to stop. "Hold your fire, you dumb sons of bitches!"

The smokescreen lifted, thinning, coming apart. Details came into view.

The blast had spooked the flatbed wagon team, sending them plunging west down the trail in an irresistible rush that tore the handbrake loose. They clattered out of sight into the distance, taking the cartload of corpses with them.

Strongman Neal had been standing near the gunpowder keg when it exploded. The blast picked him up and flung him aside. A tree got in the way. His limp, broken body lay draped around it.

One of the metal hoops that ringed the gunpowder keg, holding it together, had been turned by the blast into a white-hot streaking scythe. It hit Dutchie Hiltz in the head, taking off the top of his skull above the eyebrows.

Smoke drifted out, unveiling two outlined figures. They were on their feet, coughing, eyes tearing. Streamers and swirls of smoke drifted past them.

Remy and Gordy became aware of each other at the same time. They pivoted, leveling their guns on each other.

"Don't shoot!" That last came from Jeff Parr, who lay prone on the ground, gun in hand.

Remy and Gordy held their fire. Jeff rose to his feet. "Where's the stranger?" cried Remy.

"Damned if I know," Gordy said. "Maybe we got him —"

Sam Heller stepped into view a half-dozen paces away from the trio. They all saw each other at the same time.

Sam worked his gun, levering and firing, burning down Parr and Gordy. They spun as they were tagged, throwing their hands up in the air and falling backward. Their shots went wild.

Remy, quicker, got off two shots. One laid a hot line along Sam's left side; the other fetched him a stunning blow to the left shoulder, knocking him off-balance.

Recovering, Sam squeezed off another round, drilling Remy a few inches above the belt buckle. Remy fell.

Sam stood swaying, reeling. He spread his legs, planting his feet farther apart in an effort to stay on them. He looked around. The ground was strewn with debris and dead men. No one left to kill.

A hole in Sam's shoulder oozed warm redness that soaked his shirt with a fast-spreading stain. He felt light-headed. His vision swam in and out of focus. He missed his footing. The earth rushed up to meet him —

Blackness.

SEVEN

Johnny Cross and Luke Pettigrew came to Mace's Ford. Native sons both, they knew the country, knew that with Flatbridge out, the ford was the nearest way across Swift Creek.

The two men on the chestnut horse paused at the east bank of the ford. A thin film of smoke lay like a filter across the opposite bank, veiling the other side. Johnny sniffed the air. "Smell that, Luke? Gunpowder."

They crossed to the west bank, encountering a scene of death and destruction. Bodies littered the muddy ground. Combat veterans of some of the war's bloodiest battles, the two Texans were unfazed by the carnage.

Johnny Cross whistled soundlessly. Luke said, "Some shooting match!"

"More than a gunfight. Looks like a bomb

went off. You can smell the cordite in the air."

"They had themselves a party, all right. But who are they?"

"Beats me," Johnny said, shrugging. "You've been back longer than I have. Recognize 'em?"

"I don't know 'em from Adam," said Luke.

"Hold the reins, I want to take a look around." Johnny stepped down from the saddle and eyed the scene.

One of the fallen was apart from the others, off by himself over to one side of the clearing. He lay on his side with his back to Johnny, his legs together and bent at the knees. A handsome steel-dust horse stood beside him, its head down, nuzzling him. Nearby lay an unusual weapon, a sawed-off repeating rifle.

Johnny went to him, toeing the body. The man lay curled on his right side, a wide dark patch of blood staining his left shoulder and chest. His face was white.

"That gray's a good-looking animal," Luke said.

"This hombre don't need it no more." Johnny put a boot on the stranger's up-turned left hip and rolled him over on his back. He went down on one knee beside

94

him, reaching for the other's pockets to turn them out for valuables.

Click.

"Uh-oh," Johnny said.

"I heard that," said Luke, drawing the gun from his waistband and thumbing back the hammer.

Another *click*. Sounding identical to the first.

"Easy, Luke. Don't do nothing rash now."

"I got him covered, Johnny."

"He's got me covered," Johnny said.

Sam Heller's eyes were open. He held a pistol in his right hand. It had been hidden from view beneath him until Johnny rolled him over. A Navy Colt .36.

The clicking noise had come from when he thumbed the hammer back. The gun was pressed to Johnny's midsection. Sam's face showed signs of strain. He propped himself up on his elbows.

He'd passed out earlier from shock and loss of blood. The sound of the approaching horse splashing in the creek and the voices of two men woke him. He didn't know how long he'd been out. Not too long, though — the sun hadn't appreciably altered its position in the sky.

The mule's-leg was out of reach, and he wasn't sure he could wield it properly from down on the ground. His left arm wasn't working so good. While the newcomers were crossing the creek, Sam eased the the Navy Colt from where it had been stuck in his waistband, and half-rolled over on it, hiding it under him. He played dead until Johnny Cross knelt down beside him to pick his pockets. Movement started the wound in his shoulder bleeding again.

"Whoa," Johnny said. "My mistake."

"Don't make another, it could be fatal. Keep your hands where I can see them," said Sam. "Tell your friend not to get trigger-happy."

"Hear that, Luke?" Johnny called.

"Yup. I hear me a damned Yankee, too."

"No need to go into that now, Luke."

"Pull that trigger and you're a dead man, Yank."

"That ain't gonna do me much good, Luke," Johnny said. "I ain't looking for trouble, mister."

"You shouldn't have been looking in my pockets," Sam said.

"What good's money to a dead man? I thought you was dead."

"Well, I'm not," Sam said, voice husky through clenched teeth.

"Me and Luke were just riding through," said Johnny. "You should've kept going."

"I'm on my way, if that's okay with you."

"Vamoose."

"Mind taking that hogleg out of my belly first?"

Sam eased his gun hand back, pulling the muzzle away from where it had been pressing Johnny's midsection. Johnny rose slowly to his feet. Sam kept him covered with the gun.

"You look pretty bad hit, mister," Johnny said.

"Don't worry about it."

"It ain't you I'm worried about, it's me. You're kind of shaky. Wouldn't want that gun of yours to go off by mistake."

"If it does, it won't be a mistake."

"I'm gonna start walking toward my horse now so's I can ride out of here."

"Git."

Johnny turned his back to Sam and slowly started toward his horse, keeping his open hands in plain sight and away from his guns. Luke held the reins wrapped around his left hand as it gripped the top of the saddle horn to hold himself steady. His right hand held the gun pointed at Sam.

Johnny stepped around a dead body in his way and went to the chestnut. "Let that hammer down easy, Luke. I don't want you shooting me. That'd be a hell of a note," he said.

Luke uncocked the hammer and stuck the gun in the top of his pants. He moved back to make room and Johnny climbed up on the saddle. Johnny glanced back over his shoulder.

Sam sat upright, legs extended on the ground. He leaned forward, gun in hand, leveled on Johnny and Luke. Cold sweat misted his pale, haggard face but his gun held steady, without a tremor.

"If you don't mind my asking — what happened here?" Johnny asked, indicating the carnage.

"A little disagreement about the right of way," Sam said.

". . . We're riding out now."

"Nobody's stopping you."

"Maybe we'll meet again, stranger. If you pull through."

"I will."

"Then we'll meet again, be sure of it," Johnny said. He started the horse forward at a slow walk.

"Want to take him?" Luke said, under his breath.

"Let's not press our luck," Johnny said, low-voiced. "That's one ornery cuss. Take a lot of killing to put him down." They rode west along the trail, rounding a bend that put the stranger and the west bank clearing out of sight behind a screen of brush.

They came into view of a line of horses tied up to a hitching line strung between a couple of trees. These were the mounts belonging to the raiders who'd remained behind to clean up the massacre site. The explosion and gunfire had spooked them but the rope had held, preventing them from running away as the team pulling the corpse wagon had done. The animals were anxious, spooky, sidling and pawing the ground.

"You see what I see, Luke?"

"That's some mighty fine horseflesh."

"My thoughts exactly. They ain't doing those dead men back at the creek no good, neither," Johnny said. He swung down from the saddle. "You stay on my horse, Luke. Keep an eye out for that Yank."

"I'll do better than that." Luke shucked the carbine out of the saddle-scabbard and turned the chestnut to face back along the trail the way they came, toward the creek bank hidden behind the trees. "Sure you don't want to take that Billy Yank?" he asked.

"This is no time to go looking a gift horse in the mouth," Johnny said. A veteran horse thief, he got right down to business. Taking a clasp knife from his pocket, he unfolded a blade and began cutting loose the hitching-rope to which the line of horses was tied.

He mounted up on a fast-looking roan with good lines, securing one end of the rope to the saddle horn. The line stretched behind him, trailing a string of seven horses.

"We can switch horses later, Luke. Something damned funny happened here. Something big. Best we clear out of here pronto."

"Let's ride, Johnny."

They rode, taking the string of stolen horses with them, and were soon out of sight.

Sam Heller struggled to his feet, holding on to the gray's saddle for support.

Somewhere along the way he had holstered the mule's-leg and stuck the pistol in his waistband.

The gray turned its head toward him, regarding him with moist, dark, expressive eyes. Sam Heller stroked the gray's muzzle. "Good boy, Dusty. Didn't run out on me, did you? You're a good horse," he said.

It nuzzled him with its snout, almost knocking him down. Sam was shaky on his pins. His shirt stuck to his shoulder and chest due to dried blood. Blood that was not so dry trickled in warm rivulets down his front. The wound in his left shoulder was bleeding again. The shoulder was stiff, numb. His left side where a slug had creased it felt like a hot iron had been laid across it.

It had taken plenty for him to rise. Without Dusty standing there beside him to give him something to hold onto, he wouldn't have been able to stay upright. He might fall on his face yet. If he did, he might not get up. What strength he had left was pouring out of him fast.

Experimentally, he wriggled the fingers of his left hand. They seemed to work okay. He made a fist, opening and closing it. The bullet in his shoulder hadn't cut any nerves or tendons.

Something nagged at him, a sense of incompleteness. Something was missing — what?

His hand went to his head and he realized he was without his hat. It must have fallen off during the action. He looked around for it, spotting it a half-dozen paces away.

He guided the horse to it, walking beside the animal, holding on to the saddle. Clutching the stirrup, he hunkered down and picked up the hat.

He straightened up, a wave of dizziness washing over him, a torrent of darkness glittering with little colored lights. He held on to the saddle while the darkness passed, fading away as the scene faded in.

Sam pulled the hat down on his head. The Texas sun could be cruel to a bareheaded man. Besides, it was his hat and he wanted it. It had seen him through a lot of scrapes and across a lot of ground.

He had things to do, important things, but his top priority was to get back up on the horse while he still had the strength to do so. He climbed up into the saddle; a long, hard climb. It left him breathless and trembling. After a time the worst of it went away, but he was still weak.

Taking the mule's-leg in hand, he reloaded it with cartridges from the bandoliers crisscrossing his torso. Now he was ready for whatever might come at him. As ready as could be, under the circumstances. He holstered the weapon.

Sam Heller had been wounded a number of times in the past, both before and during the war. He knew that proper first aid often meant the difference between life and death. No medic, he, but he had a working knowledge of the necessities learned on the trail and battlefield.

He undid the bandanna knotted around

his neck and wiped his face with it, mopping up cold sweat. As soon as he wiped it clean, more fresh sweat oozed out to replace it.

Sam opened the top of his shirt, unbuttoning it, fingers feeling thick and clumsy. Gore plastered the garment to his flesh. He peeled back the fabric, freeing it. The entrance wound in his shoulder was an ugly puckered crater. No exit wound — the bullet was still in him.

A raw red furrow was plowed diagonally across his rib cage on the left side where Remy's first shot had creased him. It hurt like hell but wasn't as serious as the shoulder wound.

Folding the bandanna into a fat square, Sam placed it against the wound. He pressed down on it. Pain waves spasmed through the numbness, stabbing deep into the inside of his head. Blood soaked into the compress, wetting it, helping hold it plastered in place.

Sam leaned forward, fumbling open the top of his right-side saddlebag pouch, groping inside it. He pulled out a length of rawhide cord. He knotted a sliding loop in one end of the rawhide strand and stuck his left arm into it, drawing the loop up to his shoulder. Placing it so that it set across the bulge of the wadded bandanna compress, he pulled it tight, cinching it into place.

He wound the free end of the cord several more times around the shoulder to further secure the compress from slipping. He knotted it in place, careful not to make it so tight as to cut off circulation. No tourniquet, this. Lack of proper blood flow could also be damaging, leading to loss of the arm.

He checked the rig; it seemed crude but serviceable. Sam sipped some water from his canteen, washing out the inside of his mouth before swallowing. Shadows flitted across his face and eyes. He looked up.

The buzzards circling overhead were flying low.

Sam dug his heels into the horse's flanks and rode on. He continually scanned the walls of brush lining the trail, looking for lurkers, hand resting on the butt of the mule's-leg.

The trail plunged west through a half-mile of woods before breaking out into a stretch of wide, open country, rolling hills dotted with trees and brush. Sam paused at the treeline at wood's edge, surveying the scene. The vast, sprawling landscape seemed empty of any other humans. The hill country lay north, the plains south.

Sam rode into the open, out of the shade

into the hot sun. The openness increased his sense of vulnerability. He followed a course that minimized his exposure, leaving the trail to strike a zig-zag route/path that took advantage of what cover there was. He angled toward a stand of timber, a low mound, a rocky knob. He kept to the low-land, threading the washes and draws, avoiding crossing the ridges where possible.

Sam knew from previous studies of the map that the main trail west was the Old Mission Road. Hangtown lay to the south-west, more south than west, far from sight. Going to town was his best bet. He needed doctoring. Entering Hangtown in a weak-ened condition presented its own dangers, but it was still the best worst option.

He looked back at the woods between him and Swift Creek. The buzzards were slowly but surely descending on the west bank clearing he had quitted.

He didn't have to see the scene to know what would happen. The airborne scaven-gers would soon be at their work, touching down to begin the feast. The big birds would batten on the dead, bringing sharp, tearing beaks into play to rip and tear. Usually they went for the eyeballs first, pecking out the delicacies and gulping them whole. Left undisturbed, they wouldn't quit until the carcasses were stripped clean of every shred of flesh, leaving only gleaming white bones.

"Eat hearty, boys," Sam muttered.

He meandered southwest across the plains. This was the open range; no fences here to mark property lines. Streams and rivulets spilled south out of the hills to lace the prairie with winding silver veins. It was well-watered country, prime grazing land.

Clusters of quadrupeds dotted the landscape. Longhorn cattle by the hundreds, running free and wild. Weird-looking creatures with long faces and narrow sides. Sam kept his distance from them; they were ornery critters with no fear of man. The bulls sported horns spanning four feet across and more, with wickedly pointed tips.

In this land of vast vistas, distances seemed endless. No sign of town yet. The westering sun was bright and and blazing, but curling around the edges of the big sky lay boiling, bubbling darkness. The darkness was in Sam, light-headed from loss of blood.

His awareness drifted, fading in and out. A lurch of the horse jarred him, shaking him awake. He realized he'd been semi-conscious. That scared him.

In the distance, several hundred yards away, a many-legged black blur of motion swarmed down a long, low ride toward him.

Sam's eyes stung from sweat in them; he rubbed them to clear his vision. The many-legged blur resolved itself into a group of riders. About a dozen of them, maybe more.

The newcomers were ahead and to one side of him. They halted when they saw him. His course would take him past them so that they'd be fifty yards to the right.

They started downhill, swinging left to intercept him. Some of them shucked rifles out of scabbards. One shouldered a rifle to fire but was forestalled by a shouted command from another of the group.

Sam rode on, seemingly unconcerned, oblivious. Pounding hoofbeats neared.

The riders spread out in a wide arc to bar his way. They formed an inverted crescent, shaped like the horns of a bull.

Sam sighed, hoping he wouldn't have to fight his way through this bunch. He didn't have much left. It was all he could do just to stay in the saddle.

Nearing, he was able to make them out. They were Mexican-style vaqueros, decked out in widebrimmed sombreros, white shirts, bell-bottomed pants, brown leather chaps. Armed with six-guns and rifles. They reined in hard, their horses' hooves kicking up dirt as they halted a stone's throw away.

At the center of the crescent was the trim

figure of a woman. She was flanked by a shaggy-headed ogre and a gypsy with a gold earring.

The woman filled the field of Sam's vision. She was a beauty, with dark, flashing eyes and vivid red mouth. Full-bodied and long-legged. A black bolero hat was worn tilted rakishly to one side. Masses of inky blue-black hair were pinned up at the back of her head.

She wore a long-sleeved white blouse, black vest, black wrist-length gloves, black jeans and black leather riding boots. Vest and gun belt were trimmed with decorative silver conchos that sparkled and glinted in the sun.

The scene pulsed with shadows and light, the pulsing synchronized to the labored beating of Sam's heart. Was it love?

No. He'd run out of everything that had kept him going up to now. With his last flickering reserves of energy, he managed to lift an arm to courteously touch thumb and forefinger to his hat brim.

"Howdy, ma'am," he said. Her face was as impassive as that of a carved stone idol.

Sam slid sideways off his horse. The ground rushed up to meet him, fetching him a terrific jarring blow.

He lay on his back on the ground, as if at

the bottom of a deep well. At the top was a blue disk of sky.

The well shaft resolved itself into a circle of bodies surrounding him, hemming him in. Looking down at him. Faces were featureless orbs floating high above, impossibly distant.

Blackness returned, swallowing up Sam Heller.

EIGHT

Long shadows of late afternoon were falling across the landscape when Johnny Cross came in sight of the Cross family spread.

Johnny lay prone at the top of a ridge several hundred yards east of the ranch. It was in his nature to look before leaping. Growing up on a frontier plagued by outlaws and warlike Indians will do that, if one wants to live to grow up at all. Subsequent years of war and outlawry had only confirmed him in the habit of caution. He rarely came at a thing directly, preferring to approach it sideways — a trait that promotes longevity.

Luke was down at the foot of the ridge, minding the string of stolen horses. Johnny had dismounted and climbed to the top of the rise for a looksee. He was careful not to show himself above the crest; a skylined figure could be seen from a long way off.

He now set eyes on the family homestead

for the first time in over five years, since the day he had ridden off to go to war.

The Edwards plateau came down from the northeast, slanting southwest across the plains to intersect the Broken Hills. The Broken Hills, commonly known as the Breaks, was a belt of rough country, a rocky rampart stretching north-south for many a mile. The Breaks was a maze of hills, ravines, gullies, valleys.

The Cross spread was the westernmost ranch in Hangtree County. It stood midway between the Old Mission Road in the north and Hangtown Trail in the south. It sat on a flat covered with green grass at the foot of the Breaks, near the eastern mouth of Wild Horse Gulch. A stream ran through the property, splashing and sparkling.

The lowering sun grazed the western hills, casting long shadows across the plains. Blue-gray gloom pooled at the foothills, creeping east across the land.

A rocky spur thrust out into the range. At its tip rose a a moundlike hill with a jagged top. The ranch house nestled at the base of the hill. It was a flat-roofed, square-walled blockhouse.

A line of smoke rose not from within, but from somewhere near it. Human figures moved around in the yard in front of the house. They were too far away for Johnny to make out any details.

Whoever they were, they weren't Crosses. Johnny was the last of the family. He went downhill and got on his horse.

"What's up?" asked Luke.

"Somebody's home," Johnny said. "Any idea who?"

"Nope. I ain't been out this way since I came back home last fall. I'll tell you this, though: chances are it's a bunch of no-goods. The Breaks was always wild but it's outlaw country now. They make their hide-outs there and raid out on the plains."

"Squatters or outlaws, they're on Cross land."

"What're you fixing to do, Johnny?"

"Serve notice on 'em — it's moving day."

"How many are they?"

"I don't know, I couldn't make out much detail."

"Well, what's the plan?"

"We'll circle north into the Breaks, swing around and come out of the gulch."

Johnny and Luke had come down from the north, turning left off Old Mission Road and riding south below the ridge for cover. Now they partially retraced their route, pointing north along the ridge trail. They rode at a slow pace, almost a walk, to avoid having their string of horses kick up a dust cloud that would alert those at the ranch to their presence.

The ridge broke up into a line of low hills. The duo turned left, riding west through a gap to emerge on the plains at a point where the hill with the jagged top stood between them and the ranch house, screening them. They crossed a long open stretch to the foot of the Breaks. They saw no one from the ranch and were apparently undetected.

What looked like a solid rock wall from a distance became a jumble of hills, ridges, ravines, arroyos, boulders, knobs and stone needles. This was home turf to Johnny Cross, who'd spent countless boyhood hours ranging the Breaks and making it his. He'd roamed its myriad hills and ways, searching for stray cattle, seeking wild mustangs, hunting the game trails.

The terrain was unchanged from the way he'd remembered it. People come and go, the works of man fall into ruin, but the land abides.

He and Luke entered a ravine, one of many feeder routes through the hills into Wild Horse Gulch. The cut was thick with shadow, the sun hidden behind the hills. The path wound west, then south, opening into the gulch. The gulch was an oval valley comprising many square miles of well-watered grassland ringed by rock walls. Many smaller ravines and gullies fed into it. It was home to several hundred wild horses.

Johnny and Luke swung east, making for a gap opening on to the plains. The setting sun was at their backs. Nearing the gap, they reined in to make some final preparations.

Johnny reached into a saddlebag and took out a pair of gun belts, each carrying a holstered gun. He fitted them on over his shoulders, so the guns hung butt-out under his arms.

Luke's eyes bulged, staring. "Damn, Johnny, how many guns you got?"

"Never enough," Johnny said, "but these should do for now. Back with Quantrill, we never went on a raid with less'n six guns each." He dipped into another saddlebag and brought out two more revolvers. "Take these, Luke. You want to make sure you're dressed for the party."

Luke hesitated. "I'd just as soon use the carbine, if you can spare it. I'm a better hand with a long gun than a pistol."

"Suit yourself." Johnny shucked the carbine out of the scabbard and handed it to Luke.

"Much obliged," Luke said.

"Take another six-gun, might come in handy."

"All right." Luke took the pistol. He already had a gun stuck in the top of his pants, so he stuffed the second in the side pocket of his Confederate gray tunic. "What about the horses?" he asked.

"We'll picket the string here and come back for them later," Johnny said. A cleft in the rocks about ten feet wide and fifteen feet deep served as a place to pen the spare horses, who were hitched and hobbled to keep them from straying.

Darkness was drawing in when Johnny and Luke rode side by side out of the gap, east onto the flat. The sunset was a bright red band slashing across the western horizon. Gaps in the rock wall allowed shafts of lurid red light to pour out of the mouth of Wild Horse Gulch.

The two riders were black outlines against a red sky. Dusky gloom settled on the flat, pierced by red beams fanning out across the plains.

The Cross ranch was near the mouth of the gulch. Firelight showed in front of the ranch house.

Even in the best of times, the ranch was only marginally a going proposition. The

Cross family had barely been able to eke out a subsistence living from the property. It was a threadbare patch of civilization on the edge of a howling wilderness. Nobody settled in the Breaks. The broken land was the haunt of Indian war parties, outlaws, and bandits up from Mexico. Apparently it had only gotten worse since the war.

The ranch house was a stone-walled cube, a single-room structure with a flat timbered roof and dirt floor. It fronted south, its rear wall butted up against the side of the jagged-topped hill, protecting against attack from that direction. It was built as a strong-point, with thick stone walls, a massive door and windows with thick wooden shutters. Strategically placed gunports and loopholes dotted the walls. The roof was covered with blocks of sod to guard against Indian fire arrows.

That was then. Johnny was the last living member of the immediate family, and at the time he'd gone off to war, the scant remaining livestock had been sold off and the ranch abandoned to time and the elements. Now, much of the spread had gone to ruin. The barn was a mound of charred timbers and an ash heap. The ranch house was a gutted shell. Its timbered roof had collapsed, opening it to the sky. Windows were blank, gaping square holes. No door remained, only an empty doorway. A platform boardwalk fronting the house was a litter of broken planks and beams. The yard was littered with empty whiskey bottles and other trash.

The one part of the homestead that was in decent shape was the corral. The wooden rail fence had been patched up and repaired. Penned inside it were eight to ten good horses.

The squatters were gathered in the yard between the house and the corral. In the center of the space was a campfire. Firelight stood out in the gathering gloom. Overhead, the sky was going from a colorless void to deepening dark.

Johnny and Luke rode in, making for the fire. It blazed in a shallow pit ringed by large, round stones. The gutted, headless carcass of a freshly butchered longhorn hung on a spit roasting over the flames. The air was filled with good food smells that made Luke's mouth water and his belly rumble.

Three men were grouped around the fire, two more stood leaning with their backs against the corral's wooden rail fence. They were loafing and idling, eating, drinking, smoking and talking. Violent, profane men, talking loud, bragging big. They hadn't even bothered to set a sentry, Johnny noticed. Bunch of damned fools, he thought.

The newcomers got pretty close before being noticed. One of the squatters caught sight of them and called out to the others. Heads turned toward the intruders as if swivel-mounted with a single control. Their chatter faded away into silence.

The riders neared, their horses coming steadily at a slow, deliberate walk. Sunset had settled into a single red razorline streak across the western horizon. The Evening Star glimmered in the darkling sky.

One of the men at the fire stood holding a rifle stretched horizontally across the back of his shoulders, bent arms raised with hands clutching the piece. He was bare from the waist up, with a solidly muscled torso and brawny arms. A single decorative eagle's feather was stuck in the hatband of his hat; a second, similar feather was secured to the muzzle of his rifle by a length of rawhide. He started forward, swinging the rifle down along his side.

One of the loafers by the corral reached for a rifle that stood beside him, leaning upright against the fence. All the squatters were armed with six-guns; several wore braces of pistols.

Johnny and Luke reined in a few paces away from the group. They were outside the circle of firelight, their faces shadowed. Johnny's hands rested on the pommel of his saddle horn. Luke held the carbine to one side across the front of the saddle.

The man with the feather in his hat stepped forward, the others falling in in a loose line behind him.

"Psst! That's the bunch that jumped me!" Luke said, in a stage whisper.

"Wait for me to get the ball rolling," said Johnny, smiling.

The man with a feather in his hat raised his left hand in casual greeting. When he opened his mouth to speak, firelight glinted off a gold front tooth. "Howdy, boys. What's new at the hideout?"

"Evening, Monty," Johnny said.

Monty thrust his head forward, squinting up at Johnny, trying to make out his face in the dimness. "Do I know you?" he asked.

"I'm Johnny Cross."

"Never heard of you," Monty said.

"This's Cross land you're on."

"What of it?"

"Monty, look!" one of the men said, pointing at Luke. "It's the cripple!"

Monty turned his attention from Johnny to Luke, staring at him. "Why, so it is . . .

119

Well, I'll be damned! Talk about someone who don't know to leave well enough alone — !"

Monty stroked his chin, marveling. "You sure must have a hard head. I thought I busted your skull wide open. What do you want, crip?"

"I come to even up," Luke said, tightly.

"Forget it — you ain't got a leg to stand on." Monty guffawed, glancing back at his sidemen. "Get it, boys? He-ain't-got-a-leg-to-stand-on, haw haw!"

Luke swung the carbine toward Monty. Monty was ready for it. He dropped into a crouch, pointing his rifle at Luke. His sidemen reached for their guns —

While everybody else was reaching and getting set, Johnny Cross went into action. He drew. Fast.

One instant his folded hands rested on top of the saddle horn. An eyeblink later, both guns were in his hands. He opened up, guns blazing, his face underlit by muzzle-flares.

Most shooters find a horse's back an unstable platform for shooting, compared to having both feet on solid ground. Not Johnny Cross. Years of riding and raiding with Quantrill made the technique second-nature to him. Gunshots hammered as if they were being ground out by a mill with machinelike precision. The chestnut horse danced a little, just a little, with no effect on the accuracy of Johnny's shooting.

Twin streams of lead burned down Monty and his gang. Monty was the first to fall, the others dropping in rapid-fire succession. Few of them lived long enough for their guns to clear the holster.

Shots, shouts, shrieks — bodies whirling, flailing, and flopping to the ground. Sudden silence.

Smoke curled from the muzzles of Johnny Cross's guns. The chestnut pawed the earth, sidling a bit. Johnny holstered one gun, freeing a hand to take up the reins. Luke sat stupefied in the saddle, slack-jawed, and with mouth gaping.

Two of the fallen stirred in the dirt, moaning and groaning. Johnny fired twice. The two stopped thrashing and lay still. Dead still.

It was done. Johnny hadn't even needed the pair of guns shouldered under his arms. Luke's mouth opened wider.

"You're catching flies, hoss," Johnny said.

Luke's jaws closed with an audible click, only to open them again to exclaim: "Damn, that was fast!"

Johnny shrugged, smiling with his lips.

"I didn't even have time to shoot," Luke said. "Damn it, I wanted to get Monty myself!"

"Sorry," Johnny said, looking sheepish. "Once I start shooting it's hard to stop. Force of habit, I reckon."

"Well, what's done is done," Luke grudgingly allowed.

Johnny stepped down from his horse, walking it to the corral and hitching it to the top rail of the fence. He went to the campfire, where the savory beef carcass was roasting on a spit. "Smells good," he said. "Tonight we feast."

Luke got down off his horse, no easy process for the one-legged veteran. He was aided by the tremendous upper body strength he'd developed after a year of getting around on crutches. Placing both hands on the saddle horn, he lifted himself out of the saddle and got down on the horse's right-hand side.

He loosed the tree-branch crutch where he'd fastened it to the saddle flap above the scabbard where he'd sheathed the carbine. Wedging the crutch under his left arm, he planted himself firmly on solid ground while hitching the horse to the rail.

Luke limped over to join Johnny at the campfire. The beef carcass was nicely roasted, fat dripping from the seared flesh to fall on the hot embers of mesquite firewood, each droplet vaporizing in a hissing puff of smoke. Luke's mouth watered.

"It's chow time," Johnny said. "If we look hard enough I'm sure we can find a whiskey bottle or ten to wash down the grub."

"It was all I could do to keep from tripping over the empties," said Luke. "Loan me your pocket knife."

Johnny handed it over. Luke went to Monty's body and sat down on the ground beside it. Luke unfolded the jackknife, opening the blade.

"What're you fixing to do, Luke?"

"Some dental work." Luke pried open Monty's jaws and set to work with the knife. A moment's labor and he was done. He gripped his prize between thumb and forefinger, holding it up to the firelight: Monty's gold tooth. Solid gold, too.

"I promised myself I was gonna make a watch fob out of that gold tooth of his. Now all I got to do is get me a watch," Luke said.

"Mebbe you'll find one on one of the deaders," suggested Johnny.

"I'll look later. Right now I got to get me some food. Only thing I et in the last day and a night and a day was that beef jerky of yours."

Luke pocketed the gold tooth. He unfolded the knife and put it away. He put his hands flat on the ground and rose to his knees — his left leg had been taken off below the knee. He got the crutch under his left arm, bracing it into the ground at an angle. He straightened out his right leg, pushing up at the same time until he was standing upright.

He went to the campfire.

"Didn't you say something about coming back home for some peace and quiet?" asked Luke.

"It's peaceful enough now."

"Welcome home, Johnny."

"It's the kind of homecoming I should have expected — with gunfire," Johnny Cross said, looking around at the dead bodies sprawled on the ground.

"And you know, Luke, that suits me just fine," he added.

The ranch house was a wreck, a hollowed-out shell of a ruin. The inside was filled with the rubble of the collapsed timber roof. The structure was probably a haunt for snakes, but Johnny and Luke had no intention of finding out tonight.

Johnny's bedroll was tied behind his saddle and Monty's gang had left plenty of blankets behind. Johnny and Luke made up their bedding beside the campfire. The corpses had been dragged off to one side, downwind and out of the way.

Monty's gang had left behind plenty of whiskey, too, including an unopened case. Johnny and Luke each took a bottle with them as they sacked out on their makeshift beds on the ground near the fire. A stack of firewood, enough to keep the blaze alive throughout the night, was heaped up beside the fire.

After filling their bellies with loads of barbecued beef washed down with red whiskey — a real Texas meal — Johnny and Luke had gone back to the mouth of Wild Horse Gulch to fetch the string of horses from Mace's Ford. The animals now resided in the corral, adding their numbers to the ten horses penned there by Monty's group.

Now, Johnny and Luke lay stretched out by the fire, heads propped up on saddles serving for pillows as they smoked Johnny's long, thin cigars and sipped whiskey. Their guns were right at hand.

A purple-black sky was speckled with stars that glittered like diamond dust. A waxing, bone-white half-moon hung at the zenith. As was the way in early Texas spring, the day had been hot but the night was cool.

The campfire warded off the chill. Flames crackled, embers occasionally popping.

Luke puffed on a cigar, thoughtful. "We should've searched them bodies. Thieving bunch like this probably got some money laid by," he said. "Lord knows honest folk ain't got a pot to piss in nowadays."

"I'm too full of meat and redeye to move. Tuckered out, too. We'll search 'em tomorrow — they ain't going nowhere," Johnny said.

"Not unless coyotes git 'em and drag 'em away."

"Fire'll keep the coyotes off."

"I dunno, they's bold rascals," Luke said. He drank some whiskey. "I feel bad that I didn't fire a shot tonight. I was about as useful in the showdown as teats on a boar hog."

"Don't vex yourself. From the looks of things in Hangtree County, there's plenty of hombres who need killing," said Johnny.

"Ain't that the truth."

"Maybe we'll tie into some sooner than you think."

"How so?"

"You catch how Monty said something about 'the hideout'? That was right before one of his boys recognized you and things started getting hot."

Luke sat up. "Now that you mention it, I do recollect him saying something along those lines. I forgot about it till now."

"They saw us riding out of the gulch, so the hideout must be out there in the Breaks," Johnny said.

"You could hide an army in there."

"Mebbe somebody has. We was able to come up so close on Monty's bunch because they thought we were part of the same outfit, whoever that might be. By the time they knew different, it was too late."

Luke nodded. "Makes sense."

"Others from that outfit must be in the habit of riding back and forth between the hideout and here," Johnny said. "We'd best sleep light in case some come by."

"Okay by me. I don't sleep too good anyhow, what with the pain in my stump," said Luke. "Come sunup we can make tracks for my place, if you're of a mind to. Stay as long as you like."

"Much obliged, Luke, but I believe I'll stick. This old place ain't much but it's mine and nobody takes what belongs to Johnny Cross."

Luke nodded. "Figured you'd say that. If you need somebody to cover your back, count me in."

Johnny laughed. "And I figured you'd say that."

"Hell, this peacetime thing ain't working out too good for me anyway."

"Glad to have you aboard, partner."

"Let's drink on it."

They clinked whiskey bottles together in a toast and drank. Drank deep. Somewhere in the darkness, a coyote howled.

NINE

Torture!

Sam Heller lay stretched out across a long wooden table while a raven-haired beauty worked on him with knives and sharp-pointed instruments. A gang of men held him down. He lay spread-eagled on his back, bare from the waist up. The men gripped his limbs, pinning him to the table.

It was a struggle. Sam was big and strong, and even in his weakened condition he was a handful. A couple of times he came close to throwing them all off and breaking loose.

He was drunk, too. The better part of a bottle of tequila had been poured down his throat. It burned in his veins, belly and brain. Frontier anaesthesia.

Sam was already off his head thanks to his wound, feverish and delirious. The treatment he was getting didn't help any. It was a living nightmare.

He was in a white room: white walls, white

ceiling. One white wall held a tall oblong that was a deep-set window opening on a night-black sky. Above were wooden rafter beams, black-brown, dark with age and smoke. A wheel of light hung from the ceiling. A wagon wheel, suspended by a rig of black iron chains. It had been turned into a kind of chandelier by attaching lamps at fixed intervals along the rim.

The men holding Sam down were of Mexican descent, vaqueros. The woman looked Mexican, too.

Standing at the head of the table, leaning over it, looming large, was an ogre. He stood behind Sam's head, pawlike hands gripping Sam's shoulders on either side of his neck, pinning them down to the table. His face was upside-down from Sam's point of view, adding to its grotesqueness and distortion.

The ogre was a fat hulk — hard fat — with shaggy, curly gray hair, dark eyes, and a straggly iron-gray beard. He was grinning.

The vaquero holding down Sam's right arm had dark, almond-shaped China eyes in a nut-brown, clean-shaven face. A golden ring pierced his left ear. He looked like a pirate, a Gypsy pirate. A pirate Gypsy.

The ogre, the Gypsy — Sam remembered seeing them riding with the bunch who'd swept down on him on the plains before he'd blacked out.

The other men holding down Sam's left arm and legs had black hair, brown skin, strong hands. Vaqueros, too, no doubt. They might have been part of the bunch that rode him down, but he had no specific memory of them.

Two women stood at the table, a knife-wielder and a lamp-holder. The knife-wielder had ridden at the head of the vaquero band. No forgetting her! — not even in fever dreams fanned by tequila drunkenness.

Temptress: golden skin, dark liquid-orb eyes, high cheekbones, a hawklike nose and a ripe, red-lipped slash of a mouth. The face of an angel for Satan and a body to match.

She wore a white blouse and tight black pants. Her sleeves were rolled up above her elbows, baring her arms below. The top buttons of her blouse were open, showing a golden V of flesh and a tantalizing glimpse of the soft fullness of the tops of her breasts each time she leaned over Sam to resume work on him.

She held a long, thin, sharp-pointed instrument that looked like something between a stiletto and a silver knitting needle. It glittered and glinted in the lamp-light.

She worked the needle point into the puckered bullet-wound in Sam's left shoulder, digging, probing.

Her face was carefully composed, neutral, showing only intense concentration on her work. Sometimes she leaned in so close that Sam could feel her breath on his face. It was warm, sweet-smelling.

Standing behind and to one side of her was an aged crone: small, shriveled, almost sexless. She was white-haired, her face a nest of wrinkles, with a wide, flat nose and lipless, toothless mouth. Black marble eyes were shiny and alert. A living mummy.

In one hand she held a lamp, a tin candle-holder with a thin, round disk of shiny, polished metal behind the candle flame. The disk was a reflector, focusing the candlelight and beaming it in a ray of brightness that shone on Sam's wound. Despite her appearance of extreme age, her hand remained motionless, holding the lamp in place without twitch or tremor.

Sam Heller had a head full of fire and a body full of pain. The tequila heightened the derangement of his senses. A node of pulsing awareness in some corner of his brain remembered the beauty's voice murmuring, "It will ease your pain, gringo," as the tequila was being poured down his throat earlier.

His vision swam; above, the lights on the suspended wagon wheel fixture rushed toward him and receded away from him.

His body was taut, rigid; each muscle, vein and tendon of his powerfully built physique standing out in bold relief. His upper body was marked by old wounds: knife scars, a scattering of raised, clawlike burn streaks, and several nasty-looking dimples in the flesh that were long-healed bullet-holes. The planked wooden tabletop was slick with his blood and sweat.

The vaqueros holding Sam down were enjoying the show. It was something different, a break in the routine. It was interesting to watch the gringo suffer and see how much he could take; amusing, too. They were hard men steeped in strength, tenacity, the ability to endure pain; they appreciated those qualities in others. They watched the spectacle avidly, faces intent with cruel relish.

All but the Gypsy. His features were composed, masklike, except for alert, dark eyes; his emotions unreadable.

Sam was determined not to give his tormentors the satisfaction of seeing him suffer or hearing him cry out. His frozen face was a grimace of silent pain, breath hissing through clenched teeth. The hissing in-creased in volume as the probe went deeper. The point touched a nerve or something.

Sam spasmed, thrashing around on the table. At a few words of command from the beauty, the men holding him down tight-ened their grip, immobilizing him.

"Ah," the woman said. She withdrew the probe. Its absence brought Sam blessed relief, a release from his writhings on the white-hot griddle of agony. The respite was short-lived.

The raven-haired woman took up a long, thin needle-nosed instrument resembling an oversized pair of tweezers about twelve inches long. It smelled of the tequila which had been poured on to disinfect it.

The woman rested her free hand on the bare flesh surrounding the wound to steady Sam. She worked the tips of the tweezers into the ugly punctured crater of the bullet-hole, cold steel burrowing into living flesh.

She dug deep, twisting and probing for what seemed like an eternity. Finding what she was looking for, she battened the grip-ping jaws around the object and retracted the instrument. Generating a supreme high note of pain as it stretched and mauled tortured nerves.

It popped free from Sam's flesh, bearing

its prize with it. Clutched by twin tips of the tweezer-like instrument was a shapeless lump of lead trailing bloody tendrils of tissue. The woman held it in front of Sam's face. A number of hammering heartbeats passed before his pain-dulled eyes focused on the object.

"The bullet, *hombre*," she said.

Sam's nod of recognition was almost but not quite imperceptible. In a husky, rasping breath he manged to gasp, *"Gracias . . ."*

He didn't hear the metallic chinking sound as the bullet was dropped into a tin cup. He had passed out.

The woman who'd dug the bullet out of Sam straightened up, stretching. The muscles in the back of her neck, shoulders and upper back were stiff from tension. She put her palms at the small of her narrow-waisted back and leaned backward, stretching to work some of the kinks out.

Her name was Lorena Castillo. "You men can take a break but stay where I can find you later. I'll need you to move the gringo after I've finished cleaning the wound and stitching him up," she said.

The vaqueros grouped around the table nodded, several saying, *"Sí, Señora."* They went to the door, opening it and filing outside for a stretch and a smoke. They spoke among themselves:

"The gringo took it well, no?"

"For a gringo."

"Bah, he's drunk."

"You get drunk and see if you can stand it."

"I would like to get drunk, *sí.*"

"The gringo is *duro,* tough. *Muy hombre.*"

"We will see," said the ogre with shaggy gray hair, breaking his silence to join the conversation. His name was Hector Vasquez, the ramrod of Rancho Grande.

Inside, the withered crone was at Lorena's side, handing her a square of fresh white linen. Lorena said, "Thank you, Alma."

"It is nothing, my lady," said the old one.

Lorena used the linen to blot some of the sweat off her face. They were in a workroom of a storehouse at the Castillo ranch, Rancho Grande. The structure was a thick-walled one-story rectangle, square-edged, flat-roofed, its stone-and-timber walls plastered with stucco and whitewashed.

A polite knocking sounded on the outside of the door through which the vaqueros had exited into the plaza. One of the vaqueros stuck his head inside. "Señora Lorena? Don Eduardo is outside. He wishes a word with you," he said.

"Tell him that I will be there in a moment, after I have washed up. I would not come to him with blood on my hands," Lorena said.

"*Sí, Señora.*" The vaquero stuck his head back outside, easing the door shut.

"Though bloody hands are nothing new to the *padrone*," Lorena said when the messenger was gone.

Alma pursed her lips, her only reaction to the comment. She stood next to a side table on whose top sat a washbasin and a pitcher of water. Lorena went to it, stood facing the basin. Alma poured water over her mistress's hands into the basin. Lorena made brisk handwashing motions. The water filling the washbasin took on a red tinge.

Hands clean, Lorena dried them with a towel handed to her by Alma.

"Clean the gringo's wound, Alma. I will return presently to finish stitching it up in a moment," Lorena said.

Alma nodded.

Lorena crossed to the door, opening it, and stepped out into the night. The vaqueros who'd been holding the gringo down stood at the corner of the storehouse, smoking and talking in low voices. They fell silent until Lorena was out of earshot.

She crossed the plaza toward the hacienda of the Rancho Grande, one of the largest and oldest established ranches in Hangtree County, Texas. Or in this part of the state, for that matter.

It occupied many acres of prime grazing land bordered on the north by the foot of the Edwards plateau, the east by Swift Creek, the south by the upper branch of the Liberty River, and the west by a tributary stream that came down from the plateau to join that same upper branch of the Liberty.

This had been Mexican land when first settled by the Castillos a hundred and twenty-five years ago, given to them as a land grant by the king of Spain's imperial viceroy in Mexico City and registered in the Royal Archives in Madrid. A proud and ancient line, the Castillos.

The plaza was a wide, unpaved circular space ringed by the storehouse, the bunkhouse for the unmarried vaqueros, a mess hall where the men ate, and similar structures. At its center was a fountain and basin.

Dominating the space from the north end was the hacienda, a fortified Spanish Colonial–style mansion housing Don Eduardo Castillo, his family and servants. A two-story building that fronted south, it had a ceramic-tiled peaked roof and a hulking, thick-walled construction that had successfully repeated assaults by Indians, bandits and marauders over the decades. Its imposing white bulk gleamed in the moonlight. It was trimmed with ornate black iron grillwork.

Lorena entered through the high, arched portal of the front double doors, crossing the tiled floor of the entryway and passing under an archway into the Great Hall.

The hall was long, with a lofty ceiling. It was centered by a long banquet table with chairs. On the right-hand side, a long wall was lined with portraits of Castillo forebears and distinguished ancestors. Some of the paintings were several hundred years old and had been brought over from Spain.

The opposite wall was lined by tall, narrow windows that opened on a western view. The windows were each hung with a double set of dark, iron-banded wooden shutters several inches thick, thick enough to stop bullets. The shutters were now open and folded back against tan stucco walls, framing the windows like pairs of dark wings. The walls between the windows were decorated with religious-themed paintings and carved wooden statues of various saints.

At the opposite end of the hall was a stone fireplace big enough for a grown man to step into without bowing his head. It could hold a blaze mighty enough to heat every inch of the spacious room, but tonight only a modest-sized fire was laid there, sufficient to heat that end of the hall. Several throne-like armchairs were grouped around the hearth.

The fireplace was flanked by a pair of suits of antique armor worn by the conquista-dors, complete from helmeted head to iron-booted toe. Armatures inside the suits held them upright. On the wall above the top of the fireplace was mounted a crossed pair of spear-bladed lances. The lances bore ban-ners, one the flag of Spain and the other bearing the Castillo coat of arms.

A man stood facing the fireplace, holding a pumpkin goblet of brandy in both hands. He gazed into the glass in a kind of medita-tive reverie, watching the serpents of fire curling around the blazing hearth logs through the medium of rich, reddish-brown brandy in the cut-crystal goblet. Hearing Lorena approach, he turned to face her.

He was Don Eduardo, patriarch of the House of Castillo, *padrone* of Rancho Grande, and Lorena's father-in-law. She'd been married to his first-born son Ramon, dead these last seven years.

Now in his mid-sixties, Don Eduardo remained every inch the aristocrat, ever-aware of that status. Pride of rank and

140

heritage of blood showed in his straight-backed, stiff-necked stance, in the aura of command stamped on the features of his face.

Tall, slim, with a full head of silver-gray hair, he had a long sharp-featured face, hooded brown eyes, and a neatly trimmed salt-and-pepper mustache and goatee. Somber black clothes contrasted with a white ruffled shirtfront.

He gave the impression of a man of strong passions held tightly in check. His eyes glared, the lips of his downturned mouth were tightly pressed. The woman halted a few paces away, facing him.

"Lorena, have you gone mad?" he demanded.

"And a very good evening to you too, Don Eduardo," she said lightly. "Greetings on your return. I hope your cattle-buying trip met with success."

Don Eduardo had been away from the ranch on an overnight trip east to Palo Pinto County, to examine some blooded stock being offered for sale by a rancher there. An escort of some of his most formidable pistoleros had guarded him against the dangers of the overland trip. He'd returned to Rancho Grande little more than an hour ago.

"My concern is what has happened during my absence," he said. "Diego told me what you have been up to."

"He would," Lorena said, her upper lip curling. Diego was the *padrone*'s younger son, long a grown man.

"Never mind about that," Don Eduardo said. "I know there is no love lost between you and your brother-in-law. That disturbs me, but there is nothing to be done about it. At least Diego keeps me informed about matters of vital importance to this ranch."

"Of that I am sure," Lorena said dryly.

"Have you taken leave of your senses, bringing some filthy gringo onto my land, sheltering him under my roof?!"

"Not so filthy. He has a nice face, for a gringo," Lorena said. "And he is not under your roof. I had him put not in the hacienda but in the storehouse."

"Bah! They are all my roofs, they all belong to me. You know how I feel about these accursed Tejanos, these self-styled Texans. They are a blight on the land, a biblical plague. Usurpers. Enemies!"

"This one is no Tejano, he's a Yanqui."

"What is the difference between a jackal and a hyena? Two branches of the same Anglo root that threatens to destroy us. More dangerous than ever, now that their war between north and south is done. At least

142

that kept them busy killing each other. With the rebellion put down, the gringos will come swarming to steal our land away from us, just as they stole the entire Southwest and California from Mexico," Don Eduardo said.

While speaking he gestured violently with his hands, causing some brandy to slop out of the top of his glass and spill on the floor. Setting the goblet down on a side table, he took a handkerchief from his jacket pocket and wiped his hand clean of the liquid.

"Stop and think, Don Eduardo," Lorena said, turning some of the force of her personality on him. "Have I ever done or said anything to dishonor the memory of Ramon? Ever acted in a way that went against the pride and power of the House of Castillo and the Rancho Grande?"

"No, never," the *padrone* said grudgingly. "Which only goes to make your current actions all the more incomprehensible!" he added quickly. "I can only think that you have taken leave of your senses!"

"I know what I am doing, as I will prove to you. Earlier today, while you were away on your journey, some of our riders stopped a runaway wagon on the Old Mission Road. It carried a cargo of corpses. At the ford were more dead men. Between the wagon

143

and the river bank, nineteen in all — nineteen!"

"Yes, I have heard of this thing," said Don Eduardo. "Vasquez told me of it. Monstrous — an infamy! No doubt some new fiendish conspiracy devised by those pigs in town — Hutto and his creatures — to destroy us and steal our land."

"Your hate is blinding you, *padrone.* Wade Hutto is greedy and ambitious, but he would hardly go to such lengths to entrap us. As many pistoleros as it took for that much killing, it would have been easier to strike directly at the ranch, if that was the purpose."

"Then what was the purpose, Lorena? Tell me."

"I do not know — yet. I know only what Sombro tells me. He's half Indio, our best tracker. No one can read signs as well as he. He can read horse and wagon tracks like a bishop reads Latin."

"That is true," Don Eduardo conceded, becoming interested despite himself. "I have not yet spoken to Sombro."

"He and some of our riders are getting rid of the dead men's wagon so that it will not be connected with us. He will not be back for some hours. I questioned him before he left."

"What did he say?"

Lorena leaned forward, intent. "He says there were two wagons, two bands of men. One band came across the river at the ford. They came with a freight wagon. The other lay in wait for them on this side of the river. The ambushers killed them and took the wagon. Sombro says the wagon was carrying a heavy load. Its wheels cut deep tracks in the ground."

"What was in the wagon?"

"Ah, that is a question. What did it carry? Something worth killing for. Something worth much killing."

"Gold?"

"That would be worth the price of all those deaths, yes — gold. Gold," breathed Lorena, her eyes glittering, ripe red lips parted.

Don Eduardo scowled, thinking. "Who brings gold here? That swine Hutto does not have that kind of money. No, not Hutto and all the merchants and gamblers in Hangtree town put together."

"What about the army at Fort Pardee? A gold shipment to pay the men and buy supplies, perhaps."

"But the dead men were not soldiers. Vasquez would have told me if they were."

"The government could have hired private

guards for the shipment, no?"

Don Eduardo stroked his mustache with his fingertips, smoothing it. "What happened to the freight wagon, Lorena?"

"It went west on the Old Mission Road toward the Broken Hills, as Sombro reads it."

"If the old one says it is so, then it is so. The other wagon, with the dead men — where does it fit in?"

"If the bandits wanted to move the bodies to cover up their trail, to hide them, it would have done for the job."

Don Eduardo made a fist, swiping it in the air. "They could have put them on our land, so we would be blamed!"

"I did not think of that, but it could be so," Lorena said.

"The law and the gringos would blame Rancho Grande, while the real culprits got away! Clever, very clever. But why didn't they? What went wrong?"

Lorena's lips curved upward in a slow, self-satisfied smile. "That is where Señor Heller comes in."

"Who?"

"The gringo, Don Eduardo."

"You know his name, then."

"I went through his saddlebags. There was a portfolio filled with papers, documents.

His name was on it: Heller, Samuel Heller."

Don Eduardo made an expression of distaste. "A name that means nothing to me."

Lorena shrugged. "The portfolio held many circulars of Wanted men — pictures of the outlaws, killers and robbers, each with a price on their heads."

"Is he a lawman?" asked Don Eduardo.

She shook her head. "The gringo has no badge, no star."

"A bounty hunter, then."

Lorena nodded. "So it would seem. No ordinary bounty hunter, either. There were seven dead men at the ford."

"So?"

"They were alive before the gringo crossed the river."

"How do you know this, Lorena?"

"The testimony of the horse tracks and the dead men, as read by Sombro.

"The bandits rode in on the Old Mission Road from the west, from the Broken Hills. They lay in wait on the west bank to ambush the freight wagon. Some of them rode west with the wagon. The others stayed behind at the river. The gringo crossed the river. He went west on the road. The bandits at the river were dead. The gringo was wounded. He rode on to Rancho Grande

147

land — we found him," Lorena said.

"How badly is he hurt?" Don Eduardo asked.

"He will live."

"Ah, but should he?"

"He could be very useful to us, Don Eduardo — to the ranch."

"How?"

"As a witness, for one thing. He can testify that Rancho Grande had nothing to do with the robbery."

"The word of a bounty killer holds little weight in the councils of the law, Lorena."

"His army discharge certficate was in with his papers. He was with the North, like the soldiers at Fort Pardee. That will carry some weight with them, more than the testimony of any Rebel, I think."

Don Eduardo considered it. "You may be right. But if what you say is true, this gringo is more than just another pistolero. He is a dangerous man."

"Is that so bad?"

"He could be dangerous to us."

"A bounty hunter kills for the price on an outlaw's head. He sells his gun for money. You have money," Lorena said.

"I would like to keep what I have. In fact, I would like more," said Don Eduardo.

"He may know who robbed the freight

wagon and where the loot is hidden. He might lead us to it. And if something should happen to him, and the gold fall into Castillo hands, the United States government would be none the wiser."

Don Eduardo showed a sharp, hard-eyed glint, like that of a bird of prey. "You have given this matter a great deal of thought, Lorena. And I must say, I like the way you think."

"My thoughts are always for the advancement of Rancho Grande and the Castillo name."

"What is the extent of this man Heller's injuries?"

"He was shot in the shoulder. No bones were broken. I took the bullet out of him and patched him up. There was a flesh wound on his side, but it is nothing. He has lost a lot of blood, but he should be up on his feet in a few days with the help of Alma's potions," Lorena said.

Don Eduardo spat and made the sign of protection against the evil eye. "That witch!"

"Witch or not, she knows how to heal the wounded and the sick. The sooner the gringo is on the trail of that stolen wagon and its loot, the better."

"You may be on to something at that, Lorena. Continue with your plan, and keep me posted of any developments. When he is able to talk, find out what he knows. But be careful not to put him on his guard."

"I know what to do."

"Of that I am sure. Oh, and Lorena —"

"Yes, Don Eduardo?"

"The storehouse is good enough for him. I want no gringo in the hacienda."

"It shall be as you say, Don Eduardo."

TEN

Legend and lore say the coming of day banishes ghosts. For Johnny Cross, first light brought them. Not the ghosts of the men he'd killed last night or in the past, but family ghosts. The ghosts of memory.

Johnny awoke before dawn, early Tuesday morning. The sky was still dark, except for that streak of pale gray radiance in the east that heralds the sunrise — the false dawn, what the Indians call the Wolf's Tail.

It was cool; dew was beaded up on Johnny's top blanket, though the ones layered below it were dry. He lay there, looking up at the stars in the graying sky. The fire had burned low. Nearby, Luke Pettigrew slept soundly, snoring softly.

This was Johnny's first time home since he'd left to go to war five years ago, in the summer of 1861. Ma had been dead about a month. She'd been the only thing keeping him on the ranch.

The war's pull was strong on him, the lure of fighting was a potent strain in the Cross blood. Cross menfolk had fought in the Mexican-American War, the war for Texas independence, the War of 1812, the American Revolution, and the French and Indian War. When they weren't fighting the young nation's wars, they fought in private wars and feuds in Kentucky and the hill country of Tennessee.

By that time Pa had been long dead. He'd died when Johnny was a boy, leaving him and his older brother Cal as mainstays to keep the ranch going. Cal had joined the Texas Army of the Confederacy almost immediately after war was declared following the firing on Fort Sumter.

Johnny would have gone too, but somebody had to stay behind and help Ma tend the ranch. She wouldn't leave the place, and even if she'd been of a mind to, where could she go? The Crosses had no kin in this part of the state. With her fierce, quiet pride, Ma would rather die than move into town and live on charity, not that there was much in the way of charity in Hangtown.

What little money the family had managed to scrape by on over the years came from the wild horses that the boys caught, broke to the saddle, and sold. With Cal gone, Johnny handled the mustanging by himself. Johnny put most of the fresh meat on the table. Ma kept a vegetable garden going, but his shooting was the difference between the two of them eating or starving.

Hunger had taught him a terrible patience even as it sharpened his aim to deadly accuracy. Hunting in the Breaks, he bagged the occasional deer or antelope when he could get it, but most often took varmints such as squirrel, possum, and raccoon. Wild quail and pheasant made a welcome change in the diet. Cal promised to send money back home, but if he had, none of it ever reached them.

Ma had been sickly that winter and never quite recovered even when the warm weather came. A summer thunderstorm soaked her to the skin; she caught a chill and soon expired. She was buried beside Pa and daughter Mandy in a plot behind the ranch house at the foot of the jagged-top hill.

Johnny dug the grave himself, did the burying and read a few of her favorite passages from the Bible over her. She'd taught him and Cal how to read. He wasn't much of a reader, but good enough to get by.

With Ma gone, there was nothing to tie him to the ranch. He'd sold off what little livestock there was, loaded up his trusty smooth-bore musket, saddled up his horse and rode east across Texas to fight for the Confederacy.

Along the way he fell in with Bill Anderson and his bunch of red-hots — a story in itself — and the hard-riding, hard-fighting Texans had gone north to join up with Quantrill. He never saw brother Cal again. He heard from more than one source that Cal had died in the fighting at Shiloh.

Now Johnny was back. He'd have to visit the family plots; they'd need tending after five years of neglect. He wasn't up to it yet. Memories — ghosts. Was there a difference?

Johnny grew tired of lying there with thoughts of times past. He wasn't much for setting around thinking. It was a new day, time to be up and doing. He threw off the blankets, sat up and stretched.

He turned each boot upside-down and shook it out, protection in case a scorpion had climbed into one during the night. Pulling them on, he rose and stretched, shivering a little in the early-morning chill. He draped a blanket across his shoulders.

The eastern sky was lightening but the sun was still below the horizon. The fire had burned down low. Johnny hunkered down beside it, stirring up the embers, feeding them some fresh kindling. Flames licked up, curling around the logs.

Luke came awake with a start, grabbing for his gun.

"Stand down, soldier — it's me, Johnny."

"Huh!" Luke said, disoriented.

"Careful you don't shoot yourself. Or worse, me."

Luke put the gun aside, knuckling sleepy eyes and yawning.

Monty's gang had been encamped at the ranch. A search of their belongings turned up some food supplies: a slab of bacon, sack of flour, some beans, and most welcome of all, coffee.

Johnny and Luke breakfasted on bacon, steak and beans. The stream provided cold, fresh water. They brewed coffee in tin cups no longer needed by the dead, spiking the iron-strong liquid with a dash of whiskey, a welcome antidote to the morning's chill.

Johnny cleared the cylinders of two guns and laboriously reloaded them with fresh cap-and-ball ammunition, insurance against morning dew having rendered the previous day's load ineffective. A practice round from one Colt set an empty tin of beans skyward; a shot from the other holed it before it touched ground.

Luke hefted his crutch and hobbled around, prowling through Monty's gang's saddlebags and pouches, riffling through them. A triumphant shout announced that he'd made an important discovery.

"Look — my wooden leg!" he cried, holding the object up for Johnny to see. The prosthetic device consisted of a carved wooden foot and shin with various leather straps and buckles for holding it in place.

"Glory be," said Johnny.

Grinning hugely, Luke sat down on the ground and wrestled on his artificial limb.

His fingers worked at the fastenings, tightening straps and pulling them into place, buckling them. He rose, walking in circles. He still needed the crutch, but moved with greater facility and surety.

"Never thought I'd see this again," Luke said. "Wonder why they kept it?"

"Thieves never throw away something of value. Wooden leg's useful, plenty of market for it since the war. They just hadn't gotten around to selling it yet," said Johnny.

"Reckon so."

"Or maybe Monty just wanted to have something to remember you by."

Luke fished out the gold tooth from his jacket pocket and held it up. First rays from the rising sun caught it, glinting off it, making the yellow metal look molten. "I got something to remember Monty by," he said.

"Hell, you got Monty hisself," Johnny pointed out. "Him and his pals didn't get up and bury themselves during the night. We're going to have to get rid of 'em."

"Not before turning out their pockets to see what's inside," Luke said.

"Let's clean 'em out and haul 'em out of here before they go to rot and ruin, stink up the place. I don't want 'em on Cross land."

"Where'll we plant 'em, Johnny?"

"The Snake Pit. We won't have to bury 'em, just toss 'em in."

There had been five men in the gang. They'd left ten horses in the corral, in addition to the seven horses from the ford and the chestnut Johnny'd been riding. Each dead man had owned a saddle and firearms, guns and rifles. A search of their corpses yielded eighty dollars in gold and silver and one hundred and sixty in paper money.

Johnny and Luke split the take fifty-fifty, even shares.

"That's more money than I made during the whole war," Luke said, face alight with cheerful greed.

"Soldier's pay ain't much, and that's when the Confederacy got around to paying it, which wasn't often," Johnny said.

"That string of horses is worth plenty, and the saddles, too."

"We got to get us a running iron to change up what brands are marked on that horse-flesh before selling it. I don't reckon that bunch was too particular about where they got their animals."

"We're rich, Johnny, rich!"

"It's a start, anyhow. The trick is gonna be hanging on to it — and not hanging."

The sun had cleared the horizon. The day was already warm and heating up fast.

"The horses will keep till later. We can water and feed 'em when we get back. Let's clear them bodies out of here quick. The hotter it gets, the more snakes there'll be," Johnny said.

Luke rubbed the lower half of his face, looking thoughtful. "Let's not be too hasty, Johnny. Could be we're throwing away good money. Bunch of no-goods like this must be wanted by the law. Mebbe they's a price on their heads we could collect."

Johnny shook his head, smiling. "You're a caution, Luke. Yesterday you didn't even have a wooden leg to stand on. Today you've got more cash money in your pockets than you've ever seen in one place and you're scheming how to drag down more."

"I always figured I'd make a good businessman if I had half a chance," Luke said.

"The first rule of business is, don't tie into the law if you don't have to. Some of those horses are stolen — hell, most of 'em, probably — and we can't produce a bill of sale for a single one of 'em. Uncharitable folk like sheriffs and judges and such might say we stole 'em. Things may be fast and loose in these parts but they still hang horse thieves, last I heard."

". . . You might have something there," Luke allowed.

"Who's the law in Hangtown these days, Yerkes?"

Luke shook his head. "He got killed fighting at Goliad. The new man's named Barton, Mack Barton."

"Don't know him. What's he like?" Johnny asked.

"He's a mean one. Hutto put him in as sheriff. Anybody gets out of line, he cracks down on 'em hard. Collects taxes and fines, too, plenty of 'em. Those who can't pay get put on a county work gang breaking rocks and clearing brush.

"Barton can take care of hisself, though. He ain't no yellowbelly. Three rannies from Quinto up in the Nations came in last winter, tried to hoorah the town. Barton cleaned up on 'em with a shotgun. Left 'em dead in the street," said Luke.

"Between him and Yankee soldier boys moving in to take over, let's not go shining a light on ourselves just yet," Johnny said. "One more thing: Monty's bunch wasn't alone. Their pards from the Breaks are liable to come along sometime, anytime, to see what happened to 'em. Don't be caught without a gun or where you can't put your hand to one right quick."

Luke waved a hand in airy dismissal. "Teach your grandma to suck eggs, you don't have to tell me twice about being ready with a gun. Nobody's gonna get the drop on me again."

"Good," Johnny said. "Let's get to work. Now that you got your wooden leg back, you got no excuse for dogging it."

It was mid-morning when Johnny and Luke set out from the ranch as part of a macabre procession. Johnny rode the chestnut. A rope tied to his saddle horn trailed behind him, leading a string of two horses. Each horse had one of Monty's gang tied face-down across its back.

Luke rode a bay horse. Roped to it was a dun-colored animal of quarter-horse proportions; a big horse, deep-chested, broad in the beam, built along the lines of a dray or farm horse, a horse made for drawing a heavy load.

Harnessed to it was a travois, a kind of land-based sled used by Plains Indians to carry heavy loads for long distances. It consisted of a fan-shaped wooden framework over which was stretched and secured a strong blanket.

Johnny and Luke had felled and trimmed saplings and branches for the wood. The pieces were strong enough to bear the load, yet light enough to avoid overly encumbering the horse.

A pair of ten-foot-long straight poles served for the outer ribs. They were crossed at one end with the tips overlapping and tied with rope, causing the poles to make a V shape. Then came the crosspieces, tied down at regular intervals at right angles to the poles. Each piece was successively longer to span the widening fan shape. A horse blanket was pulled taut over the framework. Rawhide strips were threaded through holes punched in the blanket and lashed to the woodwork.

Monty and two other dead men were loaded into the travois, cradled in its hammock-like concavity. They were tied in place to keep them from falling out.

The travois was without wheels, the draft horse literally dragging it behind itself. For all that, it was remarkably effective in transporting a load of over five hundred pounds across the terrain.

The group traveled at the rate of its slowest element, the horse pulling the travois.

It proceeded at a walk. The travois kicked up a fair amount of dust; that couldn't be helped. But the effect of the telltale dust cloud would be minimized within the Breaks, whose rock walls would screen its source.

The procession filed into the eastern pass of Wild Horse Gulch. Ridges and cliffs blocked the sun, filling the gulch with cool blue shadows.

The men had filled their canteens with fresh water and packed a quantity of beef jerky for the trip. Luke augmented his firepower with a sawed-off shotgun and a leather pouch filled with twelve-gauge buckshot shells that had belonged to one of Monty's gang.

After a few hundred yards, the eastern approach opened up into the gulch proper, a parklike space encompassing many square miles of well-watered grasslands. Rolling fields were dotted with groups of wild horses, stallions, mares, colts. They looked up from their grazing to eye the intruders, running away well before the strangers neared them. Mustangs are wary of men and devilishly hard to catch.

Johnny Cross continually scanned the landscape. Danger could come from any direction — probably from the one least expected. The file rode north along the foot of a rocky ridge running north-south.

Shadows provided cover as well as welcome relief from the steadily mounting heat. Springs in the hills spilling down the slopes, becoming brooks and streams on the flat, watering tall green grass.

The horses plodded along. Limestone deposits and rock formations took fanciful shapes: a castle tower, a crouching beast, a ship's prow. That last was a wedge-shaped protuberance on the gulch's western wall, jutting out into space several hundred feet above the canyon floor.

It was the landmark Johnny had been looking for. "The Snake Pit's yonder on the far side of the gulch," he said.

He, Luke, and the horses with their morbid burdens turned left, striking west across the gulch. The sun showed over the top of the eastern cliffs, filling the gulch with buttery yellow light and heat.

Opposite, on the west wall, the promontory shaped like a ship's bow was a marquee pointing to a gap in the rock walls. "Signpost to the Snake Pit," Johnny said.

"Ain't likely to forget it," Luke said, nodding. "Sure is different from the war, eh, Johnny? Back then we never had to clean up what we killed, just left 'em laying where they fell."

"Peacetime's shaping up as a whole lot of extra work," Johnny said.

They rode into a ravine below the ship's-bow stone marker. It began as a narrow, sandy-floored cleft in rock with sandy floor, barely wide enough for the travois to make its way through, sometimes pressing close to the sides at the base of the fan-shaped carrier. The dust had a flinty smell.

The ravine wormed its way through rock walls. They began to part, opening outward from each other. The corridor gave on to a pocket valley. It was dry, waterless. Stony soil was covered with thin, short, colorless grass. Mesquite trees, gnarly and twisted, dotted the rocky flat. There were clumps of prickly-pear cactus, too.

"Watch out for rattlers," Johnny said.

"Ain't nothing but rattlers in this hole," Luke said, with feeling.

At the far end of the valley, a slanting boulder twelve feet high sheered off from a rocky ridge. It was shaped like a hard-boiled egg standing upright, with its wider end half-buried in the ground and with one side sliced off at a slanted angle.

Johnny and Luke rode toward it, carefully eyeing the ground ahead for rattlesnakes. This was prime rattlersnake country. A rattler could spook a horse, cause it to panic, maybe blindly step into a rabbit hole, stumble and break a leg.

Nearing the slanted rock, it could be seen that at its base gaped a big hole.

Horse nostrils quivered, widening, getting the scent of snake. The animals grew skittish. Johnny reined in a stone's-throw from the hole, near a clump of stunted mesquite trees little bigger than bushes. "This is as far as the horses will go," he said.

The hole in the ground was a sinkhole, a natural vertical shaft in the limestone rock about ten feet in diameter and fifty feet deep. The Snake Pit — a den of rattlesnakes.

Rattlers thronged the stony ground ringing the hole, sunning themselves. They looked like several dozen separate lengths of thick, yellow-brown rope strewn carelessly about the rocks, except that they were moving.

Johnny and Luke got down off their horses and hitched them to the trees, making sure they were tied good and tight so the horses couldn't break away. Johnny loosed his carbine from the saddle-scabbard and handed it to Luke. "You see any rattlers coming this way, shoot 'em before they get close," he said.

"I sure will!" Luke declared.

Johnny used his knife to cut one of the dead men loose from a horse. The body hit the ground with a thud. Another followed. He cut the ropes binding the other three corpses to the travois and rolled them out of it onto the ground.

He pulled on a pair of riding gloves, fitting his hands into them. He bent down over the bodies, lining them up with their feet pointed toward the hole. Luke with his crutch and wooden leg was no good for this kind of work. Johnny did it by himself.

Luke stood guard, facing the sinkhole, holding the carbine in one hand. Johnny finished arranging the bodies to his liking and straightened up. He'd worked up a pretty good sweat. He used his bandanna to wipe his brow.

A rattlesnake as thick around the middle as a young girl's arm separated itself from the group around the hole and started wriggling toward the clump of mesquite trees. Its triangular head rose up from the ground as it moved forward.

A shot cracked. The rattler's head exploded.

Smoke curled from the muzzle of the carbine. Luke had fired holding the weapon in one hand, pointing and shooting with seeming casualness.

"Nice shot," Johnny said.

"I may not be no pistol fighter, but I'm a fair hand with a rifle," Luke said.

Those unfortunate enough to have disturbed a hornet's nest know the unforgettable sound of the hive buzzing in mounting fury. The sinister sound of a rattlesnake rattling its rattles is of an order several degrees of magnitude greater in its chilling menace.

Nature, which has equipped the rattler with venom sacs loaded with deadly poison and gleaming, sharp-pointed fangs to inject it has thoughtfully equipped it with rattles at the end of its tail. When the reptile's ire is roused, its rattle warns: *I'm dangerous! Beware!*

Now, not one, but many rattlesnakes around the sinkhole reared up, wedge-shaped heads weaving, beady eyes glittering, tails agitating their buzzing rattles. They sounded like a rhythm section of percussionists for a mariachi band simultaneously shaking their maracas.

Something primal in that rattling drone, instinctive, to make the hair stand up on the back of a man's neck, send shivers up and down his spine, and chill his blood.

Johnny held a pair of loaded revolvers he'd taken from a saddlebag, these in addition to the twin guns worn holstered on his hips.

"Here they come!" Luke warned. He took up a wide stance, bracing himself solidly on the crutch so he'd be able to use both hands to work the carbine fast.

Rattlesnakes arrowed away from the hole toward the clump of mesquite trees where the men and horses were grouped. They were swollen with venom and hostility.

"They're moving fast," Luke said tightly.

"Let 'em have it," Johnny said, opening up with the pistols. He pointed a gun at the nearest rattler coiling toward him and squeezed the trigger. The flat crack of the report sounded simultaneously with the rattler's head disintegrating into pulp. Its long, looping body writhed and spasmed, a living whip being wielded by an invisible hand.

The carbine spat, tagging another rattler in the body, slamming it sideways. More rattlesnakes came on, six, twelve, more.

Johnny squared off against the venomous horde, firing first with the gun in his right hand, then with his left, covering a wide angle of approach. Hot lead pulverized snake flesh, spraying corrosive mist into the air.

Luke wielded the carbine, potting away at the plague of reptiles. As the lead snakes halved the distance between them and the men, shots came in rapid succession, sending up their own lethal chorus of rattling gunfire.

A rattler slithering in from the side managed to get within a man's length of Johnny and Luke. It reared, wicked yellow eyes glaring, open maw gaping to display a double set of wickedly close fangs. It was so close that the droplets of venom beading on the needle-sharp tips of curved fangs could be seen.

Johnny placed a shot right between its horns, taking off the top of its head. The monster rattler continued writhing and whipsawing on the ground, minus its forward motion and hostile intent.

"That was too close for comfort!" Luke shouted.

The wave of advancing rattlers was checked by gunfire, broken. The terrible thing was that even after being shot dead, some of the reptiles continued to move, spasming convulsively.

With a dozen or more of their number shot into pieces — though the pieces continued moving — the surviving rattlesnakes got the message that their attack meant death. They peeled off to the sides, scattering, fleeing the area of the sinkhole.

It was a sullen, furious exodus of rattlesnakes, slithering and S-curving away from the shooters, darting into rockpiles and disappearing into clumps of tall, yellow-gray grasses.

Johnny squeezed off some more rounds, driving off some of the stragglers. The ground before them was littered with sections and coils of the reptiles, most of them still jerking with the convulsive half-life of spasmodic muscular reaction.

There was a lull in the shooting. Johnny and Luke exchanged glances. Luke's eyes were bulging in a face shiny with cold sweat. Johnny wondered if he looked the same.

Luke rubbed his face in the crook of an arm, using the sleeve of his jacket to wipe the stinging sweat from his eyes. "They heads is blowed clean off and they still ain't got enough sense to know that they're dead. Must be pure meanness that keeps 'em going," he said.

"Like us," said Johnny. He stuck the two

guns in the top of the gun belt, freeing his hands.

The horses were anxious, upset. Pointed ears stood straight up. Hooves pawed the ground. The animals danced, sidling. It wasn't the noise and violence of gunfire that had done it, it was the smell of the snakes and the buzzing of their rattles that had sounded deep wells of unease somewhere in the depths of their brains.

Johnny went to the chestnut, speaking softly to it. "Easy, boy, easy. Ain't nothing to get on your hind legs about." The horse quieted some at the sound of his voice. He patted its corded muscular neck, stroking it.

Luke examined the carbine. "I only got a few shots left." Johnny opened a pouch in the saddlebag on the horse's left side, taking out a box of cartridges for the carbine. He went to Luke, handing it to him. Luke tore open one end of the box and began feeding rounds into the weapon's receiver.

Johnny set about quieting the other horses. Luke finished reloading. Johnny set the two extra guns aside. The guns in his twin holsters were both fully loaded.

"The way to the Snake Pit is clear. Might as well start getting shut of the bodies," Johnny said. "Cover me."

"You're covered," Luke said.

Johnny went around the row of bodies, so that he was between them and the sinkhole. "Save Monty for last. I want to enjoy his company for a while," Luke said.

Johnny tsk-tsked. "Like I said — pure meanness."

"I had a lot of time to think about Monty while I was humping my way along the road to Hangtown without my wooden leg."

"Never mind about him, you keep your eyes open for any rattlers coming at me."

"We must have run them out clear into the next county."

"Keep watching anyway." Johnny bent down, taking hold of one of the dead men's booted ankles. He started toward the sinkhole, dragging the body along with him.

The ground was littered with dead rattlesnakes and splattered with snake blood, venom, and bits of flesh. Severed snake sections continued to writhe and jerk.

Johnny dragged the body to the rim of the shaft, stepping carefully as he neared the edge. Not too near, though, lest the hard, sunbaked earth crumble underfoot and hurl him down to the bottom of the hole.

A flash of memory recalled to him days of his youth when he and Cal and Luke and some of the other venturesome companions of his boyhood would vie to see who could get closest to the sinkhole's edge. In those days, there were no bullets and powder to waste on frivolities like killing rattlesnakes for fun. They'd driven them off with firecrackers, homemade bows and arrows, thrown rocks, slingshots, sometimes even forked or pointed sticks.

"What a bunch of damned fools we was," Johnny said to himself, smiling at the memory. He peeked over the edge into the depths of the sinkhole. Way down at the bottom lay a broken human skeleton clad in strips and shreds of rags. A nameless victim given up to the pit. A lonesome death. Had he been alive when he went in, or already dead?

He wouldn't lack for company now. Lots of it.

Johnny gave a kick-push with his booted foot and sent the outlaw's dead body tumbling into the pit. It hit outcroppings from the shaft walls several times on the way down before touching bottom.

The meaty thud was followed by a discordant hissing like steam escaping a boiler.

The floor of the pit swarmed with snakes blanketing the body, many sinking fangs into it. The pit housed a rattlesnake den. The reptiles must have some hidden tunnels and byways connecting the sinkhole to the surface.

Johnny went to fetch another body. Several times Luke had to use the carbine, drilling overly bold aboveground rattlers who were in too much of a hurry to reclaim their turf. Johnny labored at his chore, not lingering. The rattlesnakes were eager to reestablish their dominion.

Johnny toted one corpse after another to the pit and threw them in. Presently only Monty remained. Johnny took hold of him by the legs. "Sure you don't want to kiss him good-bye?" he asked, sarcastic.

"I'll wave as he goes over the edge," said Luke.

Johnny dragged the body to the sinkhole and dumped it in.

"Adios, Monty," Luke murmured, "you sombitch."

Johnny wasted no time putting some distance between himself and the pit. Those rattlers were crowding back onto the scene. He rejoined Luke. "Reckon we ought to say a few words over them hombres, hoss?"

"How about, 'Good riddance,' " said Luke.

"That'll do," Johnny said. They packed up. The travois was rigged to be collapsible, like an umbrella or folding tent. It might come in handy again, especially since they lacked a wagon. It was closed up, poles and blanket tied into a roll with ropes and secured to the back of the big draft horse.

Johnny and Luke mounted up and rode out, trailing a string of three horses behind them. They threaded the narrow gorge to Wild Horse Gulch. Johnny dismounted, breaking some leafy branches off a bush and using them to sweep away their tracks leading to and going away from the valley of the Snake Pit.

They returned to the ranch without incident.

ELEVEN

On Tuesday night, Sam Heller awoke in the steaming cauldron of a bed of pain. Not that he knew it was Tuesday night. He didn't know when it was. He was in a small room on the second, top floor of the storehouse. It was dimly lit by a flickering oil lamp placed on top of a packing box.

He lay on a narrow, wooden-framed bed that was too short for him; his bare feet hung off the end of the bed. The bed stood lengthwise along the wall in a corner opposite the door to the room. A dark wooden crucifix was nailed to the wall above the bed's head.

Sam was entangled in sweat-soaked sheets. He was feverish, light-headed. He felt like he was burning up. Sweat poured from him, soaking into a thin, palletlike mattress. His thoughts were confused. He had trouble thinking straight. It took too much effort to concentrate, to follow a single line of thought.

He wanted to go back to sleep but sleep wouldn't come, only a kind of half-waking delirium. Movement nearby caught his attention. By willpower he forced his eyes to focus.

He was not alone. Two women stood at his bedside, the raven-haired beauty and the crone. Lorena and Alma.

Lorena wore a long-sleeved brown dress that was tight at the waist and reached down to her ankles. A crocheted black shawl was wrapped around her shoulders.

Alma held a brown ceramic pot with a lid on it, gripping it in both hands by twin handles that protruded from the top. She set it down on a square-topped table that stood beside the bed's head.

Lorena held something at her side, a wooden bowl which she set down on the table next to the pot. She leaned over Sam. "Gringo," she said.

". . . The lady with the knife," Sam murmured.

"You remember that? I took a bullet out of you."

"I remember."

"Good. Listen to me. You have a fever, a high fever. I have some medicine that will break it. You must drink it, all of it. Otherwise, you will die. Do you understand what I am saying?"

"Yes."

Lorena turned to the crone. "Alma." Alma took the lid off the pot. A wooden ladle with a curved handle was hung over the pot's lip. Steamy wisps of vapor rose from the potion within.

Alma had brewed the stuff earlier. It contained distilled extracts from certain medicinal plants and vegetables from her homemade pharmacopia. Powdered roots and weeds, a variety of tree fungus, exotic mushrooms and strips of cactus. The mixture was slow-cooked for hours over a charcoal fire. When it was ready, she notified Lorena and the two of them went to the upper room in the storehouse. The brew had be taken quickly to avoid losing its potency.

Alma ladled the potion into the shallow wooden bowl, filling it.

"Sit up, gringo," Lorena said. Sam tried but couldn't do it. He lacked the strength. Lorena held the wooden bowl in one hand. She reached the other behind the back of his head, lifting it upright. "It will taste vile but drink it all," she said.

Sam made a noise signaling assent. He had no fear of being poisoned. The woman could have killed him earlier if she'd been of a mind to. She wanted him alive — why, he didn't know.

Lorena held the bowl close to his mouth. The potion was a watery, gray-green color. Swirls of rainbow-colored grease floated on the surface. It smelled musty, like a damp root cellar.

She put the edge of the wooden bowl to his lips. "Drink, hombre. Drink deep," she said.

Sam swallowed, his throat working. The stuff was warm. It tasted awful, like soup made from clay.

"Don't stop, drink it to the last," Lorena said.

Sam gulped it down. The dregs of it spilled down the corner of his mouth. It left a bitter aftertaste on his tongue. He gagged, choking.

"Keep it down. If you throw it up, you will die," Lorena warned.

Sam clamped his jaws shut. His stomach churned, knotting. It rebelled at the contents but Sam held it down. After a moment, the spasm passed. His head sank back down on the pillow. Lorena straightened up, looking down at him, studying his reactions.

The warm liquid sank into Sam's belly like a paving stone. His tongue and the inside of his mouth tingled. The tingling spread down his throat, worming through his innards. Hair rose on the back of his neck.

Sam shuddered. He felt alternately hot and cold. He breathed shallowly, panting.

He'd drunk worse stuff, but he really couldn't remember when. Numbness came to his hands and feet. The skin of his face felt taut, stiff. A strange sensation came over him, a sense of forward momentum, as if he were sitting still on a moving train.

The oil lamp on the packing box swam in and out of focus. The room wavered.

An effect of the lamp's flickering glow, or of the potion?

Sam took a deep breath, hoping to steady his reeling senses. Several times during the war when he'd been treated for wounds, the doctors had dosed him with laudanum or morphine. This was like that and yet not like it.

His vision swam as he eyed Lorena. She was a sinister madonna, beautiful and dangerous. Alma was impossibly old, a living mummy.

Sam's eyes closed. Fireworks erupted on the insides of his lids, unrolling in slow motion. He felt like he was sinking deeper and deeper into the bed. It had no bottom; it was bottomless.

The fireworks behind closed eyes became the sun, moon and stars. Sam was off on a comet —

Fever dreams!

Heat? The agony of a living, sensate being suffering the merciless torments of an inferno? Sam Heller had known his share and more. Now, in his mind, he relived some of those incidents:

There was the time a few years before the war, when a war party of Apaches had been rampaging throughout south Arizona. Sam was one of a party of gold-seekers prospecting a likely claim in the high desert mountains when the Apaches struck. He'd been one of the few to survive the initial onslaught on the miners' camp and flee on horseback.

The fleeing miners took shelter in a Butterfield stage station on the overland route. The station house was made of thick stone walls. Some travelers and local ranchers and their families were forted up there.

Apaches generally liked to hit and run, but this raid had been coordinated among several tribes, laying waste to the whole southern tier of the territory. The red raiders besieged the station house. They stole all the horses first thing and settled in to wait out the defenders.

They avoided a head-on charge. No sense in that. They were there not to be killed, but to kill. Lurking in the surroundings just out of sight, they were elusive, phantomlike, rarely showing more of themselves than the shadow of an overflying bird.

For one of the defenders in the station house to show himself for even an instant in one of the windows was to risk death. The station had solid walls; the besieged had plenty of guns and ammo. But the water supply was outside: a well in the dirt front yard. The only water inside was a single, small cask that was half-full when the attack struck.

Eighteen souls, men, women and children, were penned in the stone house under the blazing Arizona sun. The water went fast, rationed or not. The well was less than ten yards from the front door, its tantalizing nearness even more maddening once the water ran out. And run out it did, early.

Water is like breathing: one of those those things you never think about until it's suddenly cut off. Funny how thirsty a man becomes the instant he realizes he can't have a drink of water when he wants one . . .

Stalemate. The Apaches couldn't storm

the place without suffering too-costly casualties, but the besieged were pinned down with no escape.

Apaches prefer not to fight at night — but they will, if necessary. On the second night, several volunteers tried to make a rush to the well to get some water. The lucky ones died in a salvo of bullets. One poor devil was taken alive. He lived for a day and a night and a day, fiendishly tortured out of range of any merciful death-dealing bullets.

Thirst. Sam's throat closed up; he couldn't swallow. His tongue swelled up in his mouth. Unquenchable thirst lit a fire in the brain.

A mother was found dead in the morning, throat cut by her own hand, but not before she first had quietly smothered to death the infant at her breast when she could stand its piteous cries no longer.

A tough desert rat, a prospector who was all rawhide and sinew and bone, threw open the door in the heat of the day and strode boldly to the cistern. It took all his strength to keep from staggering. Hauling a full bucket out of the well, he raised it in both hands to his lips before Apache bullets drilled it, knocking it out of his hands.

He dropped to the ground, scrambling for what water was left in the bucket. Unseen

Apaches shot him to pieces.

Days dragged on with no help in sight. A scant few of the toughest remained alive in the stone house. A single, concerted rush by the Apaches would have overwhelmed them.

Sam felt that the end was near. There was a roaring in his ears, fading vision; his heartbeat fluttered in his breast like a little bird trapped in a closed fist. When suddenly sounded the sweetest sound he'd ever heard: The ringing brass of a cavalry trumpet sounding the charge.

An army detachment came thundering toward the stone house. The Apaches melted away long before relief arrived.

Sam's first sip of life-giving water was so sweet it hurt . . .

Heat that made the fever now wracking Sam's body seem like a spring breeze by comparison?

Fort Fillmore, New Mexico, July 1861. Sam Heller joined the Union Army early in the war. He'd been assigned to the command of Major Lynde's 550 troops stationed at Fort Fillmore on the Rio Grande. The area swarmed with Southern sympathizers. An invasion by a column of Lieutenant Colonel John R. Baylor's 2nd Texas

Mounted Rifles threw Lynde into a blind panic.

Beaten in a few tentative engagements with the Rebels, Lynde convinced himself that Fort Fillmore was indefensible and decided to abandon it, retreating to Fort Stanton far in the north of the territory. Lynde overrode the wishes of his subordinate officers and the vast majority of the troops, who wanted to stay and fight. Fearing that Confederate sympathizers in towns along the Rio Grande would make that route untenable, Lynde "led" his men on an alternate route through the desert — a 140-mile trek.

The retreat — rout is more accurate — quickly turned into a torturous death march through a raging inferno hell. No springs along the way, no fresh water. Some of the troops had been foolhardy enough to fill their canteens with whiskey instead of water. They were the first to go mad and die. Soldiers fell out at the side of the road and in the road, some being trampled by other poor devils too sunstruck to stagger around them.

The final death knell was struck when the Federals made the climb to the San Augustan pass in the foothills of the Organ Mountains. Covered with dust, the stumbling, shambling troopers looked like crumbling statues from antiquity given some scant semblance of animation. They'd been beaten down by a hammer sun on a desert anvil.

Baylor's troops started to close in. By this time they were looked upon as saviors by the Unionist stragglers and dropouts who'd fallen by the wayside for miles along the trail. The Confederates took them prisoner and gave them water.

As Baylor's Texans surrounded the remnants of the Yankees' main body, Major Lynde decided to surrender. Officers protested, outraged. "Stand and fight, you yellow cur —" they demanded. Some would have wept tears of rage if they'd had even that much moisture left in them.

Sam Heller and a handful of like-minded stalwarts had had enough. They were not of a mind to become prisoners of war to the Confederacy. Mostly desert-wise Westerners, they'd rationed their thin supplies of water long enough to keep going. A dozen or so, they now rode off, deeper into the desert.

Desertion? They thought not. Not when their commanding officer surrendered what was left of 500 men to Baylor's 300 without firing a shot.

The fugitives took cover in arroyos and canyons with their welcoming shadows. They traveled by night in the relative cool of same, making their way through a dusty desert hell. Even more than Rebel patrols, they were wary of marauding Apaches out hunting for stragglers.

For much of the grueling trek, they went on foot to spare the horses, holding on to the saddles to keep from falling. When they were lucky enough to find them, they carved up barrel cactuses for a few precious drops of moisture. Parched, sun-cracked tongues strained to lick up morning dew drops.

In the end, only a handful survived to meet a friendly patrol from Fort Stanton. One of the few was Sam Heller . . .

A steaming cauldron of hell?

During the siege of Vicksburg in summer of 1862, Sam had been one of a scout squad on a recon mission behind enemy lines. Vicksburg was a roadblock in the middle of the vital artery of the Mississippi River. The watercourse was open and under Union control both above Vicksburg and below it. But the Confederate stronghold resisted Northern attempts to take it.

The mission took Sam and the rest of the squad into the Mississippi backwater swamps. The swamp was a deadlier enemy than Rebel guns. The scouts waded through waist-high stagnant water and muck, assaulted by decay, distemper and rot.

It was like being slowly simmered night and day in a steaming, sweltering hellbroth. Black water — hissing cottonmouths — 'gators brawling and bawling, ever ready to batten on the unwary to pull them under and away, never to rise again — by night, hordes of mosquitoes, stinging, biting, maddening —

Sam survived the mission. A few months later, he went along as an observer on a gunboat that was part of a flotilla making a sortie against the ironclad CSS *Arkansas* to tempt it to come out from under the murderously efficient batteries of cannon that protected it and the city of Vicksburg.

Sam was no sailor; he was a fighting man. It was not in his nature to just go along for the ride. He pitched in and helped out, shoveling coal in the gunboat's engine room.

Steam boilers seethed, pressure mounting so that needles on the gauges swung into the red danger zone. The open doors of the firebox were gates to hell.

Sam labored along with the black gang of coal-tenders, bodies ebony-black from head to toe with powdered coal dust, heaving shovel after shovel of coal into the flames. The temperature below decks rose to 120 degrees; strong men fainted and were carried out on deck to recover and return to the inferno below . . .

March 1865, penultimate month of the war. Sam Heller by then had long been a Secret Service operative, attached to an elite squad of Lafayette Baker's National Detective Police. Baker reported direct to President Lincoln himself.

Sam was on undercover assignment with a half-dozen of the finest men — and women — he'd ever had the honor of serving with. Beloved friends and comrades-in-arms. They were probing a sabotage and arson plot similar to the Confederates' earlier abortive attempt to burn down New York City.

An informant's tip brought the Secret Service operatives to Baltimore's Imperial Hotel at midnight. The lobby, seemingly deserted, was thick with the choking fumes of Greek Fire, the arsonists' hell-brew compound of inflammables that had doused all: horsehair-stuffed sofas, patterned carpets, plush armchairs —

A death trap. The trap was sprung; there was a timeless instant of impending fatality as a precariously perched oil lamp was knocked over by an opening door, falling to the compound-saturated floor, bursting with a *whoomp!*

A spreading ring of blue flames blossomed into a firestorm that turned unwary operatives into screaming human torches.

By sheer luck, Sam was at the edge of the blaze and saved himself by diving headfirst through a glass front window into the street, the only one of the team to escape alive . . .

. . . These and other incidents were relived by Sam again and again as his body and mind were wracked by the effects of the curative potion cooked up by the witch-woman healer, Alma.

The scenes played themselves out singly and together, cascading in a torrent of jumbled imagery as Sam found himself tossed from desert to swamp, gunboat to hotel, sequences runnning backward and forward until there was nothing left but oblivion. He fell into a deep, dreamless sleep.

At the bedside, Lorena and Alma kept long vigil through the stations of the night.

"The fever breaks," Alma said. "He will live."

"For good or ill," she added.

TWELVE

Wednesday afternoon found Johnny Cross and Luke Pettigrew in Wild Horse Gulch, scouting for mustangs. They surveyed the scene to get the way of things, see where the herds gathered, where they grazed, watered and ran. Mustangs numbering in the hundreds roamed the Breaks.

The western hills were blue in the distance, sunlight gilding their tops. Johnny and Luke ranged for miles, working down toward the southern end of the gulch.

Something about wild horses gave Johnny a high lonesome feeling, kind of happy and sad at the same time . . . bittersweet. A mustang running fast and free lifted the spirit in a way he used to experience as a youngster on Sundays when Ma read passages from the Bible to him and brother Cal.

Johnny liked horses anyway; always had. Liked them a lot better than he did most people. Seeing these magnificent animals on the gallop, coursing, pressing forward, sleek muscles working, manes and tails streaming, hooves pounding, digging dirt — all spoke to something deep inside him, striking a responsive chord.

At the same time, though, they spelled opportunity, a chance to get ahead. Mustangs were there for those who could catch them. Break them to bridle, saddle and rider.

Johnny was in a reflective mood. "Pa never made much of a go ranching, but one thing he knew was horseflesh. I don't remember much about him, but I do recall that there wasn't a horse he couldn't ride," he said. "Before he went to be with the Lord, he taught me and Cal about catching wild horses, breaking and selling 'em. Cal was a real mustanger, he could outride me."

"I don't know about that, Johnny. You always was a riding fool," Luke said.

"I was a damned fool, you mean. A damn fool kid. Cal was the better rider," said Johnny.

"I was the better shot, though," he added.

"I never got to know Cal too good, him being older and all, though my big brothers Eben and Andy did. The three of them ran together," Luke said.

"Raised a lot of hell together, too."

"Yes, indeedy. Them boys rode hell bent

for leather six ways to sundown across this
county and a couple more. Even the Comanches couldn't catch 'em — and don't
think they didn't try!"

"Sheriff couldn't catch 'em, neither."

They laughed.

"They was good fellows. I miss 'em," Luke
said.

"The war did in for a lot of good fellows,"
said Johnny.

"That it did."

They rode on, silent for a while. The cliffs
enclosing the gulch opened out and away,
widening into a vast, sprawling flatland. The
streams petered out, the grass shortening,
becoming stubbier, yellow-brown.

They were at the edge of Anvil Flats,
where the plains rolling east to Hangtown
gave way temporarily to stonier and more
barren soil.

In the middle distance south across the
flat, a high, rounded mound stood apart
from a jumble of rocky ridges and bald
stone domes. This was Buffalo Hump, a
landmark on the trail that stretched west
from Hangtown through the Breaks and
into the Staked Plains.

It was a clear, bright day, allowing the duo
to see from a long way off. A line of smoke
rose from somewhere in the hills northwest

of Buffalo Hump. The air was still and the long, thin line of smoke ascended unbroken high into the sky.

Johnny and Luke reined in, halting. Johnny said, "See that?"

"Yup. What do you think, Johnny — smoke signals?"

"Campfire, more likely. Looks to be coming out of Ghost Valley."

"That's real owlhoot country."

"Mebbe that's the hideout Monty spoke of."

"Mebbe."

"We should find out. Best we scout out them before they scout us.

Not today. They'd see us coming from a long way off," said Luke.

"Not today," Johnny agreed, "but soon."

They turned, riding north.

THIRTEEN

Sam Heller sat up in bed, back propped up against the headboard. The bedcovers were down around his waist, covering him below it. He was bare from the waist up, a wad of gauze bandages wrapped around his left shoulder and left side.

A small window set high in the wall beside the bed framed a square of blue sky. It was open, letting in fresh air. It was warm in the room.

Alma entered without knocking, carrying a bundle of folded clothes held pressed to her chest by both arms. On top of that was a pair of boots Sam recognized as his own. Gliding soundlessly to a massive wooden chest at the foot of the bed, she set her burden down on top of the lid and straightened up.

So old, wrinkled, and ancient was she that she seemed almost sexless. She might have been a long-haired old man if not for her shawl and long-skirted dress. The shawl was wrapped cowl-like around the top of her head, face peering out.

"Gracias, vieja," Sam said. Thanks, old one.

She nodded in acknowledgment, a quick, curt head bob. She turned, exiting the room, closing the door on her way out.

Sam tossed back the covers, swinging his feet to the floor. The wooden plank floor was smooth and cool against the soles of his bare feet. He stood up, stretching his good right arm above his head, yawning. His left shoulder was sore as hell. The wound was neatly bandaged, a nice job of doctoring. Its throbbing increased now that he was standing. His left side was stiff and aching where the bullet had creased him.

He tested his left arm, raising it shoulder-high, holding it out from his side. It hurt; sweat beaded up on his forehead. Lowering the arm, he worked his left hand, clenching and unclenching his fist, flexing his fingers, wriggling them. They seemed to work all right.

He went around to the foot of the bed, reaching for the stack of folded clothes. He knew them for his own, spare garments he'd kept inside the bedroll behind his saddle.

The clothes he'd been wearing when shot must have been too bloodstained to be worth saving.

He took a pair of jeans from the pile. Still a bit shaky on his feet, he sat down on the bed's edge to pull on his pants.

Rising, he padded over to the packing case standing against the wall. It served as a makeshift table. On it was a now-dark lamp, a washbasin, a pitcher of water and some towels. He poured some water into the basin, washed his face and hands and toweled them dry.

He finished getting dressed, donning a faded green-and-brown plaid long-sleeved shirt and a pair of thick gray woollen socks. He put his boots on.

There was no mirror in the room. He combed his long yellow hair with his fingers, brushing it back off his forehead and along the sides where it fell to his shoulders.

He opened the door, stepping out on to a dimly lit landing. At its end was a steep, narrow stairway. Descending it, he opened a door and stepped outside. It opened on to a plaza.

Alma stood nearby at the northwest corner of the storehouse, facing him. She extended one arm to point to a patio on the south side of the hacienda, a pavilion where vine-covered white wooden lattice fences and a canopy created a shady area, cool, green

197

and restful.

"The Señora awaits," she said, her voice a dry, toadlike croaking. Until then, he hadn't known she could speak English.

Sam nodded, stepping out of the shadows into the plaza's sunny, open space. He starting toward the big house. The sun's position in the sky marked it as an hour or so before noon. It was warm, with the promise of imminent heat.

This was a working ranch and, except for Sam, most of its inhabitants had been up since before dawn. Some vaqueros rode across the courtyard, heads turning toward Sam. Their glances were flat, unfriendly, coldly appraising. Sam was reminded that he was unarmed. He felt undressed without his guns.

Nearing the hacienda, he angled toward its southern side. The pavilion was set on a terrace. It was an airy, tunnel-like enclosure open at both its short ends. Its long walls and overhead canopy were made of diamond-pattern white lath latticework.

Vines with leafy green shoots grew along the walls and roof, providing decorous shade. Foliage and layered wooden framing broke up the sun's direct rays, filtering their brightness and heat inside the canopied trellis walls.

Bright-colored flowers blossomed on the vine-covered trellis, a burst of bright red, scarlet, pink, magenta, orange and white clinging to serpentine green stems and tendrils. Floral scents were heady in the warm morning sunshine.

Sam climbed a short, shallow stone stairway to the patio, entering the arbor. Within its coolly shadowed space were various items of lawn furniture, including a white-painted wrought iron-table and chairs. The table was set with white linen, plates, silverware, drinking glasses.

Lorena Castillo sat at the round white table, facing him. She wore a short, red and yellow embroidered vest, a lacy white blouse, wide brown leather belt, doeskin ankle-length skirt slit up the sides to mid-calf, and reddish-brown leather brown riding boots with sharp pointed toes.

Lorena encouraged Sam to advance with a nod and a subtle beckoning gesture, her dark eyes alive in a composed masklike face. Sam halted at the opposite side of the table, facing her. "Buenos dias, Señora," he said.

"I speak English, Señor Heller," Lorena said. "Please be seated and make yourself comfortable."

"Thanks." Sam pulled out a chair and sat down opposite her. "You have the advantage over me. You know my name but I don't know yours."

"I am Lorena Castillo Delgado, and this is El Rancho Grande, House of the family Castillo."

"How do you know my name?"

"I took the liberty of going through the papers in your saddlebags. They contained your name . . . and other items of interest. You will pardon the intrusion but you were in no condition to talk when you were brought here."

"What day is this?" Sam asked.

"Thursday."

"Thursday! And I came in on Monday. I lost a couple of days there."

"Be glad you did not lose your life. When you first arrived, some here thought we might have to bury you. Not I. You are strong and your wound was not mortal. Still, you are lucky to be up and about. Your powers of recovery are formidable."

Sam studied her through narrowed eyes. "Seems to me I remember you working on me with a knife."

"You had a bullet in you. I took it out." Lorena reached into a side pocket of her vest, taking out a handkerchief folded into a square. Placing it on the table she unfolded and opened it, revealing a deformed lump of lead metal. "Here it is. It belongs to you."

"It belongs to the man who shot me," Sam said.

"Apparently it did him little good, if he was one of the men found dead at the ford. The men you killed. It is yours now, you earned it."

Sam picked up the slug between thumb and forefinger, weighing it in his hand, eyeing it.

"Keep it. For luck," Lorena said.

Sam shrugged without thinking, sending pain shooting through his left shoulder. He dropped the slug in the left breast pocket of his shirt. "You did a good job of patching me up."

"I have had much practice doctoring bullet wounds for the riders of Rancho Grande," Lorena said.

"I thought I remembered you digging out that slug. And a potion brought in by you and the old woman. Strange brew! After drinking it, I'm not sure what was real and what wasn't. Everything mixed all together, dreams, memories, fancies," Sam said. "It was a wild ride, like a witches' sabbath."

"Alma is no *bruja*, no witch. She's a *curandera*, a healer. Her potion broke your fever. Without it you would have died."

"I owe you my life, then. And her."

"Alma is my creature. She does what I tell her. Otherwise your life or death is a matter of no interest to her."

"But it is to you, eh? Why?" Sam asked.

"A fighting man can be useful to have around," Lorena said, making eye contact with Sam, pinning him with an intense, unblinking gaze.

"I hate to disappoint you, but I'm nothing more than a simple stockman, looking to buy horses and cattle."

Lorena smiled thinly, her expression one of frank disbelief. "Let us have something to eat, gringo; you will tell lies better on a full stomach. I have been waiting breakfast for you. You must be hungry, I know I am," she said.

"I could eat," Sam allowed.

"Good. Another sign of your recovery," Lorena said. Red lips peeled back, flashing a smile of many teeth. She made a beckoning gesture, summoning a pair of serving women who'd been waiting on the other side of the trellis wall closest to the house.

Passing under a wooden archway, they entered the shady, green-tinged patio, each carrying a serving platter. One was prematurely aged, impassive, heavyset; the other was a nubile young girl in her mid-teens, hair parted down the middle and tied in two braids, her face piquant and pretty, her body high-breasted, slim-waisted and rounded-hipped.

They laid out pitchers of fresh fruit juices, dishes and bowls of food, corn tortillas, omelettes, steak, bacon, spicy chorizo sausages, sliced tomatoes, bread still warm from the oven, cheeses and fruit. The youngster covertly examined the big gringo, glancing at him through the corners of her eyes.

Sam dug in. He was hungry, ravenous, but remembered his table manners and slowed down fast. He tucked away the food with relentless methodicity. It was good and tasty, but he ate in moderation, not wanting to slow his mental acuity and reaction time with a too full belly. He needed his wits and speed about him.

Lorena went to it with a hearty appetite. Once the keen edge of his hunger was blunted, Sam looked up from his plate, came up for air, and resumed the conversational sparring. "You said something about finding a use for a fighting man, Señora. But I'm a businessman, nothing more."

"Ah, yes," she said, "but what business?"

"Cattle buying, and a little horse trading on the side."

Lorena laughed without humor. "And that

black book in your saddlebag, the one with all the circulars of wanted men, outlaws with a price on their head? A most unusual stock book, no?"

Sam's smile was disarming. "An honest man doing business in these parts, a stranger, has got to know who the bad hombres are, if only to protect himself. I wouldn't want to buy any stolen stock."

Lorena glanced around, making sure that she and Sam were alone on the patio. The servant girls had gone inside, carrying a load of dirty serving bowls and dishes to the kitchen.

She reached inside her vest, plucking out from a deep inside pocket a long, slim brown leather folder, its dimensions slightly taller and thinner than those of a billfold. Its outside was stained with dried bloodstains. Whisking it out of sight under the table, she quickly, furtively passed it to Sam Heller.

He took it. His green-and-brown plaid flannel shirt was worn tucked into his pants. He unbuttoned two of his shirt buttons, opening enough space to allow him to slip the folder inside his shirt and out of sight, securing it over on his right side. He closed the buttons, put his hands back on top of the table. He reached for a cup of black coffee, sipping from it.

Outwardly, all seemed as if the covert transfer had never been.

"When you were brought here unconscious and bleeding, Alma undressed you," Lorena said. "She found that in the inside pocket of your jacket. She took it out before too much blood soaked into it — enough for me to read the warrant inside."

"And what does it tell you, Señora?" said Sam, keeping a poker face.

"That you would make a better friend than an enemy, Señor Heller."

"My friends call me Sam, Señora."

"I am Señora Castillo — when others are about. Lorena, when we are alone."

"We're alone now."

"I meant in a more intimate setting. I have rivals in the house, enemies. They spy on me. I must be cautious, discreet."

"You're calling the tune, Señora."

Lorena leaned forward, serious, intent. "My position here is extremely delicate, Señor Heller.

"As is yours," she added.

"What of Señor Castillo, your husband?" Sam asked.

"Señor Castillo is no more. My husband Ramon died seven years ago."

"I'm sorry."

She shrugged. "The master of Rancho Grande is Don Eduardo, my father-in-law," she said. "When we Mexicans extend our hospitality to a guest, we say that 'our house is your house.' Unhappily I can make no such statement. I am none too secure here myself.

"Let me explain. I am a Delgado, once the first family in this land. I am a Castillo only by marriage to Ramon, Don Eduardo's firstborn. There was a child, a daughter — the angels took her when she was two years old. Ramon was killed soon after that — by gringos, Tejanos. Texas Anglos.

"I am the widow of an elder son too long dead; she who failed to produce a male heir to the House of Castillo. Don Eduardo tolerates me, nothing more. His younger son and heir Diego hates me and would like to see me sent away from here forever with nothing but the clothes on my back.

"As for the vaqueros, the ranch hands and pistoleros, they ride for Don Eduardo. They belong to him, like his horses and cattle. All but a few, who are loyal to me."

Sam dug into some steak and eggs while she talked. He was still hungry; the food was good. Lorena ate little, picking at her food, mostly pushing it around on her plate. She had business to transact.

"So much for my situation," she said. "Now for yours. You are sitting on a powderkeg."

"Not the first time. I'm used to it," Sam said.

"The only thing Don Eduardo hates more than Indios is a Tejano, a Texan."

"That lets me out. I'm from Minnesota, way up north."

"He hates all Anglos. Texans most of all, but other Anglos almost as much."

"But you don't share his sentiments?"

"I have no love for the Texans. If Don Eduardo were not a hard man, they would have run him out long ago and stolen Rancho Grande for themselves. But unlike him, I know that all Anglos are not alike. After all, you Yanquis fought a war with the Texans."

"Because they were part of the Confederacy, trying to break up the Union," Sam said. "With all respect, Señora, the war is over. We're all Americans now."

"That includes the folk of Rancho Grande, too," he added pointedly.

"That presidential warrant you carry is no peace treaty," Lorena said.

"Keeping the peace is my business," Sam countered.

"Is that what you were doing at the ford

207

when you killed those men?"

"Who says I killed anybody?"

"Sombro. He is half Yaqui Indian and the best tracker in these parts. No white or red man can read signs better. And he served the Delgado long before coming to Rancho Grande," Lorena said.

She put down knife and fork, all pretense of eating forgotten. She leaned forward, intent. "What really happened at the crossing?"

"Some outlaws jumped me. I was lucky; they weren't," Sam said.

"That is all of it?" Lorena pressed, openly skeptical.

"What else could there be?"

She sighed, shaking her head. "And here I thought we were getting along so well."

"Aren't we?"

"We need to come to a mutual understanding, hombre, and time is running out. It is lucky for you that that warrant came into my possession. I am the only one who knows what it is and what it means. A man who bears a commission from the president of the United States is a man worth knowing. As for Alma, she cannot read. But she knows how and when to keep silent.

"Don Eduardo and the others think you are nothing more than a professional gun, a bounty hunter. The *padrone* took note of that strange weapon of yours, the half-rifle and the box of parts that go with it."

"I'm a sportsman, and that's nothing more than a custom-made hunting rifle," Sam said.

"Hunting what? Men?" Lorena said, scoffing. "And that black book of circulars of wanted outlaws. There was no way to keep Don Eduardo from seeing that. It was well; it helped convince him that you are nothing more than just another bounty killer. Of which the county already has more than its share. Each rustler or robber you take will be one less thorn in his side.

"He may even have a use for you himself, if he can hire you to kill his enemies. Wade Hutto, the man who runs Hangtown, is a deadly rival of the *padrone.* He has many guns, too many for the Castillo to go up against directly.

"But if Don Eduardo or Diego should suspect that you are more than just another gringo pistolero — much more — it would not go well for you," Lorena said.

"And the reason why you don't tell him?" Sam asked.

"Why should I? What's in it for me? A saying I learned from you gringos, by the way," said Lorena.

"Somehow I doubt the sentiment is new to you."

"What of it? That is the way of the world. But the truth of it was brought home to me living on this ranch as a poor relation."

"Is it as bad as all that?"

"Don Eduardo tolerates me. I can go nowhere, do nothing without his permission. Diego hates me but hides it in the presence of his father. He lives for nothing except the day the *padrone* dies and he becomes master of the ranch. On that day he will throw me out with nothing more than what I can carry by myself."

Sam's plate was clean; he pushed it away from him. He poured himself a cup of coffee from a silver pitcher. "What can I do for you, Señora?" he asked.

"I am no fool," Lorena said. "Change is coming, I know that. With the war done the Union Army will come here in force, they will be the power in the land. A friend with influence in those circles would be most useful indeed. As that warrant shows, you are that man.

"If you live," she added.

"I'll do my best," Sam said.

"I will keep your secret. But true friendship resides on a basis of mutual trust and equality."

"What would persuade you of my sincerity, Señora?"

"To start with, tell me what really happened at the ford."

"You already seem to know plenty."

"Only what Sombro told me of the signs he read," Lorena said. "A wagon with many guards made the crossing at Mace's Ford. They were ambushed by bandits. The guards were killed and the wagon stolen. Some of the bandits stayed behind. They loaded the dead men on a second wagon to take them away and hide them. A man came along and killed the bandits — you."

"That's pretty close as far as it goes," Sam said, nodding.

"What did the bandits steal?"

"Just between the two of us, an army wagon was making a secret shipment to Fort Pardee. The guards were disguised as civilians to throw robbers off the scent."

"That did not work so well."

"Somebody must have talked out of turn to the wrong people."

Lorena was excited now, dark eyes flashing, high color blazing in her cheeks, red lips parted. She breathed hard, her chest rising and falling. "What were they carrying? Gold?"

"Something better than gold," Sam said.

"Bah! What's better than gold?"

"Guns."

"One thing our poor county has in abundance is guns," Lorena scoffed.

"Not like these," Sam said. "A gross of brand-new Henry rifles — one hundred and forty-four repeating rifles and the ammunition to go with them. Enough firepower to set the Southwest ablaze, in the wrong hands."

"Who were the robbers?

"I wish I knew."

"You must have some idea, gringo."

"The ones I tangled with at the ford were white men, outlaws. It was a big job, well-planned and carried out. Only a handful of bandit chiefs could have pulled it off."

"The guns must be worth much money."

"To the army they are. You can imagine what would happen if they came into the hands of Wahtonka and his Comanche bucks. The cavalry at Fort Pardee would be hopelessly outgunned, they wouldn't stand a chance. They'd be wiped out. There wouldn't be a town or a ranch left unburned between here and Dallas.

"The army will pay plenty to get them back," Sam said.

"How much?" asked Lorena, her expression both dreamy and calculating.

"It's too early for them to have posted a reward. If I had to guess, I'd say Washington will go anywhere from five to ten thousand dollars."

Lorena's mouth turned downward at the corners, pouting. "That is not so much."

"That's for the recovery of the guns," Sam said. "There's sure to be a price on the heads of the outlaws who took them, too. They robbed an army convoy and killed a lot of soldiers. The bounty on their heads could total another twenty, twenty-five thousand dollars."

Lorena brightened up. "A not unworthy sum, gringo, even when split two ways."

"Sure," Sam said, "all you've got to do is find the robbers and take them. That's all."

"That is what you are here to do, no?"

"It is now."

"You will hunt them?"

"Me and every other lawman and man-hunter in the west."

"But they do not have your connections," Lorena pointed out. "A big job for any man, though, and that man a stranger to Hangtree."

"I'm a quick study," said Sam.

". . . We could help each other, eh, gringo?"

"What do you bring to the table, while

213

I'm getting shot at?"

"I have lived here all my life. I know much about Hangtree and those who live here. Things that could save a man's life or end it," Lorena said. "And even if you find the bandits by yourself, what then? They are too many for one man. You were almost killed the first time you went up against them, and that was only part of the gang."

Sam said, "Next time I'll be more careful."

"And if you call in the army, they will get the reward money, not you."

"Sounds like you've got a plan, Señora."

"Always," Lorena said. "We could work together. My position on the ranch is not an enviable one, but it is not without certain assets. I command a handful of followers loyal to me. Sombro alone is worth a posse of ordinary men. If anyone can find the guns, he can. And there are others, pistoleros, bold and unafraid.

"What do you say, gringo? I make a good friend."

After a pause, she added, "And a bad enemy."

"Man can't have too many friends," Sam said. "How much is this friendship going to cost me?"

Lorena began, "I am not greedy —"

breaking off when she saw the look Sam was giving her.

"No more than is necessary," she continued.

"How much?" Sam asked.

"Half. Half of everything taken: bounties, rewards, incidentals," Lorena said.

"That's not an alliance, it's a full partnership."

"Is that so bad?"

"It's a mite steep."

"I already saved your life twice. Once by taking that bullet out of you. And again by keeping silent about who you really are and why you are here. So far I have done all the giving and you the taking. You hardly have reason to complain, gringo."

"I'm not arguing," Sam said.

"Trust is so hard to come by in this unhappy world. But we have a basis for mutual understanding. I keep your secrets. By the same token, I must rely on your discretion," Lorena said. "Don Eduardo must never know of our plans. Once he learns of those stolen guns — and he will, he has a talent for finding out such things — he will move heaven and earth to get hold of them.

"The same goes for Diego. Like me, he would do anything to have money of his own and be free of the *padrone*."

"When it comes to money — or a lady's confidences — I'm a closemouthed man," Sam assured her.

Lorena's expression took on a faraway look. "With enough money I could leave this ranch, these godforsaken plains. Go to San Francisco, Mexico City. Europe, even — Paris."

"I wish you luck."

"It will take more than wishing," she said, once more all business. "Do we have an agreement?"

"It's a go," Sam said. "One or two points I'd like to have cleared up, Señora. What happened to the wagonful of dead guards?"

"Our men found it on Monday. When night came they put it far from here on the road to Hangtree town," Lorena said. Her expression was cynical, knowing. "Don Eduardo judged that it would not do for it to be found at or near Rancho Grande. That would give the Texans an excuse to blame it on us."

"Good thinking. And the bodies at the ford?" Sam asked.

"Of the men you killed? We left them there. On Tuesday a posse from town came and took them away."

"Has the army come in yet?"

"No."

"They will. Soon, and in force."

"If they find the stolen guns first, no gold for us."

"Time for me to get to work," Sam said.

FOURTEEN

On Thursday noon, two riders approached the Cross ranch.

Johnny Cross and Luke Pettigrew had made some improvements around the place, but the ranch house was a long way from being habitable. It was a wreck, a gutted, stonewalled shell filled with masses of rubble. They hauled out some fallen roof timbers, using them to build a lean-to and to patch up the corral, now well stocked with close to twenty horses. The two men slept outdoors at night in the lean-to.

The horses were a windfall that had come easily, practically falling into their laps. Johnny and Luke were determined that they wouldn't go the same way. "With all the horse thieves and rustlers hereabouts, we need to safeguard our stock," Johnny said.

"Dirty crooks!" Luke said with feeling.

"I got an idea," said Johnny. "There's a box canyon a couple miles north of here in the eastern slope. A good hiding place, hard to find if you don't know it's there. Me and Cal used to pen our stock there when we'd be away from the ranch for any length of time. There's a spring there and good grassland. The mouth of the canyon is narrow; we closed it off with a gate fence. The two of us should be able to fix it up and get it back into shape pretty quick. We can hide the horses up there when we go out mustanging."

They spent a long, hard Wednesday repairing the five-bar timber gate that sealed off the covert grazing land of the upland spread.

Thursday morning they labored at various chores and knocked off at midday for lunch. While Luke sat in the shade massaging some of the stiffness out of his sore half-leg, Johnny went to the family burial plot for a few moments of quiet time.

A patch of land stood between the back of the ranch house and the foot of the south slope of the jagged-top hill. Johnny had fixed it up, weeding it, clearing away the dead leaves and bramble bushes that had gathered during years of neglect.

There were three graves: those of his father, mother, and sister Mandy. Pa was the first to die; then Mandy, carried off by scarlet fever at age ten; and finally Ma in the spring of Sixty-One.

The thin wooden headpieces carved with their names and dates and placed at the gravesites had long ago succumbed to the elements and come apart. Johnny replaced them with three simple wooden crosses. Wildflowers grew over the grave mounds.

Johnny let them be, leaving them where they were. It seemed fitting somehow.

No grave here for brother Cal, though; he was buried in a mass grave with thousands of Confederate and Yankee dead who'd fallen at the battle of Shiloh.

Johnny wondered where his final resting place would be. "Boot Hill, most likely," he said to himself, smiling wryly.

He was already living on borrowed time. He'd narrowly escaped death countless times during the war and afterward. Every day since then was a gift: pure gravy. "And that don't bother me a bit," he said.

It was a nice day. The sun was high, hot and shining. Birds roosted in the shady tree boughs. East of the hill, a stream meandered through grassy meadows, sunlight glinting on its surface.

Johnny thought about saying a prayer, but the only one he knew was the one about the Valley of the Shadow of Death, and that didn't fit the mood. His folks and Mandy had no need of prayers anyhow. They were good people and without doubt had gone to their just reward.

He was the one who could use the prayers. "I'd rather rely on my guns," he told himself.

He turned away from the graves, looking south. He saw two riders coming north, toward the ranch. They were still a long way off.

Luke must have seen them, too. He rounded the corner of the ranch house, coming into view. "Hey, Johnny!" he called.

"I see 'em," Johnny said. He went down to the yard in front of the ranch house, joining Luke in watching the newcomers.

Two black blurs crawling across the plains. They came openly, with no attempt at stealth. They came from the southeast, moving diagonally northwest toward the ranch.

"Looks like they come from town on Hangtree Trail," Luke said.

The trail ran west from Hangtown into the plains, across Adobe Flats into the Breaks just south of Buffalo Hump, continuing westward into the Staked Plains and beyond, clear into New Mexico.

"They're making a beeline for the ranch," Luke noted. "Only two of 'em. Wonder what they want?"

"We'll find out," Johnny said.

Twenty minutes passed before the two riders rode into the ranch house's dirt yard.

Johnny Cross sat on a crude three-legged stool that had been salvaged from inside the ranch house. He was positioned in a patch of shade in front of the structure, sitting with his back against the stone wall to the right of the empty doorframe. Nearby stood a wooden barrel filled with stream water. A rusty iron dipper was secured by a rawhide thong to a nail in the barrel's upper rim.

Luke was nowhere in sight.

The newcomers were covered with trail dust from what must have been a long, hard ride. They looked tough, hardbitten. Nothing unusual about that. Most of the folk of Hangtree County were hardbitten types. If they weren't, they usually didn't last long.

Sometimes they didn't last long if they were, either.

One was thirty, redheaded, with a same-colored mustache and long, narrow green eyes. He wore a black hat, black leather vest, and a low-slung gun on his left hip.

The other had a thick head of oily black hair and blue-black beard stubble. A handsome man in an overblown way, whose looks were spoiled by narrow eyes and a tight, mean mouth. He wore a round-topped, flat-brimmed hat, and red bandanna. His dark, fancy-patterned shirt would have been more at home in a gambling hall than out on the range. Two guns were worn tied down, gunfighter-style.

Johnny rose, standing up to face the newcomers as they reined in, hands resting easily at his sides, not far from his twin holstered guns. His manner was calm, untroubled.

The redhead's dirty face was split by a broad, white-toothed grin. His partner scowled like he was sucking on a lemon.

"Howdy," the redhead said.

Johnny nodded. "What can I do you for?"

The mean-faced man frowned, spat. "Who're you?"

"Seeing as how you're on my land, I'm the one who should be asking you that," Johnny said, his outwardly amiable demeanor unchanged. "Who're you?"

"You loco or something?"

"He must be new to the outfit," the redhead said.

"Yeh? Well, he ain't gonna get much older if he don't learn some manners."

"Easy, Reese."

"Nobody tells me what to do, Red, not even you. And especially not some punk

223

kid." Reese looked around, his scowl deepening. "Where's Monty and the rest of the boys?"

"Y'all friends of Monty?" Johnny asked.

"We're with the outfit. I'm Dan Oxblood," the redhead said, "and this here's Reese Kimbro."

"Kimbro," Johnny said, thoughtful-like. "You the one they call Killer Kimbro?"

"Looks like some sense is starting to sink into that thick skull of yours, and not a moment too soon," Kimbro said, smirking. "I reckon the name Killer Kimbro means something even to a snot-nose like you."

Johnny shook his head. "Nope."

Kimbro's thick black brows knitted together in a furious frown. His hand hung poised above the gun on his right hip. "You just bought the farm, sonny. You got your guns on. Go for 'em!"

"Whoa now, Reese —"

"Shut up, Red. This is between me and the kid."

"Not hardly. Take a look at that set of double-barrels peeking at us from the corner of that window," the redhead said.

"Shucks, now you went and spoiled my surprise," Luke said. He was inside the ranch house at the window to the left of the doorframe, sheltered behind the wall, holding a sawed-off double-barreled shotgun that rested on the lower corner of the windowsill so the big holes of the twin bores covered the two horsemen.

Kimbro's face paled beneath its tan, going sallow. His hand drifted away from his gun, moving well clear of it.

"Hesh up, Reese, and let me me do the talking; mebbe we can get out of this without getting our heads blowed off," Red said. He turned his face toward Johnny. "You seem like a sensible enough fellow. We ain't looking for trouble."

"What are you looking for?" Johnny said.

"Some jaspers we know were camped out this way. We come by to pay them a visit. Social call, you might say."

"Monty and friends?"

"That's right. They around?"

"Not any more. They done moved on."

"Where to?"

Johnny shrugged.

"When're they coming back?" asked Red.

"Not in this lifetime."

"So that's the way of it, huh? Looks like we made this trip for nothing," Red said. "We'll be riding out then."

"You do that," Johnny said.

"Hope your friend with the scattergun ain't got no itchy trigger finger."

"Oh, he won't shoot at nothing less'n he's got a mind to. Ain't that right, Luke?"

"That's right," Luke said.

"He's a peace-loving type," Johnny said. "Me, too."

"Fine. That's fine. Okay we go now?" Red asked.

"Yup."

"Well, that's fine," Red said. "By the way, I don't believe I caught your name."

"Cross, Johnny Cross."

Red stroked a crescent-shaped scar in the corner of his chin. "I heard tell of a fellow name of Cross who rode with Cullen Baker down East Texas way a while back. Cullen, Bill Longley and some other good ol' boys. Any relation?"

"Could be," Johnny said.

"Fast crowd. Man'd have to be pretty quick to keep up with that bunch."

"I like Hangtree better. It's nice and quiet."

"You think so? Well, mebbe."

"You seem like you got some sense, Red," said Johnny.

"I try."

"This here's Cross land. It's been Cross land for a long time and that's how it's gonna stay. You might spread the word around."

"I'll do that."

"That's fine," Johnny said. "Y'all can go now."

"We're on our way," Red said.

"Next time we meet, kid, it'll be even-up. You won't always have a shotgun covering you," Kimbro said.

Johnny laughed. "If that's all that's bothering you, climb down off that horse and we'll settle it now. Just you and me."

"No, thanks. I'll pick my own time and place."

"No time like now."

Kimbro sneered. "Betting against a pat hand is a sucker play. I'll wait till my deal comes around."

Red turned his horse's head away from the ranch house, toward the south. "You do what you want, Reese; I'm riding out." He touched spurs to the horse's flanks and started away, the animal moving at an easy lope.

"You talk big, sonny. Got enough sand to keep from shooting a man in the back?" Kimbro said.

"The last thing you'll ever see is me looking you straight in the eye," Johnny said.

"Until next time, then," Kimbro said. He spat on the ground. "See you soon."

He turned his horse and started after Red,

who'd already put some distance between himself and the ranch house.

Johnny stood there, watching the two of them ride away. Luke came out of the ranch house and joined him. "We should have cleaned up on them two when we had the chance," Luke said.

"It's a hot day. I didn't feel like getting rid of any bodies this afternoon," Johnny said.

"That Kimbro got a nice fat reward on him."

"Now you tell me. Well, he'll be back. We'll bag him yet."

"Just so he don't bag us."

"Kimbro? I heard of him, sure. I made like I hadn't to rile him up. But it's the other one, Red, who's the dangerous one in that combination."

"Who's he?"

"Dan Oxblood, from west of the Pecos, a real hellbender. He knows some people I know. Did some gun work with Cullen Baker down in the bosky East Texas country. Moved on before I came along so I never met him. Cullen spoke well of him, though, and he don't have much good to say about most folks."

Red and Kimbro angled west, entering the pass to Wild Horse Gulch.

"What'll you bet they're heading down to

228

Buffalo Hump, Luke? To that hideout in Ghost Valley?"

"No bet."

"Dan Oxblood, Kimbro . . . a couple of high-powered gunhawks to be hunkered down in the Breaks. I wonder who else is part of that outfit Red spoke of, and what they're up to out there."

"Knowing you, Johnny, I'm sure we'll find out the hard way. You made Kimbro look small. He'll be back and he won't be alone."

"He'll get what Monty and his pards got. I'm through drifting. Nobody's bulling me off my land."

". . . 'Course, that don't mean we can't make a strategic retreat," Johnny added. "Let's herd most of the horses to the upland park where they'll be safe out of sight. Then we go into town tonight. We'll pick up some information and see which way the wind's blowing."

"Hot damn! That ain't all I'm gonna pick up," Luke said. "You know how long it's been since I had me a woman?"

"Judging by the steam coming out of your ears, I'd say too long," Johnny said.

FIFTEEN

Gunfire sounded on Thursday afternoon at Rancho Grande. It came from behind the back of the hacienda, the big house.

Sam Heller and Lorena Castillo went toward it, Lorena leading the way. They walked side by side, a respectable arm's-length of distance between them. The sun's strong heat felt good to Sam. His left shoulder and side ached, and the soothing warmth soaked into him.

Somewhere beyond the north face of the hacienda, a pair of handguns was blasting away. Sam and Lorena rounded the north-west corner of the house. "Here is where our pistoleros practice their skills," Lorena said.

The area behind the back of the house was a stretch of open, empty space, far removed from the corral, stables, bunk-house, outbuildings, and the little ranche-ria, the handful of shacks belonging to married vaqueros with families. The space had been turned into a shooting gallery.

A tiled patio aproned the north face of the hacienda. Beyond its far edge lay a broad, grassy yard enclosed by a chest-high adobe wall covered with a white limestone wash. Behind the wall rose an eight-foot-high earthen mound that served as a kind of a bullet-catching berm, a backstop for target practice. The earthen mound showed a face of bare dirt; no blade of grass grew upon it.

The top of the wall was lined with a row of empty glass bottles, pieces of pottery, water jugs, empty flowerpots and the like. The bullet-pocked adobe wall was cratered like the face of the moon. It evoked in Sam's mind the sinister impression of a backdrop for a firing squad. Perhaps it had been used for just that, he thought, though the wall was bare of bloodstains. Don Eduardo reigned supreme on Rancho Grande; he was the law here, wielding the power of life and death.

It was mid-afternoon. The sun hung halfway between the zenith and the western horizon. A man stood at the ornate stone balustrade at the far end of the patio, facing the adobe wall. An oversized figure in a big sombrero, he cast a long, angular shadow that slanted east.

The effect was a trick of the light, for there was nothing angular about this big bear of a man. Shaggy-haired, some of his graying locks were entwined into long, snaky braids with little bows of colored ribbons knotted into the ends. The lower half of his face was covered by a bushy iron-gray beard.

He stood facing the adobe wall, a six-gun in each hand, blazing away at the bottles and pottery lined up on top of the wall bordering the yard. Alternating from one to the other, he fired the gun in his right hand, then the one in his left. Each shot scored, shattering a bottle or pot.

Lorena halted where the patio edged the house, Sam stopping beside her. She moved her mouth close to his ear to be heard over the gunfire. "That is Vasquez," she said. "Do not let his size fool you. He is quick with a gun — lightning fast. The jefe, the chief of Don Eduardo's pistoleros."

A boy stood facing a wooden plank table in the upper left-hand corner of the patio. A slight youth with glossy black hair and bird-like features, he was loading one of a line of pistols laid out on the table.

A door opened in the north wall of the house and a man stepped out on to the patio. He was carrying some of Sam's gear:

the mule's-leg sawed-off rifle in its custom-made leather rig; a bandolier whose loops were filled with cartridges for the weapon; and a long, flat, dark wooden box with a suitcase-type handle.

He made brief eye contact with Lorena, inclining his head slightly in an almost imperceptible bow. Was there a touch of courtly formality there, a sign of obeisance? Or had Sam imagined it? The gesture was quick and subtle, and he was unsure of its meaning, if any.

"That is Gitano," Lorena said, low-voiced. "Mark him well, hombre. He is one of mine. His family has served the House of Delgado, my people, since long before the Castillos came to this land. Like Alma, he was one of my retainers who came here to stay with me at Rancho Grande when I married Ramon."

Sam recognized Gitano as the piratical-looking Gypsy from the night Lorena had doctored him. In his mid-twenties, he had straight hair, matte black, parted in the middle and reaching to his jawline. It framed a sharp-featured, dark-eyed, clean-shaven face.

Sunlight glinted off the gold hoop-ring piercing his left earlobe. The cheeks of his mahagony-colored face were pitted with smallpox scars.

He had broad shoulders, a tapering torso, lean hips. He wore a white ruffled-front long-sleeved shirt, thin black vest, black bell-bottom pants, and good boots. A scarlet sash was wrapped around his middle like a cummerbund, a gun stuck in the top of it.

The hammer of the gun in Vasquez's right hand clicked on an empty chamber. The gun in his left also came up empty. The top of the wall was cleared of bottles and ceramics, only pieces of broken glass and potsherds remaining. Vasquez set the empty pistols down on the table so the boy could reload them.

Gitano crossed to the far end of the patio, bootheels clicking on the tiles. Vasquez glanced over his shoulder, saw Gitano coming. Saw, beyond him, Sam and Lorena.

Gitano set down Sam's hardware on the wooden table.

Sam and Lorena climbed three shallow stone steps to the patio and crossed toward the opposite end. Vasquez turned to face them. Here was the ogre from when Sam had had the bullet pulled. He was all heavy upper body and torso, bandy legs seeming stunted by comparison.

Vasquez doffed his big sombrero in a gesture of respect. "*Buenos tardes,* Señora

Lorena," he said.

"Good afternoon, Hector," she said.

Vasquez's eyes glittered as he gave Sam Heller the once-over. His face split in a big, toothy grin. "Back on your feet, eh, gringo? The last time I saw you, you were flat on your back. I thought we would have to bury you."

"Hope you're not too disappointed," Sam said.

"Ha ha, you make the joke, yes? That is good."

A man exited the house on to the patio. In his mid-thirties, of medium height, he was trim, athletic, with wavy brown hair slicked back and shaped into a pompadour. His chiseled oval face featured almond-shaped moist brown eyes and an eyebrow mustache.

He wore a short chocolate-colored jacket with black frogging and trimmings, matching pants that flared at the cuffs, a pale yellow shirt with ruffles at neck and wrists, a hand-tooled brown leather gun belt with an elaborately engraved gold buckle, and a holstered gun worn low on the left-hand side. Expensive imported boots of fine cordovan leather showed off his small, narrow feet to good advantage.

Vasquez, Gitano and the boy reloading the

guns acknowledged his entrance with respectful head-bows. The newcomer crossed to Sam and Lorena. He smiled from ear to ear, exhibiting a gleaming mouthful of pearly teeth.

"Senor Diego, meet Samuel Heller," Lorena said, pronouncing Sam's last name with the H silent: "Ay-lair." "Senor Heller, this is Diego Castillo, son of Don Eduardo and my brother-in-law."

Diego made no motion to shake hands, nor did Sam make the mistake of expecting him to. Sam acknowledged the introduction with a slight inclination of the head, not a bow but a nod.

Diego's beaming grin remained undimmed. "Ah yes, the mysterious stranger in whose well-being our beloved Lorena has taken such an interest."

"My interest is in all things affecting Rancho Grande," she said.

"Quite so. It is a tribute to your healing skills that our guest is back on his feet so soon."

"For which the Señora has my gratitude and thanks — as do you, Señor, for the hospitality of your house," said Sam.

Diego made a dismissive gesture, as if brushing away a bothersome insect. "It is of no matter."

"Of considerable matter to me, Señor. I hope to thank Don Eduardo for the kindnesses shown to a stranger."

"I doubt that will be possible. The *padrone* is of a most retiring nature and rarely grants the privilege of a personal audience to outsiders."

"Then perhaps you will be so good as to convey to him my deep thanks and appreciation."

"I will endeavor to do so — when the Don finds the time to condescend to meet with me, his own son." Diego laughed somewhat self-consciously, as though aware of having revealed perhaps too much of the Castillo family's inner workings.

He pointedly turned his attention to the weaponry arrayed on the table, displaying a special interest in the mule's-leg. "So this is the unusual firearm I have heard mention of! A most formidable-appearing instrument. I have never seen one quite like it. A cut-down rifle, no?"

"That's right, Señor," Sam said. "It's a Winchester, the latest make. It's a breech-loading, lever-action repeating rifle. Cutting it down makes it more compact than a carbine but with greater firepower. It can be worn as a sidearm. It's what's known as a mule's-leg."

"A 'mule's-leg' . . . ?" Diego said.

"Because it's got a kick like the hind leg of a Missouri mule."

"Most amusing. Perhaps you would be so good as to give us a demonstration. I am sure we all would like to see it in operation."

"If you like."

"Please."

Diego spoke to the boy. "Pablito, put some fresh targets up." Near the table was a wheelbarrow whose hopper was full to overflowing with empty bottles and earthenware pots. "Mostly tequila and whiskey bottles, Señor Heller. And those are just the ones our good Vasquez drank."

"If only I had, Señor Diego!"

"My little joke, of course," Diego said.

Pablito carried a double armful of bottles and reddish-brown jugs to the wall. He lined them up on the top, side by side in a row.

"Some of the melons too, boy," said Diego. Several honeydew melons stood on the table. Pablito set them on top of the wall at opposite ends, bracketing the line of bottles and jugs. The melons were a pair of pale moon faces peeking over the wall.

Sam picked up the mule's-leg, running his fingertips lightly across it, examining it.

It hadn't been cleaned since last he'd used it. That offended his sense of fitness; he was a stickler about cleaning his weapons after use. On the other hand, he preferred that no one handle the piece but himself.

The weapon's heft, its well-wrought metal felt good in his hands. Right. The mule's-leg was still armed from when he'd reloaded it after the dustup at Mace's Ford.

Pablito scampered back to the patio, getting behind the firing line.

Sam took up a stance facing the adobe wall. His left shoulder and side were hurting, but that shouldn't affect his performance. It was against his nature to show off his skills, but sometimes it was necessary to make an impression. This was one of those times. In Texas, in the West, as most everywhere, a display of marksmanship could only resound to the shooter's credit.

Holding the leveled weapon in both hands, he fired from the hip, working the lever and squeezing the trigger in one fluid motion again and again. Working from left to right, he cleared out the bottles and jugs one after another, each of them flying into pieces.

Spear blades of flame lanced from the muzzle, accompanied by a cloud of gunsmoke.

He saved the melon at the extreme right-hand side for last. It disintegrated in a mass of spewing pulp, rind and juices. Sam ceased firing.

Reaching into the wheelbarrow, Vasquez grabbed a bottle by the neck and heaved it into the air, sending it high and arching. Winking, glittering, it pinwheeled in midair. A round from the mule's-leg blew it to pieces.

Vasquez used both hands to toss up two bottles at a time. Sam blew them both out of the sky.

Diego gave a sardonic little bow, lightly clapping his hands. "Bravo, Señor. Most impressive."

Lorena's eyes glittered, spots of color glowing in her cheeks. She felt reassured that she'd forged an alliance with the right man.

Diego arched an eyebrow. "With such skills, I wonder how you happened to be wounded at the ford."

"Bottles don't shoot back, Señor Castillo. Badmen do," Sam said.

"This new Winchester is the first one of its kind that I have seen. It seems criminal somehow to mutilate it by cutting off its parts, amputating it."

"Modified, not mutilated, Señor." Sam unlatched the brass fastenings at the front edge of the wooden box and opened its hinged lid, folding it back. Within the bottom half of the case in special mountings were a wooden stock, a long barrel, and a telescopic sight, all fitted with attachments allowing them to be fastened onto the piece.

"A few quick adjustments and the mule's-leg becomes a long-range, precision rifle," Sam said.

"Most intriguing. I see that you are a specialist in your line, Señor. In this land such skills should serve you well," Diego said.

He turned to Vasquez. "Take two guns."

"*Sí, Señor Diego,*" Vasquez said. He picked up two loaded guns from the table and holstered them.

"Gitano — the knives," Diego said.

"*Sí, Señor.*" Gitano reached inside his red sash. Beneath it, wrapped around his flat belly like a waist cincher, was a tall leather belt, circling him from his hips to just below the rib cage. It sported a row of vertical sheaths, each holding a flat, slim throwing knife. Gitano reached in and withdrew three shiny daggers, holding them in one hand.

Diego told the boy to take two bottles from the wheelbarrow. Pablito obeyed, holding one in each hand.

"Señor Heller has been good enough to

leave one melon on the wall untouched. That is for you, Gitano," Diego said. Gitano nodded.

"Vasquez, you take the bottles. The boy will throw them both up in the air when I give the word," Diego said. "Now!"

Pablito tossed the bottles skyward. Vasquez drew both guns and fired, two shots sounding almost as one. The bottles burst.

At the same time, Gitano's arm was a blur of motion. Three daggers protruded from the melon on the wall. Two were placed where the eyes would be. A third stuck out from what would be the middle of the forehead.

"My compliments, gentlemen," Sam said dryly.

"At Rancho Grande, we, too, are not without specialists, Señor Heller," Diego said.

A hint of motion from the hacienda caught Diego's attention, causing him to look up. Following the direction of the other's gaze, Sam saw that Diego was staring at a second-story window overlooking the patio and grounds.

French-door windows opened out onto an iron-railed balcony. Floor-length gauzy white drapes veiled the opening. They were parted, one having been lifted by a clawlike hand. It belonged to a figure that stood framed in the portal.

An elderly man in a somber black suit, tall, slim, straight, stiff-backed. Lead-colored hair crowned a long, rawboned face, sunken-cheeked, with a silver-gray mustache and goatee. Eyes burned in the depths of hollow sockets, looking down with chill hauteur.

The hand released the edge of the curtain it had been holding, freeing it to fall in place, veiling him behind a scrim. He stepped back, swallowed up by the room's gloomy shadows.

"Don Eduardo," Lorena breathed.

Sam had the feeling of having been weighed in the balance. From the stiff, frozen faces of Diego and Lorena Castillo, he knew that he was not alone in experiencing that sensation of remote, icy scrutiny.

But the verdict of the *padrone* was yet to be determined.

Like the rest of Hangtree County, like all of Texas, Rancho Grande was open-range, free and unfenced, allowing for the unhindered passage of cattle herds to fresh pasture lands and water. But the heart of the ranch, the inner citadel of hacienda and outbuildings grouped around the central plaza, was enclosed behind adobe walls ten feet high and several feet thick.

The ramparts were a defense against Indians and bandits. The barrier was interrupted by several strategically placed portals, each sealed by massive, ironbound wooden gates.

Opposite the hacienda, across the plaza, was a high, arched main gate. Its double doors were open. Beyond the archway, a dirt road stretched straight across Castillo land, running south for miles before meeting the Hangtree Trail at a right angle. The trail ran east to Hangtown and west to the Breaks.

Lorena Castillo stood alone, inside and to the right of the portal, as Sam Heller made ready to ride out.

Sam was mounted up on Dusty. The steel-dust had been well-groomed and well-tended in the Castillo stables while his master was laid up. The mule's-leg was once again holstered on Sam's right side; a .36 Navy Colt was worn butt-out, tucked into the top of his pants on his left hip.

Like his horse, his belongings had been secured and looked after during his stay.

His gear was now stowed to the saddle. Inside a pouch in one of his saddlebags was his black book of circulars of the Most Wanted outlaws in the West. Topping things off, his head was covered by his battered but serviceable slouch hat, the same type worn by General Ulysses S. Grant and given by him to Sam as a gift.

Sam was free to leave. None of the folk of Rancho Grande hindered his departure. In fact, he had the feeling his hosts were eager to see him go, for various reasons.

Lorena stood just inside the main gate, waiting for him as he rode out. Sam reined to a halt, doffing his hat in a courtly gesture. "A thousand thanks, Señora. I'm in your debt," he said.

"Indeed you are," she said, "and I expect your thanks to exceed many thousands."

"I always pay my debts in full, for good or ill."

"Your way is hard, hombre. I do not envy you. The Texans will hate you because you are a Yanqui. The Mexicans because you are a gringo. The Indians because you are a white man. Respectable folk will shun you as a killer. Outlaws will hate and fear you for the same reason," Lorena said. "And if they really knew what you were about, none of them would rest until they killed you."

Sam laughed. "The way you tell it, I might as well lay down and die."

"You had your chance to do that when you were shot, but you chose to live. Make the most of it. Find the guns and we will split the reward."

"I'll do my damnedest."

"I trust you, gringo. You know why?"

"Is it my honest face?"

"Hardly. I know what you are and you know what I am. You need friends, allies. So do I. We are joined by self-interest. One false step for either of us and we are through, finito," said Lorena. "We can use each other, gringo."

"That's the best offer I've had in a while," Sam said.

"You are a man, I am a woman."

"So I noticed."

"More than anything else, I want to be free. Free of Rancho Grande, of House Castillo. To do that, I need to be rich," Lorena said. "Do this for me and you will not find me ungrateful. Betray me and I will kill you myself."

Sam let that pass without comment. "If I need to contact you, how do I reach you?"

"I will get in touch with you. Gitano will be our go-between. I trust him with my life," Lorena said.

"But can I trust him with mine?"

"As long as you are faithful to me. Any messages you have for me, give them to Gitano and he will pass them along. As he will relay any messages I have for you."

"How do I find him?" Sam asked.

"He will find you. He will be near. Very near," Lorena said, smiling thinly.

"Not too near. I might take him for an enemy and shoot him by mistake."

"If you do, make sure you kill him. The Gypsy is a bad enemy."

"I'd rather have him as a friend."

"Keep your bargain with me and he will serve you well."

Sam touched his hat brim in a parting salute. "Until we meet again, Señora."

She raised a hand in farewell. "Luck, gringo. And try not to get shot this time."

Sam rode out.

Sixteen

A U.S. Army cavalry column stood halted in the middle of Trail Street. It was made up of about fifty horse soldiers, riding in tandem. The column faced west, its vanguard abreast of the Cattleman Hotel.

The troops had done some hard riding. They'd been on patrol in the field, night and day, for ten days. Horses and men alike were dirty, tired, hungry and thirsty.

The cavalrymen were not in the best of humors. A grueling, fruitless search for the raiders who'd sacked and burned Midvale had brought them to a hostile settlement.

That's what Hangtown was to these Unionist troops: a stronghold of unreconstructed Rebels.

The war had officially ended in April 1865 with General Robert E. Lee signing the articles of surrender at Appomatox. But now, almost a year later, much of Texas was still in a state of siege.

These cavalrymen from Fort Pardee were part of an army of occupation. Their mission was as much about suppressing any flare-up of secessionist rebellion as it was about curtailing Comanche, Kiowa, and Lipan Apache war parties.

Townsfolk who crowded the boardwalks on both sides of Trail Street were surly, sullen and unfriendly at best. The troops resented having to risk their lives fighting Indians on behalf of a population that until recently had made war on them and, given half a chance, would do so again. Their bad mood was not improved by the thought of the mouthwatering nearness of mugs of frothy beer and tumblers of red whiskey available in the many saloons and bars lining the street — places now off-limits to them, since they were on duty.

As for the folk of Hangtown, they found the Yankee soldiers about as welcome as skunks at a garden party.

In command of the cavalry patrol was Captain Ted Harrison. A decorated combat veteran of the war, he was in his late twenties, with curly blond hair already thinning on top, bushy side-whiskers and a mustache.

The unit's top noncom was Sergeant Carlton Oakes, a tough, leathery fighting soldier who'd been in the army since the Mexican-

American War.

Wade Hutto, with Sheriff Barton in tow, went to the van of the column to palaver with Captain Harrison. Hutto's position was a delicate one. During the war, he'd been appointed chief adminstrator for the district. It was not a military but a civilian post, exempting him from the victorious Federals ban on ex-Confederate officers holding positions of authority during the occupation.

Hutto was also the preeminent man in the county, the biggest landholder and richest magnate in Hangtree — and the one who had the most gunmen at his beck and call.

But he lacked the will and the firepower to buck the United States Army.

It served his interests to position himself as the middleman, the intercessor between federal troops and the folk of the county. He had to walk a fine line between placating the Yanks while maintaining the respect of the local citizenry.

As for Barton, he was Hutto's man. Hutto had put him in as sheriff; he'd do as Hutto told him.

Hutto and Captain Harrison had had official dealings before. Hutto went out into the street where Harrison sat on his horse. Barton tagged along, hanging back a few paces behind Hutto.

"Wade Hutto here, Captain," Hutto said.

"Yes, I know you," said Harrison, his neutral tone masking any feelings, positive or negative, he held about the town boss.

"What brings you to Hangtree?" asked Hutto.

"It was reported that a wagonload of dead white men was found on Tuesday on the trail west of town," Harrison said. "Also that some other dead men were found at Mace's Ford around the same time."

"Yes, that's true."

"I want to see them."

"That'll be difficult, Captain. They're all buried on Boot Hill."

Harrison frowned. "Already? That seems a bit premature."

"Been a spell of hot weather lately. We had to get them into the ground fast," Hutto said.

"They've got to come out."

Hutto's broad face expressed puzzlement. "Not sure I get you, Captain."

"We're going to dig them up."

"When?"

"Now."

"At nighttime?"

"This is Army business. I'm in a hurry.

We didn't come out here on any pleasure trip."

"Anything you say, Captain. We're cooperating."

A fight between two dogs would have drawn a crowd in Hangtown. Dark doings on Boot Hill at night proved to be a powerful attraction. It seemed that most of the townsfolk had come out to watch the show.

The graveyard on the west edge of town was beyond the zone of light cast by the lamps and lanterns of the settlement. A waxing moon hung overhead, flooding the scene with silvery light. Thin clouds stretched streamer-like across the night sky. Torches lit up Boot Hill.

Soldiers and townspeople gathered around the knoll on the north side of Hangtree Trail. The cavalrymen picketed their mounts on a grassy field off to one side at the base of the rise, out of the way. The troopers not on gravedigging detail were massed around the horses. They were off by themselves, isolated/separated from the townsfolk.

A large number of the inhabitants had turned out to watch the cavalry dig up fresh graves. Outdoorsmen and town dwellers, cowboys and bankers, the gentry and the sporting element, respectable types and saddle tramps, gamblers and whores were among those thronging the area.

The saloons had largely been emptied of their clientele who'd come out to watch the proceedings. Many brought whiskey bottles with them and passed them around, adding a carnival-like air to the macabre setting.

That was north of the trail out of town.

On the south side it was quiet, peaceful and more or less unpeopled. The white-painted wooden church with its pointed steeple looked monumental in the moonlight, as if made of marble.

Standing vigil on the front steps were the pastor and sexton of the church. The pastor was there to make sure that these devilish Yankees committed no sacrilege or blasphemies in the churchyard's hallowed ground. Let them do what they liked on Boot Hill; none of his parishioners were buried there, only outlaws and the indigent.

The sexton, a club-footed white-haired man who served as handyman and gravedigger, was charged with guarding against drunks and whores sneaking into church grounds to practice their indignities and indecencies.

On the other side of the trail, the soldiers grouped with the horses smoked, chatted and stretched their legs.

"Keep the men together, Sergeant Oakes. No wandering off," Captain Harrison said.

"Yes, sir," Oakes said.

He addressed the troops. "Listen up, men. I know most of you would like nothing better than a drink, a woman, or both. Any man fool enough to try is more than likely to wind up dead before getting a dozen paces away. These Rebs'd do you in with a smile and their whores would knife you in the back for your loose change."

One of a group of whores standing nearby on the sidelines spoke up: "Hah! Everybody knows you bluebellies ain't got two pennies to knock together in your pockets. You drink up all your pay!"

Her associates responded with shrieks and cackles. "That's telling 'em, Madge!" one cried.

A cavalryman said to his buddy, "She's got your number, Rourke."

"And yours too, Bill!" Rourke replied.

Hearing the byplay, Wade Hutto frowned, turning to the sheriff. "Put a cork on that kind of nonsense," he said. "We don't want this turning into more of a circus than it already is."

"Okay, Wade," Barton said. He passed the word to Smalls. The deputy went over to the whores.

Madge, defiant, stood facing him with her hands on her hips. She had a mop of orange-red hair, a horse face, and a flat-chested, long-legged body with knobby elbows and knees. "Well, looky here, if it ain't the li'l deppity!"

"Pipe down, y'all," said Smalls.

"Sez who!"

"The sheriff. Try and act like ladies unless you feel like cooling your round heels in the calaboose," Smalls said.

"If I do that, how's the sheriff going to collect his cut?"

"Keep talking like that, Madge, and you're gonna get your bony ass run out of town."

"You ain't man enough to do it!"

Another whore in the group tried to mediate. "Don't mind her, deputy. She's had too much to drink."

Madge turned on her. "The hell I have! You mind your own business, Annie —"

"We'll see that she's well behaved," Annie told Smalls.

"I'd like to see you try —"

Klonk! Annie neatly clipped Madge behind the ear with a rawhide-wrapped sack pulled from a skirt pocket. Madge's eyes rolled up in her head, showing only the whites. She dropped like a puppet whose strings have all been clipped at once.

Another burly tart with limbs brawny as a lumberjack's caught Madge under the arms and held her limp form upright.

"Like I said, deputy — Madge had a little bit too much to drink. We'll take her where she can sober up," Annie said.

"Nice work," Smalls said admiringly.

"Be sure and tell the sheriff who he can count on."

"I'll do that," Smalls said, moving on.

Captain Harrison, Sergeant Oakes, and a gravedigging detail of eight troopers followed Hutto and Barton to the top of Boot Hill. The men in the detail variously carried picks, shovels and torches.

Hutto halted at the edge of an oversized mound of fresh dirt unmarked by cross or headstone. "The men from the wagon are buried here," he said.

"You put them all in one mass grave?" Harrison asked.

"What were we supposed to do? They're strangers, nobody knew them from Adam. Nobody stepped up to claim them. Or pay for their burial," Hutto said, defensively. "There's not enough money in Hangtree to rightly take care of the living, never mind the dead."

"No? Looked like the saloons and whorehouses were doing a pretty solid business when we rode in."

"Life goes on, Captain," Hutto said, shrugging. "With this hot spell the main thing was to get them into the ground quick. Along with that bunch from the ford, it was a heap of work."

"Where are the ones from the ford buried?"

"That mound over there, by those bushes." Hutto pointed to a second mound a half-dozen paces away.

Harrison turned to Sergeant Oakes. "We'll start with this one first."

"You heard the man. Get to it," the noncom told the detail. The troopers took up positions around the mound, some wielding picks to break up the earth, others shoveling it aside. Oakes and two others held torches for the rest to see by. Captain Harrison stood watching with his arms folded over his chest.

"Put your backs into it, men. Some healthy exercise'll do you good, after you've had it soft sitting in the saddle day and night scouring this godforsaken country for Indians," Sergeant Oakes said, by way of encouragement to the diggers.

"Terrible thing about Midvale, those murdering savages slaughtering a defenseless town. Terrible," Hutto said. "You pick up any sign of their trail?"

"We're working on it," Captain Harrison said, stone-faced.

". . . You reckon the same bunch of Comanches wrecked Flatbridge and killed all these fellows?"

"I'm going to find out."

The soldiers dug deeper into the mass grave. Moonlight threw solid, dark shadows, chiseled, sharp-edged. Torchlight created the opposite effect, blending and blurring them. So each lone man of the detail cast the shadows of many men, a multitude; the entire group working together wove an intricate, ever-shifting web of light and dark across the forlorn summit of Boot Hill.

Towering over all was the cruciform pillar of the gallows tree.

"Helluva way to spend the night, digging up dead men," Bill said.

"Be glad you're doing the digging and not the one being dug up," said Rourke.

Sergeant Oakes had picked them as part of the detail.

"More work with your picks and shovels and less with your mouths, unless you're looking for a boot up the tail," the noncom told them.

The diggers neared their goal. They paused to tie their yellow kerchiefs over their faces, covering noses and mouths against the stench of death.

"I just hit something soft and it ain't dirt," a trooper said, voice muffled by his bandanna.

Harrison gave Hutto a hard look. "No coffins?"

Hutto held out his arms in an imploring gesture, hands palms-up, as if mutely asking for divine compassion. "This's a poor town, Captain. We can't afford pine boxes for free for nigh on to twenty men. Ten here from the wagon and seven more over there from the ford. We wrapped each man in a blanket for a shroud. Wouldn't be decent to throw them in and cover them with nothing but dirt," he said.

"It was the least we could do," he added piously.

The excavation had uncovered an eerie heap of podlike objects like monstrous cocoons nestled in the bosom of the earth.

"Careful now, men. Watch how you dig. Don't damage these pore fellows any worse than what's already been done to them," Sergeant Oakes instructed the detail.

"Why not? Hell, they're dead," Bill said.

"Show some respect, trooper," Captain Harrison said. "If what I suspect is true, these are — were — our comrades in arms.

Brother soldiers."

The digging was about done. A massive hole had been gouged out of the earth. The soil was hardpacked clayey ground, but the real work had been done by the diggers when the bodies were first interred. With picks and spades they carved out a basin of yellow-brown hard ground, breaking it up into pieces and clods that were used to refill the hole.

Unearthing it was far easier, though still a chore. Now a pile of oversized, dirt-covered cocoons was exposed to view, heaped one on top of the other.

"Sergeant, have the men haul out the bodies and lay them out side by side so we can identify them," Captain Harrison said.

Oakes gave the orders to the detail, who began to comply. Guards had been set around the top of Boot Hill to turn back curious civilians. A crowd of them, male and female, drunk and sober, milled around the perimeter, pushing, shoving, craning for a better look.

"Ain't that just like a Yankee? Not content to confine their botheration to the living. They won't even let the dead be," somebody said.

"It ain't decent, I say," another chimed in.

"Probably going to melt down the corpse-fat to make tallow candles. Grind the bones up and use 'em for fertilizer."

"Them bluebellies'd sell the gold teeth out of their mammas' heads if they had a buyer."

The first five blanket-wrapped bodies hauled out of the pit were laid out in a row.

Sergeant Oakes handed his torch to a trooper to hold. He covered his nose and mouth with a yellow kerchief knotted at the back of his bull neck. Captain Harrison, too, had wrapped the lower half of his face with a yellow bandanna.

Oakes unwrapped the first cocooned corpse, peeling back a folded blanket to uncover the head. "Hold the light closer so I can see the face," Harrison told the torchbearer, who moved to obey.

The cadaver's flesh was gray-white, pale, bloodless, raw-boned. "A stranger to me," Harrison said, shaking his head. "Keep going, Sergeant. Try the next one."

Oakes unveiled the next in line, whose facial wounds were so disfiguring as to render his features unrecognizeable. They moved to a third, the routine unvarying: unwrap the blanket shroud, peeling it back to expose the face, a torch thrust forward and down to illuminate the features.

"No," Harrison said. Came the fourth man:

"I know him. It's Lieutenant Greer," the captain said. He straightened up, stepping back and away from the row of bodies and the pit. "That's enough. I've found out what I needed to know," Harrison said.

Hutto stood at Harrison's shoulder, not wanting to get any closer to the bodies. "What's it all about, Captain? Who's that?"

"A soldier," Harrison said, distractedly. "He was on a mission for the army."

"They all were," he added, indicating the massed dead.

"What mission?" Hutto asked.

Harrison, ignoring him, wondered aloud, "But then who's buried over there, in that second grave?"

"I can tell you that," Sam Heller said.

Harrison turned to look at the speaker, seeing a stranger. "What're you doing here? I gave orders that all civilians were to be kept out!"

"Begging the Captain's pardon, but I passed him through the line," Sergeant Oakes said.

Harrison's reaction was a mixture of outrage and astonishment. "You did? But why —"

262

"This gentleman has important information," Oakes said.

"Information best heard only by you in private, sir," he added, indicating with a tilt of his head Hutto and Barton standing nearby.

It was unorthodox, a direct violation of orders, but Harrison had not survived the war years without learning when to listen when a veteran noncom was trying to tell him something.

"All right, we'll step over here," Harrison said. His tone of voice, posture, attitude all proclaimed: This had better be good.

Harrison, Oakes, and Sam moved off to the side a dozen paces, well out of earshot of Hutto, Barton, and the troops on the scene.

"I know you well enough to know that you wouldn't deliberately disobey a direct order without good reason, Sergeant," Harrison said. "That being the case, perhaps you'll enlighten me on who the devil this man is and what this infernal mystification is all about!"

"Glad to sir," Oakes said. "Captain Harrison, meet Major Sam Heller."

"Major, eh?" Harrison said, skeptical.

"Retired," Sam said, "officially."

"That's Major Samuel T. Heller, sir, a

hero of the Union Army," said Oakes.

Dawning comprehension showed on Harrison's face. "Heller? Not the officer whose counterattack broke the back of the Reb's artillery at the Battle of Goleta?"

"The very same, sir. I know. I was there," Oakes said proudly — pardonable pride, at having been a frontline veteran of the victorious Federals at the epochal New Mexico battle with Confederate troops that was universally regarded as "the Gettysburg of the West."

"Yes sir, as soon as I saw the major outside the perimeter, giving me the high sign, I knew something was up so I had him passed on through."

Harrison, confused, said, "An honor to make your acquaintance of course, Major, but I fail to see what bearing it has on the current situation."

"This may help explain things, Captain," Sam said. Reaching into the inside breast pocket of his jacket, he took out a long, slim billfold bound in Moroccan leather and handed it to Harrison.

Harrison opened it, noticing that it contained a folded piece of vellum paper. He unfolded the single-sheet document, holding it in both hands. "What's this? It's too blamed dark for me to make out," he complained.

Sam struck a wooden match — a self-igniting "lucifer" — on the tip of a thumbnail.

It flared up in a hissing globe of light that shone on the document. "This'll shed some light on the subject," he said.

The warrant's brief text identified the bearer as Samuel T. Heller, "Agent on Special Assignment." It instructed all relevant individuals in branches civilian and military of the government of the United States of America to render any and all such assistance in money, materiel and personnel that the bearer should require to accomplish his mission for the document's issuing authority.

It bore the handwritten signature of the president of the United States and was embossed with the official seal of state. It was also signed, sealed and notarized by the secretary of the War Department. Its lower left-hand corner was marked by what was unmistakeably a dried bloodstain.

Darkness returned as the charred ember of the stick-match was hastily discarded by Sam as the flame flickered low and out. "Ouch! Burned my fingers," he said, swearing. "Hope you got all that, Captain. If not, I'll light another match."

"No need, I'm a fast reader," Harrison said, returning document and walletlike holder to its owner.

Sam refolded the document, inserting it in its container inside the folder and putting it back inside its jacket pocket. This was the presidential warrant discovered by Lorena Castillo, which decided her on forging a secret alliance with Sam.

"If that's not enough, a coded telegram to the commanding general of the Western District referring to me under my operative's name of 'Paul Pry' will further confirm my identity," Sam said.

"I'll do it if I think circumstances render it necessary. I'm willing to accept your credentials for now, especially with Sergeant Oakes vouching for your identity," Harrison said. "But what's it all about?"

"This'll take a few minutes to explain."

"I'll make the time."

Sam took a corncob pipe and waterproof tobacco pouch from a jacket side pocket. "You a pipe-smoking man, captain?"

"Cigars."

"Sorry, I don't carry them."

"I do."

Sam filled the pipe's bowl with shredded tobacco, tamping it down. Harrison took a cigar from a pocket of his military tunic. He

266

bit the tip off, spitting it out. He rolled the cigar in his fingers.

"I'd offer you some, Sergeant, but I know you favor cigars," Sam said, sealing the tobacco pouch shut and pocketing it.

"Quite all right, Major," said Oakes.

"Do me a favor and drop the 'Major,' Sergeant. From here on in, I'm just plain Sam Heller, bounty hunter."

"Yes, sir. Uh, sorry, Maj— er, Mr. Sam."

Harrison found another cigar in his tunic and gave it to Oakes. "Here, have one of mine, Sergeant."

"Yes, sir. Thank you, sir," Oakes said, grinning.

Sam lit another match and held the flame over the pipe bowl, setting the tobacco alight. He puffed away, head wreathed with ghostly gray clouds of smoke. Harrison fired up his cigar, then held the match for Oakes to light his cigar.

"What I'm about to tell you is information I picked up working undercover, posing as a bounty hunter," Sam said. "There's nothing fake about the bounty-hunting part. I kill wanted outlaws for money. But it's a good cover that gets me into lots of hard-to-get-into places on both sides of the law. You'd be surprised how many bounty killers are crooks — or maybe you wouldn't be.

"I wouldn't be telling you this if I didn't think you could keep a secret, Captain."

"Thanks," Harrison said curtly.

"And I know Sergeant Oakes can keep his mouth shut. We worked together in the war. It would be useful for him to know the background, if you have no objection."

"Why not?" Harrison said, shrugging. "Sergeants always seem to have a way of finding out things, anyway."

"Only so we can serve our commanding officers better, sir," said Oakes.

"Save that bull pucky for fertilizer, Sergeant."

"Yes, sir."

"During the last years of the war I was assigned to the Secret Service as a member of Lafayette Baker's National Detective Bureau," Sam began. "I enjoyed some success as an undercover agent. Which is why I got picked for this job.

"I don't have to tell you the strategic importance of Hangtree County as regards the entire Southwest. It's a critical junction of a number of militarily vital corridors. It's smack-dab in the middle of the war trails used by Indian war parties to raid from as far north as Kansas south through Texas into Mexico. That's a two-way route, since it's also used by Mexican bandits and slavers to strike deep into our country. Hangtree sits on the trails used by stage and freight lines and westbound settlers, too. With the war over, the territory's more important than ever.

"Then there's the situation with Mexico. During our Civil War, French Emperor Napoleon the Third installed the Austrian Archduke Maximilian as ruler of Mexico. It was an outright violation of the Monroe Doctrine prohibiting European powers from colonial ventures in this hemisphere. They got away with it because they could. With the secession to put down, Washington had to overlook the French-Austrian takeover of Mexico and the Juarista revolution it produced. Now that the war's over, the administration's not minded to be so forbearing.

"Hangtree County is a hotbed of organized banditry and lawlessness. Comancheros selling guns and whiskey to hostile Indians; bandits and slave raiders up from Mexico; and gangs of homegrown badmen are all operating out of the Breaks, using it as a base to found an outlaw empire.

"The president and the secretary of the War Department have given me a roving commission as an undercover operative to suppress the most dangerous threats to the orderly settlement and reconstruction of the territory.

"I planned to contact you, Captain, at the fort and establish my credentials but things moved too fast for me to work through proper channels," Sam continued. "Through official channels I already knew about the secret weapons shipment of a wagonload of repeating rifles and ammuntion being sent from Fort Wolters in Mineral Wells to Fort Pardee.

"It was up in Quinto in the Nations in Oklahoma Territory, a settlement that's become a robber's roost, that I first heard rumors of a plan to hijack the guns. I found my first solid lead in Denton, Texas, from an outlaw on the dodge who'd had too much to drink and liked to run his mouth when he was in his cups.

"The strike was set for somewhere in Hangtree County, but that's all I knew. Nothing about the who, how or where. I was playing a lone hand and had no way to contact anyone at either fort. I rode here as fast as I could. I arrived about an hour too late. I stumbled into the ambush spot by luck — bad luck.

"I came down from the north and struck Mace's Ford. What I didn't know was that that was where the outlaws jumped the gun wagon. Ordinarily the convoy would have crossed Flatbridge and gone straight through Hangtown west along the trail into the Breaks. But the bridge was out, forcing the gun wagon to detour north to cross Swift Creek at Mace's Ford. That's where bushwhackers massacred the escort and stole the wagon.

"They left behind some men to muddy the trail and erase their tracks. They loaded the dead guards on a flatbed wagon to take them and dump them in the hills. That's when I rode in. We had a slight disagreement," Sam said, smiling wryly.

"The horses harnessed to the flatbed wagon went wild and ran away during the shoot-out. I came out ahead, but not before catching a bullet in the left shoulder. Lost a lot of blood. I was lucky — a local rancher found me unconscious and took me in and patched me up." Sam saw no need to go into detail here about his dealings at Rancho Grande.

"I lost a couple of days, though. Just got into Hangtown today. Since I got here I managed to do some snooping that might pay off," he said. "So there's your answer, captain. The bodies on the flatbed wagon, the ones you dug up, were the gun shipment guards."

"I suspected as much," Harrison said. "I

knew it for sure when I found Lieutenant Greer among the dead. He'd been out to the fort several times before, running messages from Fort Wolters. A bit stiff-necked, but he would have made a good officer once the shine on that military academy brass wore off."

"I'm sorry," Sam said.

"They were all good men."

After a pause, Sam went on. "The others, the ones in the second mass grave, are the outlaws I killed at the ford. But the main gang got away with the guns. My guess is that they're the same bunch that hit Midvale."

Harrison nodded thoughtfully. "You don't seem surprised, Captain," Sam said.

"I've had my suspicions for a while," Harrison said. "I was at Midvale. It didn't look like an Indian raid. It looked like the work of white men. Some but not all of the dead were burned up in the fire. Those I was able to examine had all been shot. Nothing much in that by itself. The Comanches stopped using arrows a long time ago. Not when they can get guns — and there's plenty of renegades to sell firearms to them.

"The Midvale dead were shot, not once, but many times. Indians are sparing with bullets and powder because they're never sure of where the next batch will come from. One shot from them is usually fatal.

"None of the dead had been scalped. That didn't look right, either. A Comanche war party letting all those trophies go to waste? Not likely," Harrison said. "Unfortunately, it rained after Midvale was sacked, wiping out the raiders' trail. We wasted a lot of time scouting around trying to pick up their tracks. While we were on a wild-goose chase, the gun wagon was hit."

"Seems more than a coincidence, Midvale coming right before a big arms shipment," Sam said. "The raid decoyed away troops who might otherwise have helped protect the guns."

"That's how it worked out," Harrison agreed. "We would have sent a detachment to meet the gun wagon at Hangtown and escort it to Fort Pardee. Then came Midvale. Instead we sent out patrols all over the map. Some to Midvale to track the raiders and run them down. Others went north, east and west to head off the war party if it went in any of those directions, to protect the towns, ranches and settlers in those areas."

"Flatbridge was part of the plan, too," Sam said. "The arms shipment would have crossed the Swift and come through town.

But the bridge was out, destroyed. That forced the gun wagon to detour north to Mace's Ford, where the ambushers were waiting for them."

Harrison tossed his cigar stub to the ground and angrily ground it out underfoot. "You realize what this means," he said. "An outlaw gang operating on a military-like basis, with planning, organization and numbers."

"Why not? The West is full of ex-soldiers, Yanks and Rebs alike."

"The question is, who's the brains behind it? The leader?"

"I think I know."

"Well? Who is it?" Harrison demanded. "Damn it, man, don't keep me hanging!"

"Brock Harper," Sam said.

"Harper!" Harrison's eyes widened, then narrowed, calculating, thoughtful. "I wouldn't put it past him. He's vicious enough," the captain said. "But the last I heard, Harper was in Mexico with a band of mercenaries, selling their guns to Emperor Maximilian."

Sam shook his head. "He pulled out a couple of months ago, after a failed effort to steal Maximilian's treasury from a bank vault guarded by crack French troops. He and what was left of his bunch ran north for their lives."

Harrison was doubtful. "That's the first I've heard of it."

"Well, I throw a wide loop, Captain. I've got a lot of contacts to draw on," Sam said, smiling.

"What ties Harper into Midvale and the gun-wagon job?"

"I had a few suspected persons but no real leads as to the identity of the hidden hand behind the marauders. Not until tonight, a few hours ago, when a young fast gun named Johnny Cross laid out Killer Kimbro on the floor of the Golden Spur saloon."

"What of it?"

"Harper's a suspicious bird and trusts few men. But Kimbro's been with him for years as his lieutenant. Kimbro in Hangtown means that Harper can't be very far away," Sam said. "There's plenty of nervy, ruthless bandit chiefs but few have a mind like Harper's. He's a brute, but don't let that fool you. He's a cunning devil, a thinker and a planner. He's absolutely unhindered by any shred of conventional morality. Human life means no more to him than an insect's. Less, if it gets between him and something he wants.

"My sources said he was back in the States, but I didn't know where, or what he was up to. I do now. He and his outfit must be laid up in the Breaks, probably less than a day's ride outside of town."

Harrison took off his hat, rubbed the top of his head, and put his hat back on. "The Breaks covers a lot of ground. Hard country. An army could spend a fortnight combing it and still not find what it's looking for. Fort Pardee has hundreds of square miles of territory to protect and at most about 150 cavalry troops it can put in the field at any one time."

"This is your bailiwick, Captain. I've no intention of interfering," Sam said. He was being diplomatic. His commission gave him the authority to intervene if he thought it necessary, but he preferred to operate quietly behind the scenes if possible. "I don't want to tread on anyone's corns, but I have a suggestion or two, if you're interested."

"I'm open to good ideas from any and all quarters," Harrison said. "Fire away."

"The folk of Hangtree County you're assigned to protect have only slightly less use for Brock Harper and his bunch than they do for the United States Army."

"No argument there."

"On the other hand, they don't want to be murdered in their beds by a pack of murdering outlaws, either. Most of the men-folk were in the Confederate army. They're used to bandits and Indian war parties. They're trailwise, tough, and dead shots. Why not get them on your side, Captain?"

"That'd be a neat trick. But I'm a cavalry commander, not a magician."

"You've got something that beats anything in a conjuror's bag of tricks: gold," said Sam.

Harrison's laugh was bitter. "That's a joke. You know what a soldier's pay is like. A highbinder like Hutto — or for that matter, Harper — has more cash on hand than all the soldiers in Fort Pardee combined."

"I'm talking about officially, Captain. Even the tightfisted politicians in Washington will open up their pocketbooks in a case like this. An army weapons shipment attacked by outlaws, its men killed and munitions plundered — why, man, they'll call it insurrection and pay plenty to find and punish those who did it!"

"Possibly," Harrison said. "But I have neither the authority nor the resources to post a reward."

"I do," Sam said. "I carry a presidential warrant directing all federal civilian and military authorities to render whatever assistance I require. Including financial. Send a wire or courier to the commanding general, Western District, stating that one Paul Pry requires the funds and they'll be made available in quicktime."

Harrison stared at him. "You can do that?"

"That's why I'm here, Captain," said Sam. "I sure didn't come to Hangtown for my health," he added.

Harrison's fingers stroked his chin. "If word gets out about the stolen guns, it could start a panic."

"It'll get out in any case. This way, you make it work for you. Besides, these Texans don't scare easy."

"I'm not worried about them, I meant a panic in Washington."

"That'll help get the job done, too. Post a fat reward on the marauders who wiped out Midvale, and every man and boy in the county who can strap on a gun will be out in the Breaks looking for raiders."

"It could work," Harrison said, "provided you can do what you say you can do."

"Try it and find out. What have you got to lose? If you don't catch or kill the marauders, your military career will wind up right here on Boot Hill," Sam said.

"There's one consolation. If I'm ruined, I won't go down alone. I'll make sure you go along with me."

Sam laughed out loud. "That's the spirit, Captain.

"And one more thing: Best keep Harper's name out of it for now. Publicly, at least. No sense tipping him off that we're on to him yet."

Sam had a few more ideas to go over with Captain Harrison. They spent some time scheming and planning, mapping out a campaign. Once they had it squared away, Sam took his leave. "I've still got a few things to do in town tonight. I'll be in touch," he said.

"Good luck," Harrison said. "You'll need it!"

"We both will."

Sergeant Oakes escorted Sam to a shadowy section of the perimeter cordoning off Boot Hill, quietly instructing the guards to let him slip through the line without a fuss. He descended the slope and was swallowed up by darkness.

"The major ain't changed a bit," Oakes said to himself. "Still a ring-tailed hell-bender!"

SEVENTEEN

The Dog Star Saloon buzzed with the kind of excitement associated with a gold rush.

Ten thousand dollars! That was the reward posted by the army on the mystery gang of marauders that torched Midvale and stole the gun wagon — wanted dead or alive.

Johnny Cross and Luke Pettigrew occupied a side table at the saloon. A long, narrow, flat-roofed one-story wooden shed a few blocks south of Trail Street, it was sited far enough west and away from the town jail for its patrons' peace of mind.

The narrow end fronted a side street running north-south. A scarred wooden bar, black-brown with age, smoke, stains and grime, ran parallel to one of the long walls. Johnny and Luke sat near the entrance where they could keep an eye on the comings and goings.

The place was murky, dimly lit by flickering lamps. At the rear, beyond a doorway with a dirty sheet hanging from a curtain rod to cover it, lay several cribs where paying customers could have their way with one of three house whores.

The saloon's clientele was mostly made up of local ranch hands, cow punchers, tanners, skinners — hard-fisted, hard-headed strongbacks and cowboys. A rough bunch, but more or less honest. That's why they hadn't much money. To hear them talk now, though, you'd think they'd already got their hands on a piece of that federal reward money.

Gunslingers, outlaws and tinhorns generally flocked to the fancier places on Trail Street. That's why Johnny and Luke were at the Dog Star. Anybody that came looking for them with trouble in mind would stand out.

The duo sat in straight-backed armless wooden chairs at a small round-topped wooden table. A bottle of red whiskey and two wooden cups sat on the tabletop. Wooden cups, not glass tumblers. It cut down on the breakage.

Luke held a wooden cup in both hands, staring at the liquid contained therein. Holding the cup to his lips, he tilted his head and tossed it back. He gulped, shuddering. Eyes going in and out of focus, he gasped for breath.

"Ain't so bad once you git enough of it down," he said, when he had recovered. "Kind of takes the sting out of my sore knee, what's left of it, where the stump chafes against the wooden leg."

"Not that I'm complaining, mind you," he added quickly.

"Why not?" Johnny Cross asked. "You got plenty to complain about."

Luke looked surprised. "Are you kidding? A couple days ago, I was out of a horse, a musket, and a wooden leg — just about all my worldly goods. Now I got me part of a string of horses, a mean sawed-off scatter-gun, some money in my pockets, I'm getting drunk, and I got my wooden leg back, too! No sir, I ain't bellyaching! Fate's been right kind to me since you turned up, Johnny."

"Sure," Johnny said. "All you got to worry about is stopping a bullet. You string with me and there'll be plenty of lead slung at you."

Luke showed a slow, sly grin. "Now who's bellyaching?"

"Just stating a fact, hoss."

"Folks've been shooting at me for the last four years. I'm used to it. 'Sides, I notice that most nearly everybody that slings lead at you winds up dead."

"So far."

"Let's keep it that way, huh?" Luke refilled his wooden cup. "Ready for another yet?"

Johnny shook his head. "I'm fine."

"This'll make you feel even better." Luke tossed back half a cup, his idea of moderation. After the spasms subsided and his eyes refocused, he said, "This stuff must be getting to me. These Dog Star whores is starting to look good."

"You go with one of 'em and you'll have plenty to complain about in a week or two, when your pecker falls off from the pox," Johnny said. "Don't go getting too drunk. I don't want you shooting me by mistake in case we tangle with any of Kimbro's friends."

"Haw haw! Dead gunhawks got no friends," Luke said.

"Ain't it the truth?" a new voice said.

Luke sat up straighter. Johnny was motionless, except to look up from out of the tops of his eyes. Standing on the opposite side of the table was that redheaded gunman, Dan Oxblood. He was alone, a bottle of whiskey in his right hand. Johnny was aware that Red was a left-handed draw.

"Buy you a drink?" Red offered.

"That depends," Johnny said.

"On what?"

"On whether you're fixing to even up for Kimbro."

Red shook his head, grinning. "Ornery cuss, ain't you? Fellow wants to be sociable and you figure he's looking for a fight."

"That ain't a bad way to figure in Hangtown," Johnny said.

"A wide-awake young fellow like you must've seen I wasn't siding Kimbro tonight at the Golden Spur."

"Now that you mention it, I do sort of recollect that that was the case. So?"

"Before you did for him, I was getting ready to quit Kimbro anyhow. Never much cared for him at that, the sour bastard," said Red. "So?"

"You're welcome to pull up a chair and set," Johnny said.

"Much obliged." Red hooked a booted foot around the leg of a spare chair against the wall and slid it across the floor to the table. He sat down, placing the bottle on the table. "What're you boys drinking?"

"House whiskey," Luke said.

Red gave a mock shiver. "Brrrr, that's too tough for me!" Indicating the bottle he'd brought, he said, "Here, try some of this from my own private stock. Bottled in bond."

"After you." Johnny said.

"Heh heh. Trusting soul, ain't you?" Red pulled the cork, raised the bottleneck to his mouth and uptilted it, drinking long and deep. "Ah," he said, wiping his mouth with the back of his hand.

He slid the bottle over to Johnny, who took it. Johnny took a drink from it. "Tasty," he said, smacking his lips.

"Have another," Red invited.

"Don't mind if I do." Johnny took a long pull. "Smooth."

"I been saving it in my saddlebags for a special occasion. Figured Kimbro biting the dust qualifies as one."

Luke groped for the bottle. "Pass that red-eye to me, I'd like a taste." He drank deeply.

Red's eyes widened. Luke set the bottle down, its level noticeably diminished.

"You're a drinking son of a gun, ain't you?" Red said admiringly.

"That's mighty fine liquor, mighty fine," Luke said.

"Genuine Kentucky bourbon." Red settled into his chair, leaning forward. His manner now was confidential, conspiratorial. "Fact is, I got a little matter of business I'd like to kick around with y'all," he said.

"Kick away," said Johnny.

"Heard about that ten-thousand-dollar ree-ward?"

"I believe I did hear something about it," Johnny said, too casually.

"Now supposing a fellow had a line on the possible whereabouts of those guns, just supposing mind you, where do you think that would leave him? Hmm?"

"I suppose that would leave him in the way of being a rich man."

"That's good figuring."

"What I can't figure is why that fellow wouldn't keep the secret to hisself."

Red looked thoughtful. "The shortest distance between two points ain't necessarily a straight line in this wicked world."

"You've lost me. I never was any good at geometry," Johnny said.

"How're you at triggernometry? Here's a problem: how can you trust a Yankee to keep his word? Go blab the secret to that bluebelly captain, say, and what's to stop him from double-crossing you and keeping the reward money all to himself? Yanks generally being mean-minded, money-grubbing types bent on hogging the world and stealing everything that ain't tied down?

"How does a fellow protect himself against that?"

"You're telling it, hoss," Johnny said.

"Possession," Red said. "Possession is nine-tenths of the law, so they say. If a fellow had them firearms in his possession, tucked away in a safe place where Billy Yank couldn't find them, why then he'd surely have the whip hand. If the Yanks wouldn't play fair and the deal fell through, he'd still have the rifles and cartridges. Which is just as good as money, if not better."

"Sounds like that fellow you're talking about is practically in the chips already. What's stopping him?" asked Johnny.

"Well — there's a hitch."

"There always is, somehow. And what's that?"

"Getting those guns is a mighty big job. Too big for one man. But a couple of men, good ol' boys, sons of the South, Texans who know how to shoot and don't mind pulling a trigger, could get the job done."

Johnny was silent. Red leaned forward, intent, breathing hard. "Well? What do you say?" Red asked.

Johnny said, "We still supposing, or are we getting down to brass tacks?"

"It's time for the nut cutting," Red said, all serious-like. "Some might say I'm taking a long chance but I been watching you two and I like your style."

"I'm blushing like a schoolgirl," Johnny said.

Red scowled. "Okay, let's grab the hot iron. I know where the guns are, but between me and them stands a passel of bad hombres. Real bad 'uns. Mean. But not so mean that a couple of smart, fast, tough fellows couldn't steal it away from them.

"Now, you want in or not?"

"I'm still listening," said Johnny. "How about you, Luke?"

"I'm all ears."

"This talking is thirsty work," Red said. He drank from his bottle.

"So's listening," said Luke, reaching for Red's bottle. He uptilted it, holding the bottom parallel to the ceiling to extract the last few drops. He set it down.

Red eyed it. "You killed the bottle," he said.

"What I want to know," Johnny said, "is who else we got to kill?"

The long shadow of a tall man fell across them. Red started. Even Johnny's poker face betrayed a hint of surprise that the new arrival had been able to come on them unobserved, even by him.

Red looked up at the stranger, then glanced down at his own holstered gun.

"You're doing fine so far. Don't lose your

288

head and make a fool play now," the stranger said.

Red kept both hands on the table in plain sight.

"This game sounds kind of interesting, gents. Think I'll sit in and deal myself a hand," Sam Heller said.

EIGHTEEN

Late Saturday afternoon found Johnny Cross leading a line of riders along a twisty trail in a rocky gorge of the Breaks. The sun was behind the western hills, but the waning day was still hot. The line rode single-file through a narrow, high-walled ravine.

Johnny was leagued with a strange group of unlikely allies. Which was saying something, considering some of the characters he'd been thrown together with during the course of a young but eventful life.

A thorny friendship with Bloody Bill Anderson had taken him north into the Border States to join up with William Clarke Quantrill and such long riders as Frank and Jesse James, the Younger Brothers and Manning and Arch Clements. At war's end with no amnesty for Quantrill's raiders, he rode the outlaw trail through the Nations, ultimately winding up way down south in the bosky country of East Texas, siding with the likes of Cullen Baker and Bill Longley.

Now, after long years of wandering, he'd come home only to find himself teamed with the damnedest bunch of gunhawks and adventurers ever to set out on a wild quest to trade lead for gold.

"What money will do!" Johnny said to himself. With him were Luke Pettigrew, Don Oxblood, Sam Heller and five Texas vaqueros. The only one he trusted was Luke.

Don Oxblood was all easy amiability, but who knew what lay below the surface? The redheaded, left-hand gun was an outlaw and renegade, a former member of Brock Harper's outfit who'd turned his coat and betrayed the raiders' locale in hopes of collecting a piece of that ten-thousand-dollar reward. He'd also been promised amnesty for his past deeds if his tip panned out. Still, there was no telling which way Red would jump until the moment of truth.

Then there was that smiling stranger Sam Heller, who'd horned his way into the deal. It was a case of either stringing along with him or killing him. Johnny had the feeling that Heller would be a hard man to kill. A most mysterious fellow, the Yank, but he brought a lot to the table.

He could shoot, and he had money and connections. Heller had paid for some of the firearms and explosives they were packing along on this trip. It was Heller who'd arranged with the bluebelly Captain Harrison for Oxblood's provisional pardon in return for services rendered.

It was useful to have a Yankee go-between to cut a deal with the army, cutting down the chances of a double-cross when it came to the payout of the reward money to a couple of not-so-ex-Rebels. But he was a bounty killer, and a Yankee bounty killer at that. He might get it into his head to collect on some of his erstwhile partners once the job was done.

Johnny wasn't wanted in this part of Texas, but there were other places in the West where the law would pay for his hide. Fewer partners meant bigger shares for the survivors.

If it came to that, though, Johnny trusted in his wits and his guns to see him through the showdown.

Heller had brought the vaqueros in, too, five riders from Rancho Grande: Sombro, Vasquez, Gitano, Chicory and Latigo. Johnny would have liked to have known what lay behind that unusual coalition.

Hangtree County folk generally kept to themselves and their families. Their lives consisted mostly of hard work and plenty of it, with little time for socializing with their neighbors, even if they were of a mind to — which, generally, they weren't. The neighbor you shared a drink with today, you might find yourself shooting it out with tomorrow over water rights, grazing land, or even an unbranded calf.

Anglos and Mexican-Americans mixed even less, each group "sticking to their own kind" as a matter of form, preference and self-protection. But there was some contact between the two, especially for a native son and lifelong resident such as Johnny Cross. He knew Vasquez and Sombro by sight and repute; Gitano looked familiar — he'd seen him around. Chicory and Latigo were strangers to him.

The hand had been dealt, and now there was nothing for it but to play it out to the last turn of the cards.

Johnny set their course, taking the riders on a wide, far-ranging swing way out west deep into the Breaks before heading back southeast toward Buffalo Hump on Anvil Flats. He rode point, followed in order by Sombro, Red, Sam Heller, Vasquez, Gitano, Latigo, Chicory, and Luke. Mixed in along the line were a couple of pack horses containing provisions: water, food, and munitions.

By prior arrangement between Johnny and Luke, Luke brought up the rear at the tail of the file. Knowing the country, he was less likely to get lost should he become separated from the others during the convoluted windings and turnings of their journey. Part of his job was to lay back from time to time and make sure that nobody was dogging their back trail.

Also, of equal if not greater importance, Johnny wanted someone he could trust at his back. Especially considering the bunch he was riding with.

The file moved along at a slow, deliberate pace to keep the horses from kicking up dust that could be seen from a long way off. Brock Harper was sure to have spotters posted at vantage points on the high ground overlooking the hideout in all directions.

None of Harper's outfit had been seen, though time and again there'd been signs of their presence in the area. The signs had played out as the intruders had gotten deeper into the winding, roundabout course Johnny had picked to direct them undetected to the outfit's stronghold.

For some time, the trail through the ravine had been widening enough to allow two riders abreast. Now, Don Oxblood urged his horse ahead, overtaking and passing Sombro to come alongside of Johnny Cross. He kept pace with Johnny as they proceeded.

"If you wasn't supposed to be the expert on this country, I'd suspicion that you was lost," Red said. "I rode the back trails around the hideout plenty of times but I never set eyes on this one, no sir."

"That's the idea, ain't it? To come by a way so that we ain't seen?" Johnny countered.

"Hell, I'm lost," Red admitted. "I saw the top of Buffalo Hump above the cliffs an hour or two ago but I ain't seen hide nor hair of it since."

"Which means the lookouts can't see us," Johnny said.

"Spooked me a bit, that's all. I thought I knew this country, but we could be in New Mexico for all I know."

"Well — we ain't."

Oxblood took a swig of water from his canteen. He unknotted his bandanna, folding it up into a square, and poured water on it, wetting it. He mopped his forehead and the back of his neck before retying the bandanna in place. "Hot," he said.

"Come sundown it'll get so cold you'll think you were way up north," said Johnny.

They spoke low-voiced, just loud enough for each to be heard by the other.

"I don't like being outnumbered by them Mexes," Red said, scowling.

"We needed more guns, you said so yourself. It'll take more'n you, me and Luke to bust them rifles loose off of ol' Brock Harper," Johnny pointed out.

"I figured on rounding up the sidemen ourselves."

"Heller figured different."

Red's scowl deepened. "That's something else I don't cotton to. What's a damned Yankee doing, siding with a bunch of Mexes?"

"Why don't you ask him?"

"Aw, he'd just put me off with some more of that fancy doubletalk."

"He don't crack to much at that," Johnny said. "He brung along a couple of good men, though. Good with a gun, that is."

"Yeh? Who?" Red asked.

"Sombro and Vasquez."

"Which ones are they?"

"The one riding behind you is Sombro, a damned good tracker."

"That old man? He don't look like much," Red said, scoffing. Johnny made a hand gesture, indicating not assent, but rather acknowledging the fact that Oxblood had just spoken.

"If he's that good, maybe he ought to be setting the trail instead of you," Red said.

"Then you'd be saying he's leading us into an ambush," Johnny replied.

"Think you got me all figured out, don't you?"

"Mebbe."

"Well, you're right! I would say that. Reckon I'm just a contrary cuss," Red said. "You said two were good with a gun."

"Two that I know of," Johnny corrected. "The others might be good, too, but I don't know 'em."

"Who's the other one you do know?"

"Vasquez, the one with the big hat and the big belly. He's jefe de los pistoleros, top gun for Rancho Grande, a big spread north of town."

"He's fast?" Red asked, interested.

"Killed a lot of Comanches and more than a few Anglos who was prodding him," Johnny said. "Him and Sombro've been riding for Rancho Grande going back to when I was a kid. Gitano — the one with the gold ring in his ear — he's been with 'em for some years, too."

Red licked dry, sun-cracked lips. "Reckon that ring is real gold?"

"If you're thinking of taking it, I hear he's

a wizard with the blade."

"Bah. A Billy Yank and five Mexes. Trust any of them?"

"Hell, Red, I don't trust you."

"Now you went and hurt my feelings."

Johnny changed the subject. "How come you quit Harper?"

Red looked cagey. "It's tricky."

"Keep your confidences, then. You don't have to tell me a thing."

"No, no, I don't mind. Wouldn't want you to think I quit a man cold just to collect a price on his head."

"But that's part of it."

"Sure, but not all. During the war I killed Yankees who was out to kill me and none of us saw anything wrong with it. I'll go up against a man with a gun if he's got something I want," Red said.

"That's the way of it," Johnny agreed.

"Just between you and me, Kimbro recruited me for Harper's raiders. I'd heard of Harper before — who in our line hasn't? — but I never worked with him or met him. I knew nothing of the Midvale deal, on that I give you my word.

"I hired on for the gun-wagon job. Why not? Just because Robert E. Lee — bless him! — signed a piece of paper at Appomatox don't mean I've had my fill of shooting

Billy Yanks. Especially when they're hauling a wagon filled with good guns worth mucho dinero. They knew the risks when they took the job. They took their chances same as me. They came out on the wrong end of things — too bad. If they'd've been smarter or more wide awake or just plain luckier, it could've been me instead of them.

"We took the gun wagon to the Ghost Valley hideout. What I didn't know was what Harper planned next. He's already got a small army and he's planning a bigger. He aims to do Hangtown the way he did Midvale. Go in shooting, gun down everybody except the women, girls and children to be sold down in Mexico. Steal everything worth taking: money, jewels, watches, horses, cattle, guns. Burn down the town and leave no survivors.

"Killing unarmed men, and women and children — that ain't for me. It ain't sporting."

Red looked puzzled, as if trying to work out a problem whose solution was just out of reach. "Kimbro, now, he was pure poison clear through, rattlesnake-mean. He'd rather burn a man down than bed a pretty woman. It's how he took his pleasure.

"But Harper ain't built like that. He's cold as ice. When he talks about wiping out a

299

town, he's got no more feeling in him than a bookkeeper drawing a line through a ledger entry and striking out a bad debt.

"He sent Kimbro and me and some of the others into Hangtown to scout it out for him. Like I said, I already had me a belly-ful. When Kimbro braced you in the saloon I saw my chance to shuck off the others and light out. Even though it meant walking out on a payday I'd already earned for that day's work at the ford."

"Lucky you stuck around town long enough to hear about that reward being posted," Johnny said, dryly.

"Luck is what we're gonna need to take those rifles away from Harper," Red said. "That and plenty of firepower."

Sundown. Buffalo Hump towered above the badlands of Anvil Flats. It looked like its namesake, the rounded hump behind the back of a buffalo's neck. A mound several hundred feet high, it was topped by a rocky knob. Its fan-shaped lower slopes were covered with small trees, brush and weeds; its upper slopes were jagged slabs and shelves of brown, gray and black stone.

Lookouts were posted high on the bald-domed mound. Roving bands of well-armed gunmen patrolled the area.

Three outlaw riders came circling around the mound from the southwest, curving north, then east. They rode wide around the landform, swinging out into flat, open ground to make an uninterrupted circuit without a lot of weaving and dodging around rock spurs and fans thrusting out from the mound. By so doing, they avoided the intricacies of the high hill's irregular base, scalloped and ruffled like a coastline with dryland coves and inlets.

Hidden in its recesses on the northwest was a long, narrow draw, a cut shaped like an arrowhead. A narrow mouth and plenty of brush concealed it from view.

Within it were nine deadly gunmen, waiting for nightfall.

V shapes wheeled through the sky around the top of Buffalo Hump, black kites soaring and swooping in the darkling sky.

"Looky them turkey buzzards! They've come to the right place," Red Oxblood said.

"So've we," said Luke.

Johnny Cross had led the group to the cleft in rock. In the failing light Sombro found signs only of unshod horses in the draw. "Mustangs come here, but no men," he said. In addition to his guns, Sombro had a wooden bow slung across his back and a quiver of arrows hanging at his side.

"I found this draw when I was a kid, hunting. It's a good hiding place close to Ghost Valley," Johnny said.

"Now we wait till dark," Sam Heller said.

"Then we make our move, eh, Yank?" Red said.

"That's right."

Shadows pooled, thickening, spreading like a rising tide of blackwater. The horses munched on tall grasses and low brush. The men chewed beef jerky and drank canteen water. They dared not light a campfire. The comforts of tobacco were forbidden them, too. Not only would a light as small as a match fire threaten them with discovery, but the smell of tobacco smoke could travel a long way to betray the presence of interlopers.

The gunhawks checked their weapons and hardware. Sam Heller busied himself cutting varying lengths of fuse cord and rigging them to bundled sticks of dynamite.

Johnny hunkered down beside him. "Hey, Yank," he said.

"Yeh?" Sam said, not looking up from what he was doing, working as much by touch as sight in the deepening darkness.

"That day back at the ford when I was fixing to rob you — how come you didn't shoot me?" Johnny asked.

"I don't know. Must've been your honest face."

"And why'd you take my part against Hutto and the sheriff back at the Golden Spur?"

"After you killed Kimbro, I figured you were a natural for a Harper-hunting party."

"Like this one."

"That's right."

"Remember, I never asked for no favors."

"Nobody says you did."

"And I ain't giving none, neither."

"I don't expect you to. Just do your damned job."

"I will."

"Fine."

"All right, then," Johnny said, vaguely dissatisfied. Rising, he started moving away, only to halt after a pace or two. "Something bothers me . . ."

"What?" Sam asked.

"I been studying on it but I ain't got you figured out yet."

"When you do, let me know."

Johnny went away, setting down beside Luke.

After a while, Vasquez drifted over to where Sam was. He stood with his legs spread, thumbs hooked into the top of his gun belt. He had to reach under his sloping belly to find the leather band. "Gringo," he said, "there will be much killing soon, no?"

"Yes."

"That is good. I like killing gringos."

"The real money's in getting those rifles away from Harper."

"I like killing gringos better."

Sam glanced up. "What does Don Eduardo like?"

"Money," Vasquez said. "He wants the dollars. That is why we pistoleros of Rancho Grande are here."

"Good."

"But killing gringos makes it all the sweeter."

The nine rode out of the draw at midnight. Once they were in the open, Johnny Cross and Sombro took the point in tandem.

"What're those two cooking up?" Red asked, low-voiced.

"Johnny knows the way, but Sombro can smell an enemy in the dark," Luke said.

"With Harper's crowd, that won't be hard," Sam muttered.

The horses' hooves were wrapped in cut-up pieces of blanket to muffle their tread, muting the ring of iron horseshoes striking rock.

The riders filed out, hugging the irregular

terrain at the foot of Buffalo Hump's north slope. Moving east, they avoided the open as much as possible. They wormed around rocky spurs, using ridges, shelves and boulders for cover.

It was black night. The moon was hidden behind the south face of Buffalo Hump. Starlight glinted on sharp-edged rock facets and outlines.

The riders made for Ghost Valley.

Nineteen

Buffalo Hump was a hill, a high hill, hundreds of feet tall, squatting on Anvil Flats. Its upper third was bare rock, the bottom two-thirds rock and dirt. Its northern face was bordered by jagged foothills and rocky ridges. Hidden among them was a box canyon. Inside the canyon lay Ghost Valley.

A ravine a hundred yards long led into the canyon. This pass was known as the Chute. Its mouth was flanked by a pair of towering stone pillars: the Door Posts.

Rock walls a hundred feet tall enclosed the oval-shaped valley. It was watered by a spring that became a stream winding through grassy fields. The fields were littered with boulders and slabs from massive rockfalls.

Ghost Valley was a grim, lonesome place. Built by gods or devils of the wilderness and long abandoned by them, yet somehow retaining a lingering hint of their presence.

A good place for war parties, rustlers, outlaws and fugitives.

It was now tenanted by Brock Harper and his forty gun wolves.

Here and there on the valley floor, trees had been felled and dressed to create rude lean-tos, logs and planks slanting across boulders and ledges. A corral held dozens, scores of horses. A separate enclosure penned rustled cattle to supply the outlaws with fresh beef.

A number of smoky campfires dotted the scene, groups of men clustered around them. The hour was late; many men lay stretched out on bedrolls under the open sky, sleeping. Or trying to. A handful of others were awake, drinking, smoking and chatting.

On a rise in the valley stood a rugged, barnlike wooden shed, open at three sides. Mean as it was, it was the premier shelter on the site.

Here was where Harper housed his plum prize, the gun wagon. It was kept under heavy guard night and day, and was rarely out of the outlaw chief's sight. A fresh team of horses was harnessed to the gun wagon at all times, standing ready to make a fast getaway should any unexpected danger strike. At regular intervals the team was unhitched from the traces while a fresh team was harnessed in its place, keeping the animals at full strength and vigor.

Smaller huts and shacks were grouped around the open barn, like satellites orbiting a planet. They were occupied by members of Harper's inner circle, a cadre of lackeys who conveyed his commands to the lower ranks. Around the gun wagon, the fires were hotter, whiskey stronger, horses faster, and the desperadoes more desperate.

A case or two of rifles and ammunition had been unloaded early on from the wagon and distributed to Harper's inner circle of a dozen hardcore disciples. Each was now armed with a brand-new Henry repeating rifle and boxes of cartridges.

The outlaws so gifted had already taken much practice with the prized weapons. The ground of the target-practice area was littered with empty brass shells.

Not all the bunch had received the new rifles. To possess one was a mark of favor, a badge of honor among the raiders. All those who had taken part in the wagon hijacking earned weapons.

But Harper had forbidden them to take the Henrys outside of Ghost Valley, since to be seen with one was sure proof of participation in the robbery. That included Kimbro and the others who had ridden into Hangtown on Thursday. That was why the saddle-scabbard on Dan Oxblood's horse held no Henry repeater, an absence for which the redhead was later profoundly grateful. Promises of amnesty aside, Red found it prudent not to have such incriminating evidence on his person.

Harper was miserly when it came to doling out the Henrys to the rest of his marauders. They were crooks; he didn't trust them. Give most of them a brand-spanking-new repeating rifle and ammunition and they'd likely as not take off on their own to raise hell, shoot up the territory and generally do something stupid.

He would not allow his outlaw force to be so summarily dispersed. Not when he still had use of them to pillage Hangtree County. Those rifles would have to be earned.

The main body of his pack of gun wolves would get their Henry repeaters on the day that they they set out to take Hangtown and the surrounding ranches and settlements. A day that was fast coming.

There'd been 144 rifles in the wagon; except for about a dozen he'd given out, the rest still remained crated in the hopper of the freight wagon. As did most of the ammunition.

Now, in the dead of night, Harper made the rounds of the outlaw camp. It was one of his unscheduled inspection tours, an errand that might take place at any time during the hours of darkness and help to ensure that some sort of discipline and order was maintained at all times by the gun-wagon guards.

Harper carried a Henry repeater, the first rifle taken out of the first crate; it had hardly been out of his hands since the day at Mace's Ford. He brandished it like a royal scepter, emblematic of his status as raider chieftain.

He grunted with satisfaction, pleased to note that the circle of guards ringing his prize was manned by a full complement of sentinels. Not that they were in the sharpest state of vigilance at this late hour, but at least they were awake, on their feet, and relatively sober.

A good thing, too — for them. He was not above shooting a man for sleeping or being drunk on duty. It maintained order and encouraged the others in the performance of their tasks.

No one must take his prize cache of weaponry from him. Not the United States Army. No posse of lawmen. No war party of rifle-craving Indian bucks. No Mexican bandidos. And certainly not any of his own men.

"They all want what I got but it's mine and I mean to keep it," he said to himself, unaware that his features had formed into a snarl.

The rifles would bring him men, new recruits for his fast-growing outfit, the nucleus of an outlaw army that would tear through the southwest.

He said, "Nobody takes what belongs to Brock Harper!"

TWENTY

The moon was edging into view west of the knob of Buffalo Hump as nine deadly gunmen closed in on Ghost Valley.

Sam Heller, Johnny Cross, Luke Pettigrew, Dan Oxblood, Sombro, Hector Vasquez, Gitano, Chicory and Latigo. Nine mounted men, plus a couple of pack horses carrying explosives.

The invaders took cover behind a rocky ridge about a quarter-mile north of the mound. This was the staging area, the last stop where all nine would be gathered together. Presently they would divide into groups and go their separate ways to open the way for the taking of Brock Harper's hideout.

Through gaps in the rocks they eyed the Chute, which lay on the opposite side of a gritty, boulder-strewn flat. A campfire blazed at the mouth of the pass, flanked by the towering stone buttresses of the Door Posts.

Reflected firelight from within the ravine outlined the rocky portals with a yellow-red glow. Flickering glimmers of light on stone had an eerie, spectral appearance.

"There's two men on watch at the Door Posts," Red Oxblood said in a husky stage whisper. The enemy was far away, but the need for stealth was deeply ingrained in all the nine.

Three riders appeared, rounding the eastern curve of Buffalo Hump and riding west across the northern flat. Moonlight caused them to throw long, angular shadows across the gritty plain.

"Here comes the patrol," Sam Heller said.

"The night guard," Red said. "Harper keeps riders circling the Hump all day and night."

The trio came galloping across the flat, swinging south toward the Chute. They slowed to a halt at the mouth of the pass, outlined by the yellow-red glow within.

"They got to advance and be recognized by the watchmen," Red said.

After a pause, the trio entered the Chute, vanishing from sight.

"I calculate it takes each patrol about two hours to make a complete round of the

Hump," Luke said.

"Two hours and twenty minutes," Sam said.

Vasquez made a noise of derision. "What makes you so sure, gringo?"

"My watch."

"Bah! How can you read a watch in the dark?"

"I took off the glass covering and feel the position of the hour and minute hand," Sam said.

"Pretty good," Luke said. "I got to get me a timepiece some of these days."

"I already got a solid-gold watch fob," he added, thinking of Monty's gold tooth, safe in his pocket. Johnny chuckled.

"You are full of tricks, eh, gringo?" Vasquez said.

"I better be," said Sam.

"We all better be," Johnny Cross said.

Time passed. Presently three riders appeared in the mouth of the Chute. Riding out from between stony portals, they rode west across the flat.

Sam's fingertips brushed the hands of his watch with a feather touch. "Fifteen minutes," he said. "Fifteen minutes for one set of night guards to return and a new one to go out on patrol." He closed the lid with a click and carefully pocketed the watch.

"So we got two hours and twenty minutes to get ready and do what we got to do," Johnny said.

"Make it two hours. Give the patrol that just left time to get well clear of here before we cross the flat and get into position," Sam said.

"And then we get the ball rolling."

"That's right."

The last night guard to leave on patrol rounded Buffalo Hump's eastern slope at about four o'clock in the morning. The starry sky was still a rich purple-black, and darkness lay heavily on the scene. The incoming night guards rode three abreast, starting north across the flat.

About halfway to the Chute, a line of house-sized boulders spilled out of the foothills of the high, humped hill. From the darkness of the rocks sped a dart that struck home in the breast of the guardsman riding on the left-hand side, knocking him out of the saddle.

The other two were unaware of what had happened except that the third had fallen off his mount. They pulled up short to see if he was all right.

Something punched the middle rider in the back, between the shoulder blades. He slumped forward in the saddle, sprawled facedown aross the horse, a feathered shaft sticking out of his back.

The third man opened his mouth to shout, perhaps in fright, perhaps in alarm, or possibly in some mixture of both. An arrow took him in the torso.

He looked down to see it protruding from his chest, its slender length still quivering, vibrating from the impact. It seemed absurdly fragile, so flimsy an instrument to take a man's life.

Even as he had that thought, the guardsman died, a groaning sigh replacing the frantic shout that had trembled on his lips waiting to be vented a split-second earlier.

A couple of mounted men came around from behind a boulder where they'd been hiding. Latigo, an expert horseman, was first out, racing toward the riderless horses. Overtaking them, he headed them off from running toward the Chute, herding them.

Close behind Latigo were Red Oxblood and Sombro, the latter slipping his long bow over a shoulder and across his back. Sombro had fired the bow from horseback, smoothly loosing one arrow after another, all three speeding unerringly to their targets.

"Damn! You could teach the Comanches a thing or two about bows and arrows," Red said in a stage whisper. Sombro acknowledged the other's words with a nod of the head.

Red helped Latigo round up the horses with the empty saddles. The animals were not so much scared as bewildered. It would take more than blood and violent death to spook the mounts of Brock Harper's outlaw band.

Red handed over to Latigo the reins of the horse he was leading. "Here, hold the horses."

"Where do you go?" Latigo asked.

"To make sure they're all dead," Red said, indicating the fallen guards with a tilt of his head.

"None escape once Sombro sets his mark on them," Latigo said.

Red was a man who liked to see things for himself. He rode to the nearest body. The corpse lay sprawled on its side, the shaft in his chest having splintered and broken when he fell atop it after falling off his horse. A mortal wound; nobody could have survived that.

Red went to the next guard, who lay facedown with an arrow sticking out of his back. Leaning out of the saddle, Red prodded him with the tip of his rifle. "Deader than hell," he said.

He glanced up. The third and final corpse, that of the first guard to die, lay some distance away. Latigo rode up alongside Red, having finished securing two riderless mounts to a rope string trailing behind him. Sombro took the third horse in tow.

No alarm had been raised, no hue and cry given. The two watchmen at the Chute were unaware that anything had happened. They stood inside the pass, near the campfire. Each was armed with a new Henry repeating rifle and a brace of six-guns.

They stood staring into the outer darkness beyond the campfire. The fire was a mistake, though. Its light wrecked their night vision, hampering their ability to see what was going on around them.

"Night guard's running a little late, Slim," said one.

"What do you care, Hank? They're the ones going off duty, not us. We're stuck out here till sunup," Slim said.

There was a sound of approaching hoofbeats.

"That's them. Here they come now," Hank said.

A figure stepped into view, emerging from where he'd been lurking behind the columnar pillar of the easternmost of the Door Posts. A stranger.

Gitano. His right arm bent and raised at the shoulder, hand holding a flat-bladed knife ready for throwing.

Thunk! The knife lodged in Slim's left breast, taking him in the heart. Slim groaned, sat down hard.

One smooth rush of uninterrupted, flowing motion, Gitano struck again, a second blade appearing in his hand, heaving it as a whirring pinwheel that took Hank in the middle, high in the belly.

Hank reeled, staggering stiff-legged, the rifle slipping from his hands. It hit the ground hard but did not go off, skittering across a large, flat stone.

The slight twists and turns of the ravine that was the Chute did not afford a direct view from its mouth to the interior of Ghost Valley. Therefore, none in the outlaw camp saw the watchmen fall.

Gitano put fingers to his mouth and made a sound like the call of a night bird. The all-clear signal.

A moment later, riders appeared, materializing out of black darkness.

The Nine were gathering.

Sam, Johnny, Vasquez, Luke, and Chicory made up one group. With them were the pack horses.

They were followed by a moment later by

Sombro, Red, and Latigo. The latter trailed a string of three horses, each with a member of the night guard slung facedown across its back.

All present knew their parts and immediately began doing what they had to do. Gitano retrieved his blades, wiping them clean of dead men's blood before returning them to their belly-belt sheaths.

Red and Chicory dragged the corpses of Hank and Slim to one side, hiding them behind a cluster of rocks.

Sam and Vasquez began carefully removing gunny sacks and barrel kegs from where they were secured to the pack horses. The sacks held bundles of dynamite; the kegs were filled with gunpowder. They began stuffing the bundles of dynamite in the seams of rock underlying a massive overhanging shelf that jutted out from high on the west Door Post.

Luke measured out looping lengths of fuse cord, passing them to Sam and Vasquez, who attached them to various bundles and packets of explosives.

Sombro took a smaller burlap sack of dynamite and slung its carrying strap over a shoulder.

Gitano and Latigo armed themselves with rifles and bandoliers. They donned the bandoliers first. The rifles were rigged with straps that allowed the men to sling them across their backs. Latigo also shouldered a sackful of dynamite by the strap.

Dark eyes flashing, Gitano cut a glance at Sam. "Signal when you reach the top," Sam said. "*Bueno suerte* — good luck."

Gitano nodded. He and Latigo exited the Chute, rounding a Door Post and following the outer wall of the rocky spur that was the east wing of the pass. Going south toward Buffalo Hump for several dozen yards, they came to a place where the rock face was jagged and broken, forming a kind of jumbled, blocky stairway a hundred feet up to the top. They started upward, scaling the side of the slope.

Sombro and Red Oxblood climbed the outer wall of the opposite spur that was the Chute's west wing. Sombro secured the bow across his back and hung the quiver of arrows down his side. The redhead shouldered a sack of dynamite.

A massive seam like an inverted V opened in the rock face, accessing the summit. The lower slope was lined with a fan-shaped skirt of rocks and dirt; its upper half was stepped with stony blocks and ledges.

Sombro took the lead, ascending with the agility of a young man. Red followed, making his way but well behind.

Inside the pass, Luke and Chicory finalized the job of mining the overhang of the west Door Post. Kegs of gunpowder were set in the wide base of the vein, while bundles of dynamite were placed higher up where the crack narrowed. Luke measured lengths of cord, cutting, fixing, and setting them, while Chicory manhandled the kegs and bundled the sticks into place.

Sam, Johnny and Vasquez worked together, arranging a macabre tableau. Using ropes and pieces of dead wood, they tied each of the three dead members of the night guard upright in the saddles of their horses. Extra arrows had been stuck into the corpses to magnify the grotesqueness of the sight.

Vasquez checked his guns, various sets of which were holstered and slung on his massive form.

Johnny readied for his ride, arming himself pistol-fighter-style as he'd done prior to the start of so many other raids, during the war and after. Two guns were holstered on his hips. A second pair of gun belts were crossed over his shoulders, holstered guns worn butt-out under his arms. Two more guns were tucked in his waistband, one on the side and the other behind him, nestled in the small of his back. A loaded repeating carbine lay near to hand in its saddle-scabbard.

A pair of hands curled over the outer rim of the top of the east rampart wall of the Chute. Gitano's hands.

He pulled himself up in to the summit. The crest of the spur was flattish and about twenty feet wide, forming a pathway a hundred yards long that thrust into the heights overlooking Ghost Valley. A moment later, Latigo joined him on the top.

Gitano crossed to the far side, toeing the edge of the inner wall. He glanced down into the depths of the Chute, whose sandy floor lay a hundred feet below. He had no fear of heights. He saw the others at the mouth of the pass: Sam, Johnny and Vasquez in one group, with Luke and Chicory laboring over the explosives at the base of the west Door Post.

Distant motion caught his eye, causing him to look up and turn his gaze to the opposite side of the Chute. Sombro and Red stood on top of the western rock rampart.

Putting a hand to his mouth, Gitano imitated the cry of the night bird, a plaintive call that sounded twice in the high, empty air. The double cry signaled that both pairs of climbers had reached the summit.

Below, hats tilted upward, revealing up-turned ovals that were the faces of their *compañeros* at the mouth of the pass. Vasquez took off his big sombrero and waved it, gesturing that the signal had been heard and understood.

Gitano stepped back from the edge, turning toward the north slope of Buffalo Hump rising above them. He and Latigo started south along the top of the Chute's east wall, making for the heights overlooking the outlaw camp.

Atop the Chute's west wall, Sombro and Red also set out for the cliffs enclosing Ghost Valley.

TWENTY-ONE

"Let's go," Sam said.

Johnny held a lead rope trailing back to the string of three dead men on three horses. The men of the night guard, tied upright in their saddles, harnesseses of sticks and ropes used to brace them, holding them in place. Arrows sticking out of them.

"I'll handle the rope work, Yank," Johnny said. "I can get these plow handles of mine into action quicker'n you can loose that sawed-off rifle of yours."

Sam smiled thinly. "That's right obliging of you."

"That's me. I'm an obliging fellow," Johnny said. He, Sam and Vasquez mounted up, climbing into their saddles.

Vasquez glanced sideways at Sam. "Ready to ride, gringo?"

"Yup. Hope you can keep up," Sam said.

"Don't worry about me!"

"I'm not." Sam swung around in the saddle, facing Luke and Chicory over at the base of the west Door Post. "Ready, men?"

Chicory nodded.

"All set," Luke said.

"Better light up now," said Sam.

Luke struck a match, holding it cupped in his hand. Applying the flame to the tip of a fat cigar held clenched between his teeth, he puffed away, getting it going.

Chicory had a cigar, too. He leaned in to get it lit, flame glow underlighting his face. The son of a Cajun father and Mexican mother, his long face with its pointy features was all knobs, sharp edges and hollows, set off by a drooping black mustache that would have done honor to one of the grumbling troopers of Napoleon's Old Guard.

"Phaugh! This cigar tastes like crud, Mr. Yankee, if you'll pardon my saying so," Luke said.

"I wouldn't know, I smoke a pipe myself," Sam said.

"You could have chose a better brand."

"This way you won't smoke it all up before it's time to light the fuses."

"These are short fuses; once they're lit they'll go up derned quick!"

"And then the walls come tumbling down," Johnny said.

"Don't light the fuses until we're clear, you goddamned crazy gringo," Vasquez said.

"Wouldn't think of it," Luke said. "Give 'em hell, y'all."

"Bonne chance," Chicory said.

"See you," Johnny said.

Sam flashed a two-fingered salute from the tip of his hat brim. He, Johnny and Vasquez started their horses forward, deeper into the Chute.

Chicory took a few more puffs on his cigar, thoughtful-like. "I don't know, it's not such a bad smoke," he said at last.

A rope line stretched back from the horn of Johnny's saddle, trailing behind him to the lead horse in the string of three. The horses' gait caused the dead men to jiggle and sway in the saddle, an eerie counterfeit of life.

Threading the rocky gorge of the Chute, the riders emerged from its far end into Ghost Valley. The box canyon was a high-walled cauldron dotted with a dozen camp-fires scattered around its stony floor. Lines of smoke rose up from them into the sky to form a hazy canopy over the scene, veiling the paling stars above.

A stillness lay over the site; at this hour, it was as quiet as a camp of rowdy, ornery gun-happy outlaws would ever get. Most of them were asleep or dead drunk.

A fair amount of activity and motion centered around the open barn on the rise. It was a patchwork quilt of light and darkness, animated by blurred figures backlit by fire glow.

The newcomers turned right, circling around under the canyon's north wall. "That big shed is where the gun wagon is, according to Red," Sam said to the others.

They pointed their horses toward the rise in the center of the valley, making for it, trailing their grisly burden behind them. A voice from an unseen speaker called out to the new arrivals. Their advent fell like a pall of gloom on those outlaws still up and carousing.

Drunken voices trailed off, falling silent. Heads turned in the direction of the newcomers. Seated men stood up. Sleepers were nudged awake by their comrades.

Sam, Johnny and Vasquez closed in on the shed on the rise. The guards ringing it stirred, moving forward.

"What y'all got there?" one said, speaking for the gun guards.

"Time to bring it on home," Sam said out of the side of his mouth. "You make the call, Johnny. That Texas twang of yours beats my Yankee accent."

"That's for damned sure," Johnny said.

He loosed the slipknot, freeing the rope line from the saddle horn, holding his end of the rope in his left hand, tugging sharply on it to urge the string of three horses forward.

The lead horse came up on his left, drawing abreast of him. Arrows stuck out of the corpse in the saddle, plain to see in the firelight.

Voice breaking uncertainly, the gun guards' spokesman demanded, "I said, what you got there? — Say, what's that?"

"Comanches!"

Shouting at the top of his voice, Johnny let go of the rope, slapping the flat of his hand down hard on the rump of the lead horse, startling the already unnerved animal. "Yee-haw, git, git!"

The horse bolted, the other two following in its wake. The trio with their arrowed riders broke into a run, charging into the middle of the camp of massed outlaws.

Johnny kept shouting. "Comanches, Comanches! The Injins are coming! Injins! Comanches!"

At the same time, Sam took off his hat and waved it over his head, broad bold gestures that could be seen a long way off, even atop the rock walls ringing Ghost Valley.

The bolting horses alone would have caused a commotion. As would the outcry of the dreaded word: "Comanches!" Three corpses with arrows sticking out of them clinched the deal.

That's when the riflemen on the ramparts opened fire. Gitano and Latigo on one side, Sombro and Oxblood on the other. Together they unleashed a murderous fusillade that mowed men down where they stood. The sharpshooters whooped and hollered in imitation of Indian war cries, shrieks echoing across the canyon which was now a bowl of confusion.

It's easy to stampede cattle, especially at night when the herd is restless. It only takes a sharp, sudden shock. A coyote howl, a gunshot, even a dropped tin pan can get the whole herd moving, running out of control in a blind panic.

The outlaws reacted the same way. In a sense, it was funny. Harper's raiders had used the old dodge of hiding their crimes behind faked Indian attacks. On the other hand, they actually were in Comanche territory, with a real threat of stumbling into the real-life counterparts of the Indians they were impersonating. They fell victim to their own buildup.

The four riflemen aloft were all armed with repeating rifles, allowing them to wreak havoc and create a clamorous roar far out of proportion to their small numbers. The impact was magnified by weird, bloodcurdling shrieks and howls. Adding to the chaos were the piercing screams of men cut down by the onslaught, the wounded and the dying.

Horses penned in the outlaw corral panicked, spooked. They collectively shuddered in a massing surge, whinnying, neighing. Milling, circling, they slammed against rail fence posts, bumping, clattering, kicking.

Sam, Johnny and Vasquez went into action, charging into the thick of the ring of gun-wagon guards.

A pistol snaked into Johnny's hand, spitting flame and lead. Spurring his horse, he rushed a mass of armed men, shooting into them. Dark figures fell to lines of light that were muzzle-flares of the bullets spearing them.

Sam kicked in with his mule's-leg, the sawed-off Winchester barking out bullet after bullet. He ripped out a concerto of concentrated firepower, mowing down a line of Harper's gun wolves.

Vasquez, with a gun in each hand and the

reins held between his teeth, peeled off at a tangent from his two sidemen. Piloting toward a clump of men around a campfire, he rode among them, cutting them down with gunfire.

The raiders for the moment were mostly thrown into a blind panic. Mostly. There were some of them so iron-nerved or nerveless, or so cunning and quick-thinking, that they kept their heads even under extreme provocation.

Such a one was Brock Harper. At the sound of shots and shouts his gun was already in his hand, ready to shoot the three newcomers. But there was no clear line of fire with the chaos and confusion now loose in the outlaw camp. His own men were in his way, his lieutenants, those of his inner circle, running back and forth to block his shots — or catch them.

Sam, Johnny and Vasquez scattered, each to a different part of camp, each sowing the maximum amount of death, destruction and discord. Their horses wheeling, veering, reversing, rearing, keeping the outlaws from getting a bead on their riders.

Harper was in the center of the storm, shouting and roaring. "Keep your heads, you dumb bastards! Can't you see what they're doing? They're hoorahing you, like we'd do to the townsfolk when robbing a bank! Hold your ground and shoot, you sons of bitches —"

He was shouting into the wind — the whirlwind. Some few of his men, very few, rallied to him, around him. They were guided by his bullish clamor, the bellowing of a gored bull. They stood their ground and started shooting at the hijackers. When they could see them, which wasn't often or easy, thanks to the evasive maneuvers of the intruders.

Sam and Johnny had the same idea. Each made for the gun wagon.

Johnny neared the open barn, coming in sight of the wagon with its team of harnessed horses. A line of gunmen formed up in front of it.

A loaded pistol in his hand, Johnny burned down several men, opening holes in the line. But the others were shooting back.

Bullets cracked, whizzing through the air around him. An edge of his hat brim was nipped off by a round. A tug at the edge of his jacket as another bullet narrowly missed him.

A stallion in a blind panic kicked down the top rail of a section of corral fence, getting its forelegs over it and jumping clear. It broke for open ground, running wild.

A mass of horses swelled against the section of fence, their irresistible weight and energy knocking it down, tearing a big gap in the corral. Crazed horses, eyes rolling, nostrils and mouths foaming, galloped through camp.

"The horses is busting loose! Don't let 'em get away!" somebody shouted.

Nobody wanted to be without a getaway horse at a time like this, marooned afoot out here at Buffalo Hump in the middle of nowhere as the hideout was getting shot to pieces.

A streaming mass of escaped horses ran between the gun wagon and the rest of the camp. His horse rearing up, Sam pulled up short, reining in to avoid running into a wall of gunfire.

The gun-wagon guards had got their bearings now. Harper's counterattack was starting to pay off. Sam and Johnny caught sight of each other.

"Time to vamoose!" Sam said.

Johnny said, "I reckon —"

Tightly wheeling their mounts around in the opposite direction, they turned, retreating. Vasquez came in at a tangent, overtaking and passing them as they all made for the Chute.

■ ■ ■ ■

Above, aloft on top of Ghost Valley's curved western wall were Sombro and Dan Oxblood. They'd set down their rifles after pouring volley after volley down into the outlaw camp, firing and reloading until the barrels were red hot.

Now Red smoked a cigar while Sombro fitted an arrow to his bow. A special arrow, with a stick of dynamite tied lengthwise by thin strips of tough rawhide to the shaft. "Ready?" Red asked.

"*Sí,*" Sombro said.

"Here goes, then —"

Red touched the glowing tip of the cigar to the end of the fuse protruding out of the stick of dynamite. The fuse came alight, sputtering and sparking its way up the cord. Sombro loosed the arrow, sending it on a high arcing trajectory that lofted it up over the canyon bowl before dropping it down. It fell in the vicinity of the gun wagon.

What order Brock Harper had managed to stabilize out of the situation vanished when the explosive fire arrow detonated nearby. There was a tremendous blast of sound, smoke and fire, a booming concussion. Sundered earth went geysering in a fiery torrent.

These outlaws weren't stupid, at least not where the basics of winning and losing were concerned. Dynamite changed the equation. Bad enough to be penned in the canyon and shot like fish in a barrel. But to have explosives dropped in on their heads turned the hideout into a death trap.

Now it was every man for himself, "save himself who can!" The rush was on.

At the gun wagon, handlers had been holding on to the traces, doing their part to keep it immobilized. The team of horses, already agitated, was maddened now by the explosion. Blindly they surged forward, obsessed solely with the urge to run.

A handler slipped, losing his footing. "Lordy, I can't hold 'em —"

He fell under the horses' hooves and was trampled to rags and jelly.

Harper bulled his way to the fore, making a beeline for the wagon, the focus of his hopes, needs and all-consuming ambition. Gun in hand, he railed, "I'll kill any man turns loose of this wagon!"

An underling pleaded, "Boss, we cain't stop 'em —"

"You must, damn your eyes!"

"Brock, they's a-gonna bust loose!"

"Get out of my way, ya yellow-bellied sons

of bitches!" Harper made his way to the gun wagon.

It rocked back and forth on its springs as men held to its sides and the traces, trying to restrain the straining team that heaved at the harness in its collective will to run, run, run!

Harper clambered up into the front seat of the wagon, gathering up the ends of the sets of leather reins, clutching them in oversized, ham-like hands. Hauling on them, he leaned back, putting all his considerable strength and weight into the effort. "Whoa! I say whoa, you horses, whoa! Ease up, damn you, whoa! Mangy brainless cayuses, pull back dammit, damn and double-damn you!"

Arkansas Claude Fenner hauled himself up and over the sidewall, pulling himself on top of the crates of rifles and cartridges. Harper almost shot him until he saw who it was. "Get up here, Fenner, and grab hold of that brake with both hands — give it all you got!"

Fenner threw his legs into the boot, landing hard on the passenger side of the thinly cushioned seat board. He gripped the axe-handle-sized and -shaped hand brake. "I got it, Brocky! I got it! The horses, they's gentling now —"

A second blast followed, coming even closer than the first. Shaking the earth, shivering the pen, it brought the timbered framework and boarded-over canopy down around and on the wagon and team of horses. Raining down on Harper and Fenton, battering, beating and bruising them.

"That does it!" Fenner cried. The team lurched forward, pulling clear of the collapsing shed. Boards and timbered uprights coming apart on all sides, horses and wagon broke free, into open air and space.

The two lead horses in tandem saw their opportunity and took it on the run. The other pairs in the team followed, obedient to the single paramount impulse to flee.

Some of the handlers and gun guards ran alongside or behind the rear of the wagon. They grabbed at it, clutching the top rails, pulling themselves on board or simply holding on for dear life.

A luckless figure loomed up in front of the runaway team, too dazed or slow to react in time to save himself. He threw up his arms and then the horses were on him. He disappeared under them, trampled by iron-shod hooves and run over by wagon wheels.

The gun wagon tore down the rise. It hit a bump on the flat that flung a couple of hangers-on loose. A sideman went under the wheels and was cut in two.

The wagon thundered east across the canyon floor. Harper and Fenner were hurled about, fighting to keep from being thrown from the wagon. The hand brake was broken, useless. Its restraining gears and ratchets had torn free, as Fenner discovered when he took hold of it, hauling back on it to no use whatsoever.

A jagged board-end had opened a wicked gash in Harper's forehead, spilling blood down his face. He pawed his eyes with the back of his hand, trying to keep the blood out of his eyes.

No ordinary man, though, he who was being tossed around in the dice cup of the gods. He was Brock Harper!

That knowledge, the high valuation apportioned to the man in the roster of his own self-worth, spurred the bandit chief to regain control of the situation. Call it pride, the Devil's own sin. Something in the man caused Harper to win through on this wild ride pulled by runaway horses.

Leaning forward in his seat — a sudden pitch of the wagon's course nearly catapulting him out of the front of the wagon — Harper braced himself to keep from falling. Groping around on the floor of the boot, he found and gathered up the reins, clutching them so their ends came out the tops of his fists.

A scream sounded as a man who'd been holding on to the side of the wagon lost his grip and went under the wheels.

Blinking through blood and stinging sweat, Harper took stock of the scene. The runaways were plunging north across the canyon floor, racing toward the near end of the Chute.

He glanced back over his shoulder. Four men were in the back of the wagon, holding on to the sides as the vehicle rocked and swayed. Sour-faced Hap Engelhardt was one, and Cy Treadwell, and two more of the gang.

Behind, Ghost Valley was a hellish scene. Smoke, fire, wild horses, bodies strewn about.

Cupping a hand to his mouth, Engelhardt shouted, "Can you stop 'em?"

"No stopping them now," Harper said. "Got to let them have their heads until they run themselves out and slow down! Could be worse, though!"

"Eh? How's that?"

"I still got the guns!"

"Yeh — there's that . . ." Engelhardt was

doubtful, his expression more bilious than ever.

One of the others cried, "Look out, we're going into the Chute!"

"Nothing to do but ride it out!" Harper shouted back. He was getting a little bit of response from the team, enough to rein in the animals a few degrees when they showed a sign of going off course.

The runaway team plunged into the Chute. Harper felt like a lead ball being fired down the length of a cannon barrel. A few feet of play opened on both sides between the wagon and the ravine walls. Noise hammered off the sides of the Chute, rising to deafening levels.

There was a chance of getting clear, though, as long as the team kept to their straightaway course, thought Harper.

The hole at the far end of the Chute widened, nearing. Suddenly team and wagon bulleted out of the pass, zooming past the Door Posts into the open.

Breakout!

Others in the wagon were cheering. Fenner clapped a hand on Harper's shoulder. "By God, Brocky, we made it! I don't know how you did it but you did!"

Harper growled, "We ain't out of the woods yet! The team's still out of control!"

"Hell, let 'em run till they's winded, now that we's in the clear —"

KA-BOOM!

The rest of Fenner's remark was lost in an eruption of noise. The biggest blast yet, an explosion that literally brought down much of the west Door Post.

Concussion battered those in the wagon, swatting Hap Engelhardt and Cy Treadwell and the other two in the back of the wagon into space, a giant invisible hand brushing away gnats.

An avalanche of crushed rocks, dirt and smoke rained down as the column of the west Door Post cracked asunder, freeing a massive overhang to come crashing down.

A torrent of rock and earth rained down on the flat. A pillar of smoke and fire unfolded into lightening sky.

All the result of the blast triggered by gunpowder and dynamite that collapsed the rocky column.

Moments earlier, after shooting up Ghost Valley, Sam, Johnny and Vasquez had fled through the Chute, reining in just outside it. As the runaway gun wagon closed in on the mouth of the Chute, the three riders joined Luke and Chicory in taking cover behind the curve of the east Door Post, putting the bulk of the rocky spur between

342

themselves and the explosives in the western column.

Luke lit the master fuse, triggering a mighty blast as soon as the wagon broke out into the flat. Thick clouds of dust and smoke obscured the scene. When they began to lift, Luke and Chicory were startled to find themselves alone. Sam, Johnny and Vasquez were nowhere in sight.

"Where'd they go?" Luke said.

Back in Ghost Valley, the dazed remnants of the pack of gun wolves were beginning to recover. Ever on the alert for the main chance, they grasped the essentials of the situation.

"Look! Harper's running out on us with the gun wagon!"

"Stealing all our loot!

"Mount up, boys, and let's get after him!"

"I'll skin him alive, the Judas!"

It took time to round up a handful of horses running loose in the canyon, some of which were already saddled. Eight or ten purposeful riders galloped toward the Chute. A dozen men on foot ran after them, hopelessly trying to catch up.

The haphazard though grimly determined pursuit was barred by sudden destruction at the far end, where a blast brought down a wall of rock and loose dirt twenty feet high.

Closing the mouth of the pass, sealing the exit, it penned the rest of the outlaws inside the canyon.

Trapped like flies in a corked bottle.

TWENTY-TWO

The team of runaway horses hitched to the gun wagon would have gladly continued running to the edge of the eastern horizon to meet the rising sun. But they lacked the stamina. They'd shot their bolt during the breakneck flight from Ghost Valley.

Nostrils and mouths foaming, sides heaving, flanks glossy with sweat, they were out of breath and exhausted. Their pace began to lag.

Harper relaxed his furious concentration on working the traces of the team to cut a sideways glance at Fenner. The rangy Arkansan sat huddled beside him, haggard, white-eyed, hunched into a ball.

Swallowing hard, Fenner dared to raise up his head, looking around. Looking over his shoulder, he saw that the back of the wagon was empty of all passengers. He began, "Engelhardt, and Treadwell, and the others —"

"Gone," Harper said flatly.

The team's pace flagged, the gun wagon slowing. Spirits lifting, Fenner managed to force a halfway grin. "By God, Brocky, we made it! —"

BLAM!

Harper was slapped hard in the face by something wet, so hard that for an instant his face was pushed out of shape. Fenner slammed into him, giving him a jolt.

Fenner now sat slumped beside him, sagging, inert. Still clutching the reins, Harper rubbed the back of a hand against his face to clear it. It came away smeared with red stuff. Blood! Mixed with tissue and bits of bone.

A big hole the size of a silver dollar showed in Fenner's left breast, wetly red and glistening.

Echoes of gunfire boomed across the flat. A shot, the single shot that had just killed Claude Fenner. Trying to look everywhere at once, Harper could discover no shooter.

Despite their fear, the horses slowed, winded. Exhausted. A horse is a fretful animal. So, at that instant, was Brock Harper.

Fenner had been pounded out of existence as though struck by the Hammer of God itself. A killing round fired by an unseen marksman.

First rays of breaking day came slanting off the planet's eastern rim. A sunbeam glinted off a reflective surface in the distance near a rocky ridge ahead of Harper and to his right.

The diamond dazzle was accompanied by a glimmer of motion. It was so far away that Harper had trouble making it out. The gun wagon continued its eastward course across the flat.

The blurred image resolved itself into a rifleman on horseback. The marksman who'd shot Fenner. The rifle was pointed at Harper.

The team continued forward, narrowing the gap between Harper and his unknown adversary. Harper had no rifle handy. He'd lost his during the ruckus at Ghost Valley. The wagon was full of crates of rifles, but none were readily accessible. All Harper had was a six-gun and at this range it would be ineffective against a rifle.

Harper reached anyway. He let go of the reins in his gun hand, clawing at the pistol in his holster.

It cleared leather. Harper leveled it at the distant figure ahead. Laughing and crying at the same time, he said, "You son of a bitch!"

A blow slammed him, knocking him sideways to the left and out of the wagon.

He lay sprawled on the ground. The riderless wagon continued east, drawing away from him, dwindling. *Stop, damn you, stop!* he thought. He tried to speak but couldn't.

The gun was still in his hand. It was too heavy to lift, though. That was funny, since he was used to having an inexhaustable reservoir of strength and energy to draw from.

Harper felt tired. He decided he'd lay where he was for a while, resting until he got his strength back. The bullet hole in his chest loosed his lifeblood into thirsty sands that soaked it up.

Brock Harper was no more.

Sam Heller lowered his rifle and began taking it apart, removing the additions that turned the sawed-off mule's-leg into a long-range rifle good for sharpshooting. Nimble fingers unfastened the bolts securing the wooden butt stock to the rear of the cut-down Winchester.

He fitted the stock into a long, flat wooden carrying case. Unscrewing the elongated barrel extension attached to the Winchester's chopped barrel, he put that in the box, too. The telescopic sight had been unneeded at this range. He closed the lid and lowered the box to where it was lashed to the side of his saddle.

The masterless gun wagon rolled past him in his place of concealment and kept going east.

West, far away but coming up fast, were two riders. Sam turned his horse, withdrawing farther behind the rocky outcropping where he'd been lurking. He reloaded the mule's-leg.

The two riders raced east, chasing the wagon. They were Johnny Cross and Vasquez. Their horses ran neck and neck. Johnny leaned way forward on his horse, bent almost double. Vasquez used a rawhide quirt to lash his horse to greater speed.

They flashed past the outcropping, oblivious of Sam on Dusty hiding behind a tangle of scrub brush. He let them go.

Johnny and Vasquez closed in on the gun wagon, Johnny coming up on its right, Vasquez on its left. Leaning out of their saddles, they each grabbed a harness strap of one of the two lead horses. Control the lead horses and the rest of the team would fall into place.

Riding along, Johnny and Vasquez slowed the horses, finally bringing them to a halt. Dismounting, they faced each other.

"The gun wagon!" Johnny said.

"*Sí,* the gun wagon," Vasquez breathed, eyes glittering.

"Here it is."

"And here we are."

They eyed each other.

"Want it all, don't you?" Johnny said.

"And you?" Vasquez countered.

Johnny smiled thinly.

Vasquez nodded, as if confirming a thought he'd had. "For such as us, there is no other way," he said. "My *padrone* needs the guns, not a mouthful of empty promises from the big gringo."

"Where'd that Yank go, anyway? I lost him after the blast," Johnny said.

"I hope a mountain fell on him," Vasquez said feelingly. "No matter. Our business will not take long."

"All the while I was growing up, I always heard you was fast. But that was a long time ago."

"You think so, little gringo? Try me."

Johnny's smile broadened into a grin of genuine pleasure. "I was hoping you'd say that."

They squared off, face to face, barely a half-dozen paces separating them.

"Anytime," Johnny said.

A bullet tore into the ground between

them, spraying them with rock chips and dirt. Startled, they both whirled to confront the shooter.

Sam Heller sat on horseback, holding the mule's-leg leveled. He had ridden up unseen during the face-off, using the gun wagon for cover.

"You're two of the most ornery cusses I ever saw," Sam said, shaking his head in mock sadness. "Haven't had your fill of killing yet?"

"Not quite," Johnny said. He stepped back, turning, positioning himself so he'd have a line of fire on Sam or Vasquez. His hands hovered inches above hip-holstered gun butts.

Vasquez did the same, stepping to the side. "It's good that you come along now, gringo. So we can finish it."

"You feel that way too, Johnny?" Sam asked.

"You ain't a bad fellow at that, for a northerner," Johnny said, shrugging. "But I'll feel better with these guns in the hands of a good ol' Texas boy like me."

"You're drawing against a leveled gun," Sam said.

"You can get one of us but not both," Johnny said.

"That's right, gringo," Vasquez said. "You

try for me, the little gringo gets you. Try for him, and I get you."

"Tell it to the army," Sam said.

They came out of the rising sun, out of the bright new dawn. An entire cavalry patrol, fully armed and fresh.

Sam had faced that way, so he'd seen them coming from a long way off. Johnny and Vasquez had their backs turned to that direction and were unaware of the cavalry's imminent arrival.

The cavalry column came forward, guidons flying, their banners bright. On command, the column parted, one file swinging left, the other right. The horse soldiers fanned out into a rank that curved around the gun wagon, barring it with an arc of armed men with shouldered carbines.

Johnny's smile melted, his face stiffening. Vasquez bared his teeth in a snarl.

"Best keep those guns holstered, men," Sam said, pleasantly enough.

Captain Ted Harrison and Sergeant Oakes rode forward. "Here we are on Sunday dawn, as agreed on," Harrison said. "The gun wagon?"

"This is it," Sam said.

"Who're these two?" Harrison said, indicating Johnny and Vasquez.

"Friends of mine," Sam said dryly.

352

"Couldn't have done it without them."

Harrison nodded. "Tell the men to lower their weapons, Sergeant."

"Yes, sir," Oakes said. He barked out the order at the phalanx of horse soldiers, who stopped pointing their carbines at the trio at the wagon. Johnny and Vasquez breathed easier.

"What about Harper?" Harrison asked.

"That's him, lying yonder," Sam said, pointing toward the body sprawled on the ground a hundred yards westward.

"Good," Harrison said, smiling, showing his teeth. "And the outlaws?"

"What's left of them are pinned in Ghost Valley. We blew up the Chute. We've got six men back there, two outside what's left of the Door Posts and another four on top of the canyon with rifles and dynamite in case there's any fight left in the gang. They each come in for equal shares of the reward money."

"I'll send some troops there directly."

"By the way, Captain, this is Hector Vasquez, foreman on the Rancho Grande, the spread I was telling you about."

"My compliments, Señor Vasquez," Harrison said. "Please send my thanks to Don Eduardo and tell him that the army would be pleased to contract with his ranch to supply fresh beef to Fort Pardee."

"I will do so, Excellency. Gracias," Vasquez said.

"This young fellow is Johnny Cross," Sam said. "He's been in it with me from the start."

"Good work, Mr. Cross."

"Thanks, Captain."

"Johnny's a mustanger and if he can catch and break horses like he shoots you can't go wrong," Sam said.

"We can always use plenty of fresh mounts at the fort. We'll work out the details when you come into my office to pick up your share of the reward money."

"Much obliged, Captain," Johnny said.

"We'll go round up the rest of the outlaws now and settle the financial arrangements later," Harrison said. "Sergeant, leave a detail here to guard the gun wagon and move the rest of the troops out to Ghost Valley."

"Yes, sir."

"I'd better come along to identify our bunch at the canyon and make sure there aren't any wrangles between them and the troops," Sam said.

"Good idea, Mr. Heller," the captain said. "And — thanks."

"All in a day's work, Captain," Sam said.

"A profitable day, between the reward on the gun wagon and the bounties posted on Harper and most of his gang."

Harrison nodded, turning his horse and riding off to rejoin his troops, who were forming up to move out. A sizeable detail would remain behind to guard the gun wagon.

"You coming?" Sam asked.

"I ain't letting you out of my sight until I get paid off," Johnny said.

"Me, too," Vasquez said. "You are too full of tricks, gringo."

He and Johnny mounted up, taking their place with Sam at the head of the cavalry column. They and the troops moved out, heading westward toward Ghost Valley.

"Do me a favor," Sam said, voice pitched so that only Johnny could hear him. "Don't sell the army any stolen horses."

"I'll try," Johnny said. "Reckon you'll be moving on once you collect your bounty money, eh, Yank?"

"Not at all. Nice peaceable place like this, I think I'll stick around for a while."

"That's what I was afraid of," Johnny groaned.

Sam laughed. "I'll put the Heller brand on Hangtree County!"

His vow held a threat, a promise, and the herald of a new day.

ABOUT THE AUTHOR

William W. Johnstone is the *USA Today* and *New York Times* bestselling author of over 220 books, including *THE FIRST MOUNTAIN MAN, THE LAST MOUNTAIN MAN, BLOOD BOND, EAGLES, A TOWN CALLED FURY, SAVAGE TEXAS, MATT JENSEN, THE LAST MOUNTAIN: THE FAMILY JENSEN, SIDEWINDERS, THE LAST GUNFIGHTER*, and the stand-alone thrillers *Vengeance is Mine, Invasion USA Border War, Remember the Alamo, Jackknife* and *Home Invasion*. Visit his website at www .williamjohnstone.net or by email at dogcia 2006@aol.com.

Being the all around assistant, typist, researcher, and fact checker to one of the most popular western authors of all time, J. A. Johnstone learned from the master, Uncle William W. Johnstone.

Bill, as he preferred to be called, began

tutoring J.A. at an early age. After-school hours were often spent retyping manuscripts or researching his massive American Western History library as well as the more modern wars and conflicts. J.A. worked hard — and learned.

"Every day with Bill was an adventure story in itself, Bill taught me all he could about the art of storytelling and creating believable characters. *'Keep the historical facts accurate,'* he would say. *'Remember the readers, and as your grandfather once told me, I am telling you now: be the best J.A. Johnstone you can be.'*"

The employees of Thorndike Press hope you have enjoyed this Large Print book. All our Thorndike, Wheeler, and Kennebec Large Print titles are designed for easy reading, and all our books are made to last. Other Thorndike Press Large Print books are available at your library, through selected bookstores, or directly from us.

For information about titles, please call:
(800) 223-1244

or visit our Web site at:
http://gale.cengage.com/thorndike

To share your comments, please write:
Publisher
Thorndike Press
10 Water St., Suite 310
Waterville, ME 04901